MW00377499

Lady Briar
WEDS THE SCOT

#1 Blakeley Manor Series

BY
FENNA EDGEWOOD

WOLF PUBLISHING

Lady Briar Weds the Scot by Fenna Edgewood

Published by WOLF Publishing UG

Copyright © 2022 Fenna Edgewood
Text by Fenna Edgewood
Edited by Chris Hall
Cover Art by Victoria Cooper
Paperback ISBN: 978-3-98536-110-6
Hard Cover ISBN: 978-3-98536-111-3
Ebook ISBN: 978-3-98536-109-0

This is a work of fiction. Names, characters, businesses, places, brands, media, events and incidents are either the products of the author's imagination or used in a fictitious manner.

Any resemblance to actual persons, living or dead, or actual events is purely coincidental.

All Rights Reserved

This book or any portion thereof may not be reproduced or used in any manner whatsoever without the express written permission of the author except for the use of brief quotations in a book review.

WOLF Publishing - This is us:

Two sisters, two personalities.. But only one big love!

Diving into a world of dreams..
    ...Romance, heartfelt emotions, lovable and witty characters, some humor, and some mystery! Because we want it all! Historical Romance at its best!

Visit our website to learn all about us, our authors and books!

Sign up to our mailing list to receive first hand information on new releases, freebies and promotions as well as exclusive giveaways and sneak-peeks!

WWW.WOLF-PUBLISHING.COM

Also by Fenna Edgewood

The Blakeley Manor Series

Two families, from very different worlds, are about to converge at Blakeley Manor...

Upstairs...

The Blakeley family is famed for their infinite fortune—and their infinite eccentricities. As the Blakeley siblings reunite to host a Christmas house party, they are plunged into scandal as each one forges a passionate new alliance that crosses the boundaries of all propriety.

Downstairs...

Four very different siblings—a lady's maid, a housekeeper, a gardener, and a groom—are tied together, not only by the love and loyalty they share but by dangerous secrets that could cost them not only their employment...but also their hearts.

#1 Lady Briar Weds the Scot

#2 Kiss Me, My Duke

#3 My So-Called Scoundrel

Prequel: The Countess's Christmas Groom

Lady Briar
WEDS THE SCOT

Chapter One

Blakeley Manor, August 1817

L ady Briar Blakeley had already suffered more than most young
ladies her age could have tolerated for longer than one
morning.

But Briar was not most young ladies, and come to think of it,
"endured" might have been a more apt term for what she was currently
experiencing.

The large watery brown eyes of young Mr. Percy Quintrell were
looking back accusingly at her.

Watery, not because of the unshed tears they might have held, had
Percy been a more romantic or sincere sort of young man. Rather
because of the great drams of liquor Briar presumed he had drunk
rather recently before arriving at Blakeley Manor that morning. On
second thought, she rather suspected there *were* a few unshed tears,
but they were tears of petulance and annoyance rather than any deep
feeling.

She had wounded Percy right where it hurt—in his pride. And what
was more, she could not feel sorry for it, not when he had wounded

hers by showing up in the first place and expecting her to accept his preposterous marriage proposal.

"You cannot be serious," Percy was saying loftily. "We have been all but betrothed our whole lives."

"Have we?" Briar wrinkled her nose doubtfully. "This is the first I have heard of it."

"Of course," Percy said, shaking his head reproachfully at her, which Briar could immediately see was a mistake on his part. He put a hand to his temple and grimaced. A hangover, no doubt. She could smell the liquor seeping off him and resisted the urge to give him a scolding. "Since we were small, our parents have held out the hope that someday we would wed..."

"Our parents? Mine have been gone for more than five years. I do recall them chattering on about how sweet we looked together when we were small. But we were what? Six years old, then? Younger? And as I recall, we were wearing matching outfits that day," she mused. "Perhaps that was a large part of it."

"Matching outfits had nothing to do with our parents' matrimonial expectations for us," Percy huffed. "And I, for one, have rested my hopes and dreams upon the expectation of our marriage for many years."

"Truly? You have?" Briar was doubtful. "You haven't visited Blakeley Manor in quite some time. Not since before your father passed."

"Of course, I have dreamed of it," Percy said, ignoring the other comment. "How I have pined, waiting until the time was finally right..."

"And is it right? Now, I mean?" Briar interrupted, raising her eyebrows.

"Of course," Percy snapped. "I do wish you would stop interrupting."

"I'm afraid that is one of my greatest failings, Percy. If we were to be married, you would become used to it, I'm sure," Briar said breezily. "Not that I truly believe that will happen."

"My becoming used to your interruptions? Or our marriage?" Percy huffed.

"Well, either. I certainly have no intention of marrying you, Percy.

You're drunk for one..."

Percy bolted out of his armchair as if he had been shot. "I am not. How dare you!"

"Do not shout at me in my own home if you please," Briar said mildly. "My brother is just down the hall. If I might continue? Second of all, besides smelling like the inside of a barrel of whisky, there are other impediments which make you quite an undesirable match as far as I am concerned."

Percy's face reddened. "Oh, really? Such as?"

"Well, you haven't shown the least bit of interest in me until now, have you? But I understand that since your father passed, your estate is in quite dire straits financially. I'm terribly sorry for you, Percy." More particularly, she was sorry for his mother and younger brothers. "But I don't see how drinking yourself to death or... well, carousing rather dishonorably is meant to help you fix things up. You're running through your wealth when you should be conserving it. And I certainly won't play your heiress wife, if that's what you came here hoping for."

"Carousing dishonorably?" Percy sneered. "Just what is that supposed to mean? What would a naïve chit like you know of what men get up to?"

Briar narrowed her eyes coldly. "A man? Is that what you are declaring yourself to be? Well, Percy, I have two brothers. And from what I have seen of the antics of young men, carousing is one thing. Behaving as dishonorably as you have done is quite another." She blushed, despite herself. "I am referring, of course, to the Brewer girl."

Percy had the grace to blanch.

"Yes, I've heard about that." Briar crossed her arms over her chest.

She watched with disappointment as Percy tried to brush off the words, his face quickly moving from guilt to stubborn condescension.

"Well, and so what?" he sneered. "As if men do not sow wild oats. She was a silly green girl. What did you expect me to do about her?"

"If she was a silly green girl, as you say," Briar said hotly. "Then you should not have dallied with her in the first place!"

"Bah!" Percy waved a dismissive hand. "What would you have me do? Marry the chit?"

Briar bristled. "That is not as ridiculous an idea as you appear to think. Certainly less ridiculous than the two of us marrying."

Percy stopped laughing at that and scowled. "I can see this has been a waste of my time."

"For both of us," Briar said coldly. "But as we are already conversing, why not do right by the girl, Percy? From what I understand, she is carrying your child! Do you not care about her in the least?"

Percy refused to meet her eyes. His scowl deepened. "I see what you're doing."

"Oh, yes? And what is that?"

"It's the pot calling the kettle black, isn't it? You're too good to marry me. As if the prim and proper Lady Briar hasn't made any mistakes."

Briar choked. "None so great as yours, certainly. Though of course, I am not a perfect..."

"No, you're not, are you? You're a prude. You're missish. Puritanical. You'd be lucky to have a man such as I to marry you. Who else is going to do it? I don't see them lining up at the door. And with the mouth you've developed, I can see why." Percy looked despicably triumphant. "But you won't get rid of me so easily. No, I know my rights."

Briar was becoming weary of the inane conversation. She glanced at the bell on the table beside her. Her brother, the duke, was just down the hall. Moreover, there was sure to be a footman or two not far away. Should she summon someone? Or see to Percy on her own?

He was a worm, she decided, and thus she would deal with him on her own. She did not require assistance to squash a worm.

That said, he was rather working himself into a frenzy.

"I won't let this go, you see," Percy said, pointing melodramatically. "You *shall* marry me, as was promised. I am not about to be made a fool of."

Briar snorted. "A little late for that," she muttered.

Percy took a threatening step forward. "What was that?"

"Percy," she said, standing up straighter. "You are being utterly ridiculous. Get hold of yourself. I am not going to marry you, and you *will* let this go, for there is nothing to be so worked up over. We have never and will never be engaged. I wish you luck in finding a more amiable young lady who is interested in your suit." Wished the young lady luck, that is. "Now, I bid you good day."

But Percy would not be dismissed so easily.

He stepped forward and grasped her arm rather roughly. Briar gasped in outrage.

"Let me go at once!"

"I will not. A man may lay hands on his own wife, and you will be that soon."

"You are a lunatic if you think so, Percy Quintrell," Briar replied. "And when my brother catches you..."

The door to the drawing room swung open, almost lazily.

"Catches you what?" a voice queried coldly.

"Your Grace!" Percy dropped her arm like a hot coal and whipped around to face the man standing in the doorway.

For once, Briar was rather grateful for the intimidating way her brother had of carrying himself.

Edmund Blakeley, the Duke of Dareford, was a handsome man of thirty who bore himself with confidence, which could at times be mistaken for arrogance. Tall and lanky, he dressed conservatively but stylishly, possessed a strong angular jaw that ladies quite admired, an elegant Roman nose inherited from his father, and the dark hair he shared with their elder sister, Katherine.

He was a wonderful older brother and frequently funny, warm, and affectionate. Though at the moment, his face was frigid and stern as he glared at Percy Quintrell.

"We have not seen you at Blakeley Manor in some time, Mr. Quintrell," the duke observed coolly.

"That's right, Your Grace. It has been some years. I had hoped to remedy that by catching up on lost time, as it were, with your sister today," Percy blustered. He glanced behind him as if hoping Briar would decide to play the saint and confirm his story.

Briar smiled blithely and looked past Percy at her brother.

"Percy has just been reminding me of our engagement, Dare."

The Duke of Dareford raised his eyebrows laconically. "Engagement? I did not realize we had been invited..."

"Our betrothal, I should say rather," Briar corrected. "He claims it is a longstanding one. Agreed upon by both our sets of parents. Do you recall this, Brother? Did our parents arrange my engagement, Dare? To Percy?"

Dare looked back at her expressionlessly for a moment. "Are you engaged to Percy Quintrell? Without your own knowledge?" His lips twitched. "I should think not. Mother did not even like his family all that much."

"I say!" Percy exclaimed. "That is not what I recall."

"Quiet," Dare commanded. He studied the young man with distaste. "Am I to understand that you came here this morning, hoping to coerce my sister into believing she was obligated to marry you?" He frowned. "Even if there had been some sort of family agreement between our parents, Quintrell, I assure you, I should have broken it for Briar's sake some time ago."

"What the devil is that supposed to mean?" Percy retorted.

"Your father did not leave his family in the best circumstances when he passed, from what I understand. Which is a pity for your mother and brothers' sake. Since his passing, your reputation for reck-lessness has not improved, Percy. Quite the contrary. In fact, a story has been circulating. One I shall not deign to mention in front of my sister..."

"About the village girl who is increasing, Dare? I already know of it," Briar offered helpfully. She ignored Percy's furious expression. "She is the Brewers' daughter, you know. Our tenants."

Dare nodded reluctantly. "It is a shameful thing to have done to a young woman, Percy. And to not even provide for her in her distress." He shook his head slowly. "Do you really think I would let my sister marry a man—of the landed gentry, no less—who could not or would not even take care of his own natural child?"

Percy opened his mouth, then closed it again.

"Yes, excellent decision." Dare narrowed his eyes. "I think it is best you leave now."

Percy nodded stiffly and, to Briar's relief, began to walk toward the drawing-room door. Then he stopped and looked back at them both, his expression returning to its earlier petulance. His eyes honed in on Briar.

"This isn't over, you know. You think to drag my name through the mud? How about some mud of your own? I'll see your name doesn't remain so very pure much longer, *Lady Briar*!" he swore nastily.

"What pathetic threats, Percy," the Duke of Dareford replied, his eyes very cold. "You'll do no such thing. You'll stay away from my sister if you know what is good for you, or you'll find yourself horsewhipped and pilloried before you can say Jack Robinson."

He gestured at the door, and for the first time, Briar noticed a tall and striking man standing there. Clearly, he had been watching all the proceedings. He was very tall indeed, even taller than Dare, who was over six feet.

"I'm afraid we'll have to conduct our meeting about the new greenhouse another time, Spencer," Dare said apologetically. "I don't suppose I could trouble you to show our unwanted guest the way out on your way back to the gardens?"

The man was a gardener then, Briar realized. And more than that, he was one of the Spencers! The name held special significance to Briar, for her elder sister, Kat, had recently married for the second time. And the man she had fallen in love with had been none other than one of the Blakeley Manor grooms, Ashley Spencer. Their wedding had caused quite the stir a few months back.

This must be Ashley's elder brother. Briar's curiosity was piqued. She had glimpsed the elder Spencer only briefly at the wedding breakfast, a tall man who she had somehow mistaken for being much older. But this man was no older than Dare. They had not had an opportunity to meet, which she now decided was very odd—for she routinely made it a point of learning all the Blakeley Manor servants' names— and must soon be remedied. After all, were they not family? Perhaps Mr. Spencer was a shy and reticent man, and that was why their paths had not yet crossed. Though as she watched him, she was not sure the word "shy" was applicable.

"I should like nothing better, Yer Grace," the man said, nodding his head. "Happened to be passing on my way to yer study and heard this one"—he gestured at Percy with a lazy shrug of one shoulder—"stirring up a fuss, so thought I'd see if my services might be required."

There was something about the way he spoke that was quite

unusual, Briar thought.

"Very good of you, Spencer," Dare said, nodding his appreciation.

"Come along with ye now," Spencer growled, looking darkly at Percy.

Briar felt her eyebrows raise of their own accord. Mr. Spencer was decidedly fiercer than his amiable younger brother. He had *growled*. Rather like a wild animal. There was a low burr to his speech that Briar was at first not able to put her finger on. Then it dawned on her—of course! He was a Scot!

Decidedly odd, for Mr. Spencer's younger brother had no such Scottish accent. Furthermore, while she had known her sister's new husband's brother and two sisters were employed at the Manor, this man was not what she had been expecting.

He was simply huge, for one. Mr. Spencer possessed the physique of a warrior, his body packed and powerful. His face was handsome, with a strong, square jaw framed by dark chestnut hair so long he wore it in an old-fashioned queue, a single tail bound with a leather strip. She was not used to seeing such hair on servants. It made him look rather roguish, a little like a pirate.

But then, he did not carry himself like most servants, either. He looked at Dare as if they were equals. His gaze was sharp and piercing.

"You are Scots," she exclaimed. "But I have met your brother, and he is..."

"No' a Scot, nay," Spencer said. He looked at her and frowned. Was he annoyed that she had questioned him? Delayed him in his task further? "We are brothers, aye. But half-brothers."

"Oh, I see," Briar said hurriedly, feeling herself blushing. "My apologies."

"I daresay Spencer would like to continue on his way, Briar," Dare said.

"Of course," Briar said hastily.

It was on the tip of her tongue to say "Farewell, Percy." Then she thought better of it and said nothing at all as the hulking gardener stood aside to let the sulky suitor enter the hall.

"Well, you have had quite the morning," her brother remarked, turning toward her as the drawing-room door closed.

"I suppose I have," Briar sighed. "I could have handled Percy, you know. I was just about to throw him out myself."

"Were you?" Dare smiled. "Well, I'm sure you could have managed him. Nevertheless, I was passing and heard raised voices." He frowned. "Really, you should not have met with him alone at all, Briar. What were you thinking?"

"He is a childhood acquaintance. I thought nothing of it. Really, Dare, do not scold me. It is not my fault he behaved so ungentlemanly!"

"No, of course not," Dare agreed. But his frown remained. "Still, you ought to have called for me or that lady's maid you are forever dismissing. You should know better than to meet with a young man alone."

"He isn't a young man. He is just Percy! Our neighbor. The boy I played with all through my childhood. Just a silly boy. Until this morning, I had never even considered him as a suitor," Briar said defensively. "I had no idea he was going to start in with all that nonsense about being engaged."

Dare sighed. "I suppose that is fair enough. It was rather... bizarre."

"Very bizarre," Briar agreed. She hesitated, then added, "Do you suppose he is so desperate for funds, Dare?"

"Do not go feeling sorry for him now, Briar," Dare said, warningly. "His mess of an estate is not your affair."

"No, but he has a mother and young brothers, as you said. If he remains on his present course and becomes a spendthrift and a wastrel, then they are at his mercy."

"His father is to blame for whatever poor circumstances his mother and brothers find themselves in, not Percy," Dare said with a sigh. "But you are correct. As the eldest son, it is his responsibility to see to those under his care with maturity and fortitude. His time for playing the rich coxcomb should have been at an end long ago." He scowled. "And no matter what, there is no excuse for not taking care of... Well, we need not speak of it."

"Oh, please." Briar waved a hand. "You know, I might at least visit the girl. After all, she is the daughter of one of our tenants."

Dare's expression hardened. "Indeed. Until you mentioned it

earlier, I am afraid I had not realized that."

Briar nodded. "They must be very worried about her. I'm sure she thought Percy would provide for her in the event that she should become... well."

"Yes. Well." Dare ran a hand through his dark hair. "Very well, pay a visit to the family. Do what you can. We can at least take care of the girl, even if Percy will not."

"Thank you, Dare," Briar said, brightening. "I'll go very soon."

Wren Spencer had no desire to become a footman, yet here he was playing the part of one.

However, the duke was an excellent employer and an honorable man. What was more, Wren could relate to the protectiveness of an older brother trying to do right by a younger sister.

And lastly, this young man was an arse.

Therefore, it gave Wren some measure of pleasure to throw—nay, *escort*—Mr. Percy Quintrell out of Blakeley Manor and onto the front drive where his barouche waited.

And that was where the matter should have ended.

But the young fool could not keep his trap shut.

He managed to remain silent as he tromped behind Wren all the way to the front door. But as soon as he stepped outside, his tongue loosened, and all his miserable self-indulgence began to pour out.

"Your duke is a damned fool. Do you know that, footman?"

Wren ignored him and said nothing.

"What is more," Quintrell continued, "his sister is an even greater fool. Passing up an opportunity to get married! You'd think they were lining up at the door for her." He paused. "As if I were so desperate to get leg-shackled to the wench. They sing her praises as if she were something remarkable, but she's just an ordinary girl. Rather plain, one might say."

Here, Wren most certainly disagreed. He was no expert on dukes, but certainly a duke's younger sister was unlikely to suffer for proposals. Especially when she was not hard on the eyes. But there was no point in saying so. This young man clearly believed himself the only expert on the matter.

"Why, she's a bit of muslin like any other bit. And I've had my bits if you take my meaning."

This was obviously a pathetic attempt to inspire Wren's admiration. But Wren did not admire men who made a sport of conquering women. Nor did he appreciate hearing the virtue of the young lady of the house disparaged by an arrogant whelp.

Despite his best efforts, Wren felt his temper beginning to rise.

"She's beneath my touch. I'll say it frankly. She's no better than a village light-skirt," the young man continued. "I should count myself lucky to have escaped, really."

Wren ground to a halt.

The young gentleman ground right into him.

Wren waited a moment for Quintrell to take a step back, then turned.

"Ye would do well," he said slowly, "to guard yer tongue and watch yer words, young sir."

For a moment, Quintrell only stared. Evidently, he was not used to being addressed in such a tone by a servant.

Then the young pup sneered. "Or what?"

Wren would not be baited so easily.

"Let us get ye to yer carriage," he said simply, turning around again and resuming his walk across the smooth, white pebbled drive.

"Briar has you wrapped around her little finger, the little trollop," the young man burst out, evidently deciding he would push his luck with Wren since he had not been sufficiently set down by the duke and his sister.

Wren stopped and turned back. "I would recommend ye refrain from speaking the young lady's name again, ye wee numpty. I willna ask a second time."

The young man sneered nastily. "Oh, so she's your lady, too, is—"

Wren decked him.

He hit him in the nose, not the jaw. This was intentionally done, for Wren decided the sight of Quintrell's own blood might have more of an impact. Sure enough, the young man began to howl, clutching his nose as the blood dripped onto the pebbled drive and hopping about in a way that forced Wren to bite the inside of his cheek to prevent himself from laughing.

"You've bloodied me!" Quintrell shrieked. "You've wounded me! You! A damned servant! I'll have your head for this, I will. Oh, you have no idea who you have made an enemy of today, you—"

"Get in yer carriage, or that willna be the last of yer blood ye'll see today," Wren instructed, marching toward the conveyance and gesturing to the driver's seat.

The young man eyed him nervously. "Y-you'll hit me again?"

"With great pleasure," Wren muttered, too low to be heard. More loudly he said, "I hope that shallna be necessary, for ye're departing. Immediately. If ye do so with great haste, perhaps I willna tell the duke the sort of language ye were using regarding his younger sister. If ye think yer nose hurts right now, ye have no idea how much more it will sting when ye've been dealt a blow with all the force of an elder brother's fury behind it."

Of course, he should not have hit the young gentleman. But he was *not* a footman. And he highly doubted the duke would have done any less. Nor that he would have disapproved.

Wren would never have to see the clot-heid again. After this, he would return to his work in the gardens. To peace and quiet.

Young Mr. Percy Quintrell was clambering hastily into the barouche. He picked up the reins and seemed to be about to use them but, of course, could not help but try to get one more nasty word in.

"You'll pay for this, whoever you are. I'll see that you're sacked. I'll see that your name is mud from here to... to... Scotland! You'll never work again. You'll live the rest of your days begging. You'll—"

"I highly doubt that," Wren interrupted. "Ye really must stop making threats ye canna see carried out, lad. It is unmanly. Now get."

Stepping forward, he gave the horse pulling the barouche a stimulating slap on the rear.

Quintrell yelped as the barouche started forward at a breakneck speed.

Wren watched until the vehicle was well out of sight, then began walking back to the formal gardens.

Chapter Two

To some, a garden was a thing of beauty. An opportunity to commune with nature. Or simply to enjoy the fresh air. Nothing more.

To others, they were expressions of the political. And thus, an English garden could communicate a sense of freedom, while there were those who saw political despotism in the stark formality of a French-styled garden.

An English landscape garden was supposed to reflect the natural beauty around it and thus imbue not only the picturesque, but a romantic wildness. In the last decade or so, trends had reversed, and now some were inclined to a more formal style.

To some, gardens were a controversial subject. The very epitome of what constituted beauty could be defined in them. Was the perfect country house landscape frigid and formal as some proclaimed? Or was it the removal of artifice, the reclaiming of passionate nature?

Wren did not really give a fig one way or the other.

A garden was a garden. What was beautiful was what lay within it. Even a simple pasture full of sheep could conjure the "picturesque" as far as Wren was concerned.

The very act of being out of doors with the wind in your face, the scent of fresh heather and moss, and all the other growing things reminded you that you were alive and part of the blossoming, wild world.

That was a garden.

Besides, Wren was not the architect of the gardens at Blakeley Manor. He was merely their keeper.

He would be the first to admit he was very fortunate to be employed in such a bonny place. The outside world had always spoken to his heart. He walked daily through open fields and wooded areas, pruning the hedges along winding paths, maintaining a variety of ornamental and formal gardens.

Someday, he would care for his own domain. Wherever that would be.

He would not be a simple gardener forever. This was a resting stop along the way to something else.

But to what, he could not yet say. His sister Laurel chided that he should not be at Blakeley Manor in the first place. That he should have returned to Scotland long ago.

But that would have been too simple. And the Spencers could not do anything simply.

No, his younger brother, Ash, was proof enough of that.

Why, the mad lad had gone and done the most incredible thing of all. He had married the duke's older, widowed sister. Now Ash Spencer resided in a country estate away from his older brother and two sisters. There would be visits, of course. But his destiny had changed. He was no longer the simple young groom he had so recently been. He was a father to an adopted son. A husband to a former countess.

And Wren? His destiny was a tangled thing. It lay sprawled before him, the possibilities muddled.

Now Ash had gone and complicated Wren's present. After all, his employer was now also his brother-in-law, was he not? And yet, he was the duke's gardener. His sister, Laurel, the duke's housekeeper.

Wren shook his head, a feeling of annoyance returning. He hoisted a shovel from a row of tools in the storage shed he had entered and began walking down the path toward a flower bed that needed turning.

Ash may have joined the duke's family by means of marriage, but as far as Wren was concerned, the Blakeleys had their world and the Spencers another. The two would not meet again.

"Mr. Spencer?"

Wren could not help it. He dropped the iron shovel he was carrying and let out an oath as it fell right on his booted foot.

"Lady Briar," he said between gritted teeth. "I wasna expecting to see ye. Again. Today. Was there something ye required assistance with?"

He glanced at her as the pain in his foot began to fade.

She was a bonny lass, he admitted to himself. He could see why that young fool Quintrell had not wanted to relinquish his claim upon her, baseless though it was. It had been a long time since Wren had even noticed a woman, but even he had to acknowledge Lady Briar Blakeley had a soft, elegant beauty.

She was the sort of girl who was striking without having to make any effort to be so. In contrast to her older siblings who had the cool, dark good looks of the family, Briar, well, *glowed.* Everything about her was warm and vibrant. With her mane of dark copper hair and her gold-dusted complexion and those rosy lips, she reminded Wren of nothing so much as a wild rose. Sharp and sweet.

He glowered down at his foot. Nothing good came from such thoughts. Aye, admire the lass, he told himself. From a vast distance.

Sharp and sweet would break the heart. He knew that well.

"Mr. Spencer, I am ever so sorry!" the girl was exclaiming, looking with a horrified expression at his foot.

"It's nothing," he said shortly.

"Well, I am glad it is not too painful. I apologize for distracting you from your work." She hesitated, biting her lower lip.

It was a rosy, soft thing, that lip. Plump and luscious. Reminding Wren of the full petals of a red rose.

"I suppose you are very busy with your... gardening tasks." He watched her suckle the lower lip again.

"Good Lord," Wren muttered impatiently. More loudly, "Aye, about to do some digging in the herb garden." He hoisted the shovel and held it aloft as a reminder of what she had interrupted. "If there is nothing else, my lady."

"Of course, certainly," she murmured, her face coloring awkwardly. "That is. I had hoped. I had thought..."

"Och, spit it out then," he snapped and saw her face fall. He was reminded of how very young a lady she was. Her expression was pitiful in its disappointment, and he felt an unexpected pang of remorse.

Clearing his throat, he tried to gentle his voice. "If there is something ye require or wish for me to do, ye need only ask, my lady. Surely ye ken this. I am at yer disposal."

Her face perked up. "Well, that's just it, really. I'm not your 'lady' anymore, really, am I? I am your *sister*. We are family now. Are we not?" Her face had lit up as she spoke, and she smiled radiantly at him.

A bonny rose, aye. But he could not have a bloody blooming rose following him about.

He understood her train of thought but decided to be obtuse.

"I'm sure I dinna comprehend yer meaning, my lady," he said stiffly. "Now, if there is nothing else..."

"But your brother—your younger brother Ash—is married to my sister," she interrupted eagerly. "How much plainer can it be? We are united, you and I, by the bonds of... Well, by their bond of... Oh dear, I am not saying this properly." She put a hand to her cheek. It was a pretty, dainty gesture for a pretty, dainty girl like Briar Blakeley to make.

A gesture that reminded Wren how out of place she was, standing there with him. He was covered with dirt from the gardens, his work boots coated in muck. While her hand was so smooth, so white.

She did not belong out here with him, in the muck. In the dirt.

Two families united by marriage? He thought of his own complicated family history. Two such dissimilar families.

While he was happy his younger brother had made such a happy match, that did not mean he had anything in common with these English Blakeleys. No, they were as dissimilar as could be.

Even his sisters seemed to agree with that much.

"Aye, they made an odd pairing, my lady, but I wish them the best. But that doesna mean that ye owe me, or anyone in my family, anything beyond what ye already bestow. Employment."

"Oh yes, that does rather make it awkward, I suppose." Briar looked distressed. "Our relationship. Employer and employee. Oh dear, yes."

Wren stifled a groan. "There is no relationship, my lady. I have my duties, just as ye must have yers. Mine lay out here. In the herb garden. Yers lay in the big house..." Where he hoped she would return after taking the not very subtle hint.

"Well, in fact, at times they lay outside of the big house," she said brightly. "Indeed, I came here not only to remind you of our connection, which I have done very, very badly, I know. But also to see if you might lend me your assistance. Though it does fall outside of your usual realm of expertise. I suppose I might have simply asked a footman but..."

"What is the task, my lady?" Wren said impatiently. "What do ye need? A new flower arrangement for yer room? Something for the front hall? A flower for yer hat?"

"Oh no, nothing like that." Briar waved a hand and gave a tinkling happy laugh. He flinched. This was unbearable. The lass was as fresh and pretty as a daisy and seemed just as oblivious to her own charms as a garden flower was, too.

She smelled much better than a daisy, however. Daisies were highly overrated flowers. When you got up close to one, they smelled disappointingly like manure. No, Briar Blakeley smelled like something delicious. Like something you wouldn't mind popping straight into your mouth. Like cake baked with vanilla and cinnamon. Or a confectionary's shop.

She was sweet as honey, probably twice as naive, and something about her was making his blood pound and his loins tighten. The sooner he could get rid of her the better.

"I need an escort," she was saying. "I mean, I don't need one. I don't think I do. But I realize that Dare will demand I have one, and if I don't, he'll make a dreadful fuss should he find out. So why not kill two birds with one stone, I thought, and ask you to escort me and give us a chance to get to know one another a little better? Of course, I wish to become acquainted with your sisters, too. But I did not think Dare would approve of my escort being anything but male and so... Well, do you see?"

Wren could only stare.

"No, I don't suppose you do. Truly, I am ordinarily much more composed," Briar said with a sigh. "I believe Percy's visit threw me off for the entire day. Listen to me, blathering away and causing you to crush your toes with that shovel and now taking up far too much of your precious time and..."

Quintrell!

Wren had nearly forgotten about young Percy Quintrell and his nastiness.

"Och, aye," he murmured, running a hand over his face with a sigh. "I suppose that would throw anyone off their day, having a wee *bampot* like that burst in on them."

Briar looked at him with interest. "I don't know what a 'bampot' is. But I agree with your general sentiment."

She hesitated, then began to bite her lip. Wren suppressed a groan. He was not sure how much more he could stand of the sight of her nibbling on that luscious appendage. He felt a familiar stirring in his breeches and quickly shifted his stance, hoisting the shovel over his shoulder.

"Aye, verra well then," he grumbled. He began to turn away to stow the shovel in a nearby shed.

"What does that mean?" Briar exclaimed. "Does that mean you'll go with me?"

Wren glowered down at his shovel. "I said 'aye' did I no'? Best get on with it, then. I'm sure ye dinna want to stand here all day yammering when there's something important ye need doing. Let me just put this away, and we'll be off." He paused, then turned to look at her. "What did ye say ye needed an escort for again exactly, my lady?"

"Oh, I didn't say. Or did I? I don't think I did..."

Wren felt a smile starting. He quickly smothered it. "No, ye didna."

"Ah, I didn't think so. Well, it shouldn't take too long. We're going to see the Brewers. You're familiar with their cottage, I'm sure?"

"Aye, Walt Brewer. Emma is his wife. And they have a daughter... I've no' seen the lass in a year or more. I suppose she's grown now."

"Yes, Bessie Brewer. She is about my age. She was living in the village for a spell, working at the tavern, but she's home again. She's going to have a baby, you know." Briar's face became a little flushed as she spoke.

Wren understood only too well. "A baby, ye say? And the father wouldna happen to be a certain no-good, yellow-bellied..."

"Yes, it's Percy," Briar said. "And as he has no plans to do anything for the girl, Dare and I certainly will."

Wren stared at her a moment, indecisively, before speaking. "It seems to me that ye might want to keep a fair amount of distance between yerself and that young man. As well as anyone who has had anything to do with him. I hope ye'll excuse me saying so, but he's a nasty piece of work, my lady."

"Oh, you've already called him 'yellow-bellied'," Briar said cheerfully, not seeming at all put out by his unsolicited advice. "So, I don't think 'nasty piece of work' is much worse. And I agree with you, mostly. Of course, I wish to stay far away from Percy. But he is staying far away from Bessie, you see. He's not helping her at all. I've asked about, even just today, amongst our own servants. The ones who know the Brewers." She flushed angrily. "He's utterly abandoned her, Mr. Spencer. He won't do a thing for her. She's carrying his child and has had to return to her parents. From what I hear, they'll support her, but they're ashamed and embarrassed. It shouldn't be this way."

"Aye, poor lass," Wren muttered. That was the way of it. The woman paid for the pleasure of two. It was not fair. "'Tis a sin to treat a woman in such a way."

"I wholeheartedly concur. So come with me then, Mr. Spencer. You may wait in the carriage if the sight of Bessie will distress you in any way. But at least I'll not have to worry about Dare scolding me later, and I won't have to explain myself all over again to a footman. Oh, please, say you will, Mr. Spencer?"

"Distress myself?" Wren's face scrunched up. "It willna distress me to see a young lass who's to have a bairn. The shame isna hers, as far as I'm concerned, but the mon who willna marry her."

Briar was staring at him with fascination. "Your Scots accent grows much heavier when you are angry, Mr. Spencer. Has anyone ever told you that?"

Wren frowned and grunted. "Aye, it may have been mentioned. Once or twice."

"The shovel, Mr. Spencer?" Briar nodded toward the instrument. "I suppose you must stow it away first. Will you meet me at the carriage in front of the house when you are ready? I'll ask for it to be brought around now."

She began to step away, then paused, and looked back at him. Even though he refused to meet her eye, he could tell she was smiling. "And thank you, Mr. Spencer. Family or not, I appreciate the assistance."

"Aye, well, ye may as well call me Wren," he said, then immediately wished he hadn't.

But from the glow on her face, he could tell she was only too pleased to acquiesce.

"Of course! Then you must call me 'Briar' rather than 'my lady,'" she said quickly.

This he would certainly not be doing, but he made a noncommittal motion with his head and stalked off to the shed.

<hr />

Well, this was not the auspicious start between herself and Mr. Spencer that Briar had been hoping for. But that was her own fault, wasn't it? Her dratted, twisting tongue seemed to be constantly muddled today.

Still, things seemed to be coming together. He had said he would come, hadn't he?

He had. In that delightful, deep Scottish brogue of his.

But that isn't all you find delightful about the man, is it now, Briar? a voice in her head teased. He was a compelling man in other ways.

She had never before thought of "huge" and "hulking" as particularly complimentary terms for a man—nor ones which would send the most delicate parts beneath her petticoats quivering. Yet, there was something about Mr. Wren Spencer which had just this effect. He was a strange contradiction of hulking maleness and male beauty. His jewel-blue eyes and dark-brown hair framed a tautly muscled face that might have belonged to some ancient warrior from a story.

But he was not her prince from a fairy tale. She did not even want him to be. He was her brother-in-law. She wished to show his family kindness, show them that the Blakeleys embraced their newfound connection by marriage rather than ignoring or shying away from it. If her mother were there, Briar knew she would have been doing the same.

The Spencers might be servants by trade, but she would bet her life they were anything but common.

After all, what little Briar was already privileged to know about Wren's sister, Laurel Spencer, would cause quite a stir from London to Paris should it ever become common knowledge.

And Kat Blakeley, Briar's elder sister, had married Ash Spencer because he was no common man. He may have been a simple groom working in the Blakeley stables, but in him, she had found the hero of her heart. He was a better father to Briar's little nephew Oliver than his own had ever been. Briar would never in a thousand years discount the transformation Ash had wrought, not only in her elder sister, but in her sister's son.

Thus, she was determined to show the Spencers her appreciation. For had not their youngest brother brought her sister the greatest happiness of all?

Gratitude was all it was, plain and simple. And fine, perhaps a little curiosity.

But in the end, while Wren Spencer may be a captivating man, he was a man, plain and simple. Though she knew many underestimated her because of her youth, Briar had dealt with her fair share of men. In spite of Percy's bluster and insults, his was not her first proposal, nor did she think it would be her last.

No, this interaction had been an anomaly. An awkward anomaly.

Going forward, Briar would handle Wren Spencer with grace and aplomb. She would cultivate a careful, casual friendship and then hand him off to Dare.

Dear Dare, who was more reserved and more reluctant to encourage a relationship between the two families, but who, ultimately, would do as she begged. Perhaps he would even find he had more in common with Mr. Spencer than he realized. Why, they could lament the annoyance of younger sisters, for one!

Smiling, Briar marched toward the carriage, feeling more composed. She had dressed for the outing in a simple but stylish dress of soft brown French cambric. Overtop, she wore a pale brown pelisse, ornamented in gold embroidery with gold Maltese buttons. Brown kid half boots decorated with tassels and soft yellow leather gloves completed the ensemble. With her freckles and dark red hair—those trying to flatter her tended to describe it as "titian" or "copper"—the earthy tones which would have been plain on another young lady were warm and flattering.

At least, she hoped they were. And that was enough of that. She would not think of her own appearance or the effect it may or may not have again that afternoon, she decided. Briar took the proffered hand of the footman and clambered up into the carriage where she saw, with relief, Mr. Spencer already sat waiting. She would think only of poor Bessie Brewer, who was, after all, the reason for their outing in the first place.

And with that, her jaw clenched a little as the carriage gave a lurch and started forward.

"Feeling unwell, Lady Briar? We can always continue the errand another day," Mr. Spencer said, leaning forward far too eagerly.

"Not at all, Mr. Spencer," Briar replied smoothly. There. That was better already. No stuttering or stumbling. "I simply had the misfortune to recall the purpose of our endeavor and to recall the unfortunate fact of Mr. Percy Quintrell's existence."

For a moment, she thought Mr. Spencer was trying to smile.

"Ah, in that case, yer expression makes perfect sense. Ye looked as if ye were about to become violently ill." He nodded sagely and settled back, gazing out the window.

"Indeed," she murmured.

Now that they were here together, she had to admit she felt oddly shy. Was it the confines of the carriage? She stole a glance at her companion. Mr. Spencer had cleaned up nicely. He wore a simple shirt of white muslin and suspenders, covered by a plain dark-wool jacket as the day was cool. His trousers were dark gray wool and exquisitely fitted...

Stop looking at them, Briar, she chided. *Stop looking. Full stop.*

She swiveled her head toward the window and racked her brain for something to say to break the silence.

Paying him a compliment on his presentation would likely not go over well. Wren Spencer seemed the kind of man who would prickle under flattery, rather than puff up from it like the Percy Quintrell sort.

"How are the gardens?" she blurted out lamely. "Coming along, I mean. How are the gardens coming along this season?" Oh dear, the awkwardness was back.

"This season? High summer?" Mr. Spencer quirked a well-shaped, bushy brown eyebrow. "Did ye have a particular garden in mind, Lady Briar, or would ye like a report on all of them?"

"I said nothing of a report." Briar blushed furiously. "And I thought we had done away with the formalities of such titles."

"Aye, and yet ye have been calling me 'Mr. Spencer' since ye climbed into the carriage," he said mildly.

"Tell me of your favorite garden," Briar said suddenly, latching on to a way to force him to speak. "Which one do you enjoy above all?"

"The herb garden," he answered, not taking the time to think it over.

"The herb garden?" She scrunched up her nose. "The kitchen garden you mean?"

"Aye, the one with all the green things that are so good to eat," he replied, looking amused. "Why? Does that surprise ye?"

"I suppose I had thought you would choose one that required careful cultivation, like one of the pleasure gardens. The Italian garden with the pergola passageway. Or the Indian one with that exquisite little folly, perhaps."

"Aye, but they are just that—for pleasure. The herb garden is practical. The food it produces feeds yer household. Provides medicines and seasoning. Cabbages and cauliflowers may no' fit yer idea of romance, Lady Briar, but they are what a person needs to live. To me, that is a more noble thing to produce than all the bonny lilies and delphiniums for a bouquet to fill a vase in some rich man's hall."

Briar was quiet for a moment. "Is that all you see us as? Rich people whose vases must be filled?"

Mr. Spencer shifted on the carriage bench. "I meant no offense, my lady."

"Call me Briar," she practically snapped. "I know you did not. I am simply asking."

He gave her a sardonic look. "Well, ye *are* rich. And ye do have many vases, do ye no'?"

"I have no idea how many vases I have," she burst out before realizing how comical this sounded. She began to laugh.

"Let us begin again, Mr. Spencer. Wren, I mean." Her heart fluttered slightly as the name passed her lips, but she pressed on, refusing to blush again before him that day. "I can see why an herb garden is a fine thing in your eyes. I suppose if I had given it more consideration, if I had been including the kitchen garden in my idea of what constituted the gardens to which you tended, then I may have listed it as my favorite first as well. It does seem like a much more useful thing to feed and care for people. Although, of course, humans need beauty, too. God made the delphiniums as well as the cauliflowers, lest you forget." She wagged a finger teasingly at him, hoping to elicit a smile.

Instead, he nodded seriously. "Man needs beauty, once his belly has been filled. He canna consider the latter without the former."

Before she could stop herself, she said, "That sounds as if it comes from a man who has known true hunger before."

There was silence.

"I have. Before."

"Were you... in the wars, Mr. Spencer?" Briar asked tentatively. She had not even considered this, but now it seemed a likely explanation.

"Aye. I was. At Waterloo and battles before that one, before ye ask, aye. I dinna wish to discuss it with ye, however," Mr. Spencer said shortly, turning back to the window. "Suffice it to say, there were no herbs with us when we needed them, then."

"I... understand," Briar murmured awkwardly. She was trying to form some apology when she realized they were slowing down. "I believe we have reached the Brewers."

"Aye," Wren grunted. He did not seem in quite the right mood for a social visit.

"You do not have to come inside with me, Mr. Spencer," she said decisively, sliding across the seat. "I will not be too long. Your presence was only required for my protection. A silly thing, I realize. I am sorry to have inconvenienced you. You need not concern yourself for me more. Rest here and..." She forced herself to stop blathering, closed her mouth firmly, and slipped down and out, wondering if she had only served to offend him more by leaving him behind.

She forced her attention to the more important task at hand— putting the Brewers at ease. For if she was correct, they were all at home and presently engaged in staring at her from out of their very clean front windows.

She walked slowly from the lane where the carriage was parked and swung open the wooden gate to the Brewers' yard.

The cottage yard was full of activity. Chickens ran to and fro while a small dog jumped around, yapping happily at its own tail. There was a calico cat sunning itself on top of a barrel. Briar smiled as the dog collided with her ankles, sat down, and looked up in puzzlement.

The cottage itself was a very homey-looking dwelling, with a thatched roof and a little wooden porch that had been added on for extra space and comfort. Of course, Briar knew that her brother, the Duke of Dareford, was an extremely conscientious landowner, who saw to maintenance and repairs for all his tenant cottages. Even so, the Brewers had clearly made improvements of their own. The yard was well swept and tidy, with flowers planted in window boxes and a garden out back. The house had been freshly painted and someone—perhaps Bessie herself?—had even drawn blue flowers upon the front door.

Everything about the yard and exterior of the house suggested a happy family. Or at least, a family that had been happy up until recently.

Briar walked up to the front door and knocked.

She could hear a murmur of voices from behind the door and did her best to wait quietly and patiently. Would they answer? Did they not wish to see her? Perhaps they did not wish to see anyone.

The voices grew a little louder. Clearly her presence was causing some kind of commotion.

And then there was the marching of feet, and the door swung open.

"Good day to you, my lady," a young woman's voice rang out.

Bessie Brewer stood before her, a small smile on her lips, her hands on her hips.

The girls were of the same age, and Briar had seen Bessie many times before at village events and festivals.

But now those hips had changed quite dramatically, and it was all Briar could do not to let out a gasp of shock. The rumor mill had not prepared Briar for just how far along Bessie was with child. Her belly was swelled out past the door. She must be very near to her time, indeed.

"Thank you," Briar breathed, trying to hide her surprise. "It is very good to see you, Bessie. Is your family at home?"

"It is all right to stare. I know I am as big as a house," Bessie said, trying to sound cheerful. But Briar caught sight of the dark red spots on her cheeks. She was embarrassed.

Impulsively, Briar leaned toward the other girl and grabbed her hand, squeezing it affectionately. "It is true. You are gigantic," she said, matching Bessie's cheery tone. "You must be very excited to finally see your little one. What a wonderful occasion that will be."

Bessie's eyebrows went up, but she gave Briar an appreciative squeeze in return. "I'm not sure how wonderful my Ma and Pa think it will be, with another mouth to feed, but I cannot say I won't be glad to have my ankles return to ordinary size," she said lightly, turning to face the older couple who stood awkwardly behind her in the little cottage sitting room.

"Mr. and Mrs. Brewer, how lovely to see you," Briar said, taking another step across the threshold. "I'm only sorry it has taken me so long to visit. I must confess, I had not realized how far along your Bessie was. And here I thought I was coming with gifts early, only to find I am late!" She smiled at them both.

Mrs. Brewer returned the smile with a small one of her own before glancing at her husband, whose expression remained doleful.

He was an older gray-haired man of about sixty who Dare had told Briar had been a hard worker all his life. Bessie was their only daughter. Their son, Matthew, had been killed in the wars with the French.

Bessie was to have been their pride and joy, then. They must have had many hopes riding on her. Not least, that she would marry and help to care for them in their old age, Briar suddenly realized with a pang.

"I have brought some things for the baby, Bessie," Briar began. "And my brother and I had hoped you might also allow us to make a contribution of another kind..."

"Accepting charity now, that's what we're being reduced to!" Mr. Brewer suddenly exploded. "Our daughter destroyin' our good name, our reputations. Bringing shame upon this family. Oh, if our Matthew could see us now. If he could see his sister now..."

The outburst was quite unexpected and very loud. Briar took a step back but found there was nowhere to go. She stepped right into something hard and firm.

"Hold on, lass," Mr. Spencer said in a low voice. "Have patience with the poor man. Miserable though he may be, have patience."

Briar could only nod, so shocked was she to realize he was there. He must have followed her from the carriage after all.

"Ye left behind yer wee baskets," he said in her ear. His voice was gruff and deep. She could feel his chest rumbling against her back. "I thought ye might need them."

"Oh, yes," Briar said faintly. "That I certainly do."

"Ye might need some other help, too, methinks," he muttered. More loudly, he spoke to the room, "Ye have a braw place here, Mr. Brewer. A fine cottage. I'm sure yer missus makes a fine cup of tea, too. I dinna suppose ye would do Lady Briar and I the honor of sharing one with us now?"

He stepped past Briar, carrying the baskets which he held aloft, as if showing he came in peace, then laid them gently down on the kitchen table.

"We ken ye've had some trouble, sir," he said, looking at Mr. and Mrs. Brewer with gentleness in his eyes. "But trouble befalls us all, does it no'? I've had my share of trouble in my day. Matthew, did ye say yer boy's name was? He's no' here now. Am I to take it he fell while soldiering?"

Mr. Brewer had quietened while Wren spoke. Now he nodded. His face was strained and pale. Briar felt a stab of sympathy for the man. Surely, he was not so filled with shame for his daughter, or she would not still be here, would she?

"Waterloo, was it now?"

Another nod.

"Aye, I was there meself," Wren went on. "Wretched day. Wretched place. An honorable mon yer Matthew must have been. I'm sure he drew great comfort thinking of ye and his mother and his sister." He glanced over at where Bessie stood quietly by. She had said nothing since her father's tirade began.

"We love our Bessie, we do," Mrs. Brewer said suddenly, as if understanding Wren's thoughts.

Briar watched as she crossed quickly over to her daughter and wrapped an arm around her waist.

"Our Bessie is a good girl. No matter what they say," Mrs. Brewer said with a little tearful hiccup. "She's a good, helpful girl."

"Of course she is," Wren said. "What a blessing to have a daughter in the house. And soon a bonny bairn, too. Perhaps it will be a boy. Ye might even honor yer son and call it Matthew."

"A cursed bairn," Mr. Brewer said woefully. "A child without a father."

Bessie gave a little sob at this, and Briar shot daggers from her eyes at Mr. Brewer. Was this what poor Bessie had to put up with every day? Cast aside by the young man she must have believed loved her, only to have to return to a father who made her feel shame?

"Nay, no' cursed," Wren Spencer said firmly. "And the child shall have a father. Ye will be its father, will ye no', Mr. Brewer? Just because Bessie's lad turned out to be a craven knave doesna mean the child will be the same. Look at ye. Look at yer fine wife and yer fine daughter. The Brewer name is what matters. Put shame aside. Think only of the future and the child. A child is a blessing."

"A blessing we cannot afford even if we would embrace it," Mr. Brewer said, sounding less angry than pitiful.

"Aye, then ye'd best listen to Lady Briar here, hadn't ye? If she has a plan, charity or not, listen."

"The man who should be providing for Bessie and her child is not here, but I am, Mr. Brewer," Briar said quietly, shooting Wren Spencer a thankful look. "My brother and I are thoroughly disgusted that Percy Quintrell is not doing what he ought. Please, Mr. Brewer, you know the Blakeley family is better off in the world than many—through no doing of ours. It is such a small thing for us, but it will help in what is perhaps such a large way for Bessie and the child. Won't you allow it?"

"Aye, he'll allow it because he loves his family. He's a provider, is Mr. Brewer. Men provide for their family. Ye've worked hard all yer life, Mr. Brewer. Now listen to Lady Briar, so when the bairn comes along, ye may enjoy yer blessing and no' feel this bitterness in yer heart, eh?" Wren said, not taking his eyes off the other man.

Mr. Brewer nodded slowly. "Of course, of course. I am..." He cleared his throat. "My apologies to you, Lady Briar. I don't know what came over me."

"Please, think nothing of it," Briar said stiffly. Though it was Bessie and Mrs. Brewer she longed to speak with alone.

Wren Spencer must have read her thoughts. "Come along with me now, Mr. Brewer, will ye? Show me that garden ye have out back. Are those cabbages ye have growing? How are the rabbits enjoying them?"

He hit on just the right thing. Briar hid a smile as Mr. Brewer immediately burst into a lively sermon on the evils of rabbits, and the two men swept out the door, leaving Briar to sit down at the kitchen table with Bessie and Mrs. Brewer over a nice cup of tea.

"I know you must think me such a fool, milady," Bessie said awhile into their womanly chatter about childbirth, the best garments for a newborn, and names for the little one. "But I really did think he loved me." She looked up with a proud expression on her pretty face. "Nay, more than that. I thought we would wed. I would not have given him my maidenhead if I had not." She blushed and put her head down quickly.

"It is none of my business, truly, Bessie," Briar said quickly. "I am not here to judge you. Only to help where I can. I know you don't want the help, but I am so glad you will accept it—for my own sake and my brother's. We feel better knowing you and your family will be cared for. And please know, you always will be. As long as there is a Blakeley at Blakeley Manor." She gave a little laugh. "And I think it is safe to say that will be for a very long time."

Then she sobered. "But I am sorry for what Percy has put you and your family through, Bessie. What he did was so very wrong. To lie to you. To betray you. It turns my stomach to know a man who calls himself a 'gentleman' could so easily do such a thing."

"Aye, that is what I told my husband," Mrs. Brewer said softly. "The blame is more on him than my Bessie. Of course she would fall for such a young man. Of course she would have no cause not to believe him. Why would he lie?" She shook her head sadly. "I suppose it is a sport of his. I pity the other girls he gets in such a way."

"Aye, I pity them," Bessie said bitterly. "But I pity me the most."

"You have a baby to look forward to," Briar said softly. "I know it will be hard work, too. But a new baby's smile... Well, I have heard it is the most beautiful thing to a mother."

"Aye, you and Matthew had such beautiful smiles," Mrs. Brewer agreed, her face sad. She tried to brighten. "You still do, of course, my Bessie."

"You have a future here at Blakeley Manor, always, Bessie. Please, remember that," Briar said.

She rose to go. "But in the meantime, I hope the rest of your confinement goes well. Please send word up to the manor should you need anything. Anything at all."

She walked back out to the yard and stood waiting for Wren, her heart still heavy.

A hand touched her arm. "Ready to go, my lady?"

She nodded, not even bothering to complain about his formality. She felt drained. Tired. It had been a long day, though it was ending better than it had started.

Back in the carriage, they drove in silence.

"You were very kind to Mr. Brewer," she said finally. "I don't know what I should have done, what I should have said, if you had not been there. You knew just what to say."

"It was nothing." Wren waved a hand. "Men like that... Well, he's a harder mon than I'd like to see, but he means well." He met Briar's eyes. "He does love the girl. He is harsh, but I think... Well, I think it will be all right."

"That's all we can hope for, isn't it?" Briar asked softly.

Their eyes stayed locked for a moment. Both thinking about the Brewers.

Briar felt an odd sense of affinity. They had departed on this quest together. He had helped her through it. Such a simple task, but it had been a success because he had been with her.

"I'm glad I—" she began, but just then the carriage came to an abrupt halt.

She flew across the bench and would have fallen—or worse, injured herself—had not Mr. Spencer caught her by the arms and stopped her trajectory.

He settled her quickly on the bench beside him, but his gaze was on the window. "What the devil..."

There was shouting from outside.

"Here," he said brusquely. "You stay here."

And then he jumped out.

Briar waited a moment. Stay here? She thought not.

She clambered out the open door and onto the road behind him.

A familiar gilded red barouche was blocking the road before them. Its driver stood, looking exceedingly unconcerned about the blockade, his arms crossed over his chest and a familiar sneer on his young face.

"Percy!" Briar exclaimed in disgust. "Ugh. Not twice in one day."

"That expresses it nicely," Wren muttered. "Lord Quintrell, yer vehicle is blocking our path. Kindly remove it."

"Awfully sorry, but I can't. Wheel seems to be jammed or some-thing," Percy said laconically, stepping forward. "Suppose you'll have to give me a ride back home, Briar. Room enough in that carriage for one more?"

"Ugh," Briar said again. "Really, Percy?" She took a sniff. "Is that whisky I smell? Have you been drinking? All day long? Have you even been home at all?"

Percy scowled. "Why would I go home? Nothing for me there. Now let's get going."

He took another step toward the Blakeley carriage only to find his way barred.

Wren stood there, his hands curled into fists, his expression quite menacing.

"I would have thought ye'd have had enough this morning," he said, glaring down at Percy who had already taken two steps back.

"Why'd you bring this one with you?" Percy slurred. "He follows you everywhere now, Briar?"

"He came with me on an errand to the Brewers, Percy," Briar exclaimed hotly. "An errand I should not have had to pay if you had done your duty in the first place. Or better yet, behaved as a gentleman in the first place!"

"Huh? What's that?" Percy looked obliviously unconcerned.

"Bessie Brewer!" Briar said angrily. "Surely her name still means something to you! She is carrying your child. She says you promised to marry her."

Percy glanced at her and gave a slow smile. "Just like you promised me, sweetling?"

"Oh really, Percy," Briar erupted. "How can you seriously compare the two things? Dishonoring a tenant's daughter..."

"Not my tenant," Percy said happily. "Yours, not mine."

"Getting her with child, abandoning yer child," Wren said in a low threatening tone, taking a step toward the young man who fell back immediately against his barouche. "Does that sound more like yers? Does it?"

"Keep him away from me, Briar, or I won't be held accountable for the results," Percy said sulkily. He had put a hand to his nose, and Briar noticed how swollen it was.

"What happened to your face, Percy?" she asked curiously, a suspicion growing.

"Had a fall. At the tavern. Quite funny it was," Percy said, but he was scowling.

"Did ye now?" Wren asked, folding his arms over his chest and looking interested. "A chair up and hit ye in the face, perhaps?"

"Something like that. Now can we leave? You can't just leave me here. It is growing dark. A deserted country road. Who knows what could happen to me," Percy said plaintively. But there was a glint in his eyes that told Briar everything she needed to know.

She made a disgusted *tsking* sound just as Wren said, "A young pup like ye afraid to be on a country road at night, with a perfectly good horse behind him hitched to his barouche. Why, ye ought to be ashamed of yerself. Ye've as good as called yerself a coward to Lady Briar's face and mine. Why, there's nothing wrong with yer barouche, I'd wager..." He took a step toward it, but Percy jumped in front.

"Don't you dare touch it! I'll have a proper servant attend to it. Not a great lump like you. Keep your filthy, sweaty hands off it."

Wren rolled his eyes, held up his hands, and looked at Briar. "If Quintrell had no' already found injury once this morning with a tavern chair—" He looked significantly at Percy, who reddened. "Then I would perhaps deal with him differently right now. But as the pup is sopping with whisky and too pathetic to argue with, I have another solution in mind, Lady Briar, if it meets with yer approval."

"Anything that gets us quickly away from Mr. Quintrell shall meet with my enthusiastic approval, Mr. Spencer. Even if we have to turn the carriage around and backtrack hundreds of miles to get home. I am quite prepared for anything. Excluding, that is, sharing any space except the great outdoors with Percy Quintrell," Briar said.

Wren Spencer nodded. "That's what I hoped ye would say."

He marched over to their carriage and leaned up to speak to the driver, who had been waiting patiently all this time.

Then he stepped over to the Blakeley carriage and, approaching the team of horses, began to unhitch one of the large stallions.

"What are you doing?" Percy cried. "What is the meaning of this?"

"Dinna fash yerself," Wren said with surprising mildness. "It isna yer concern."

When the horse had been unhitched, he led it over to Briar. "With yer permission?"

Briar felt her heart speed up. She nodded.

And then he caught her by the waist with strong, warm hands and tossed her up on the horse.

Chapter Three

Now that she was up in front of him, cradled in his arms, cupped against his body, pressed against his most intimate parts, Wren was forcefully reminded for the second time that day what a desirable young woman Lady Briar Blakeley was.

Before this, "exasperatingly sweet" would have been the first words that came to mind to describe her.

But as they left an infuriated-looking Percy in their dust, Wren reminded himself that Briar must be a highly sought-after bride. Not only by the likes of Percy Quintrell, but the many other young suitors who she had already rejected in the short time since she had been "out." She was lively and spirited, clever and capable. Though rather prone, it seemed to him, to getting her own way and managing those around her.

She was also, well, quite uncommonly pretty. Some might even say beautiful. With her dark flame-colored hair and those sandy specks upon her cheeks, which some fools might disparagingly call "freckles," to Wren they looked like the kisses of the sun goddess, contrasting as they did with the rest of the girl's sweet ivory skin. Well, she was charmed, he decided. There was a captivating quality to her which would serve her all her life. She would not simply possess a fleeting sort of beauty but would become an astonishingly original-looking woman as she matured. Even now when she looked at him, the lush curves of her lips sent tingles down his spine. Her warm, honey-tinged eyes held his own captive when he made the mistake of meeting them full-on.

In the past, some might have called a girl like Briar Blakeley more than magnificent or entrancing. They might have called her a witch, an enchantress.

But such things were foolish nonsense. It was men's own hearts— more specifically their cocks, Wren acknowledged to himself wryly— that were touched by female beauty. Whether a woman intended to touch them or not.

Percy Quintrell being the perfect example of such pigheaded male madness.

Did he even see Briar for who she was, Wren wondered? Or did he simply want her as a wealthy wife to bear his children?

He felt his body tense at the idea of the girl he held in his arms bearing children for that swine. She was well out of it.

Let her find some mild, pleasant young man instead who would cherish her, respect her, and, aye, hopefully bring her some measure of happiness in this life. The girl had a heart, a love for people, that much could not be denied. She deserved some happiness for her kind-heartedness.

He wondered now why her older brother and sister had not taken her to London for a Season already. She must be, what? At least eighteen or nineteen years old. Among the English elite, a girl like Briar should be married by now.

He was tempted to ask. Almost. But then she spoke instead.

"Well, that was exhilarating." She turned her head to try to look at him, and Wren instinctively leaned away.

Their faces were mere inches apart. They were already far too close for his comfort.

"Stay seated, turn around, hold still," he snapped, not caring for how he sounded.

"Oh, of course. My apologies," she said, hastily turning her head around again. "But really, that was such a wonderful plan," she called over her shoulder. "Did you see the look on Percy's face? He was furious. I do pity our poor driver, though, if he has to take Percy home in such a state."

"He willna have to," Wren replied wryly. "The young fop can see himself home now that we're gone."

"What do you mean?" Briar asked, turning again before remembering his admonishment and shifting back, though not before he had seen the way she had of scrunching up her nose when puzzled. It was adorable. Like an endearing baby rabbit.

He frowned. Since when did he find a rabbit anything more than a pest? And a pest was what Briar Blakeley had certainly been to him today. Perhaps she and rabbits did have much in common.

He recalled she had asked him a question and cleared his throat. "I mean there's likely nothing at all the matter with his barouche. He was simply being an ar—" He coughed. "An obstacle. To thwart ye."

"Well, I certainly hope he doesn't decide to become an obstacle for poor Bessie," Briar said with concern. "I should not like to hear he had been bothering her family next, simply because he learned I had been there. Oh dear, whyever did I mention it..."

"I'll check on them tomorrow if it would please ye," Wren said shortly. "I'm sure yer brother would approve and no' mind if I took the time."

"Oh, would you?" Briar sounded relieved. "That would be a weight off my mind. Thank you."

"Aye." Wren lapsed back into silence. Would she fill it again? he wondered, idly curious. Or let them ride the rest of the way home in peace?

He had his answer a few minutes later.

As the late summer sun drifted lazily below the horizon, Briar's body suddenly slumped against his.

"Here now," he complained loudly.

Then he realized she had fallen asleep.

"*A Dhia,*" he muttered to himself in Gaelic. Of course, the girl was tired. She'd had a long day, starting with that daft git's proposal, had she not?

With a sigh, Wren bundled her more closely to him so she would not slide off the horse.

Her brother would have his head if that happened, he told himself, so in good conscience, he could do nothing but hold her more closely to him. It was for her safety, nothing more. Certainly not because she smelled like sweet smelling hay and clean soap. Certainly not because her body was lushly curving and soft and warm, and... Oh, God, Wren felt a familiar stirring and shifted in the saddle, horrified.

He was not about to permit himself to react to Lady Briar in that way.

Not now. Not ever. Not even when the lady was asleep.

He cleared his throat loudly, hoping to wake her up.

Then coughed.

Then pretended to sneeze.

There was no reaction. At least, not the one he had hoped for. Instead, she began to snore softly.

"Gads," he grumbled. "She sleeps like the dead."

The dark red head tumbled forward as the horse cantered over a hill. It looked awkward, even painful, so Wren gently gathered the girl's head against his chest, holding it in place with his chin positioned gingerly overtop.

They were well and truly croodling now. Oh, if Laurel and Marigold could see him now, Wren thought gloomily. Wouldn't they laugh?

But before he knew it, they began to approach Blakeley Manor.

Wren tried to feel relieved. He was nearly done with Lady Briar. After this, just let her try to find him in the gardens again! He would hide in their darkest, deepest recesses for the next month to avoid her and her errands.

"Here now," he said loudly, poking her none too gently with a finger in the ribs and taking slight satisfaction when she finally jumped awake. "We're home, my lady."

He rode the horse toward the front of the house, pretending not to notice as Briar covertly wiped the drool from her mouth with the corner of her pelisse sleeve.

"I'll leave ye here and take the horse to the stable," he declared and helped her slide down to the ground.

He was turning to go when she spoke. Her voice was still thick with sleep, as if she were just beginning to fully wake, yet her tone was teasing. "Mr. Spencer! Is that really how you will say good-bye? After the afternoon we have had? The adventures we have shared?"

He turned the horse back slowly. "It is nearly evening, in fact," he pointed out. "Well, good evening to ye, my lady." He began to turn the horse again.

"Mr. Spencer!" She sounded exasperated and amused. "Thank you. For everything. You need not turn back yet again. But truly, I do thank you."

"Aye," he grunted and rode away without a backward glance.

"Oooh, that man," Briar muttered, watching him go.

"What man?" a man's voice asked mildly from behind.

She turned around to see Dare coming out of the house.

"You've missed dinner, Briar. Where have you been all this time?" Dare frowned and looked past her. "And where is the carriage? Did you not leave with it?"

"I'm sure Clifford will be back with it soon," she promised. "He could not have been too far behind us. Though I suppose we did take some short cuts over the hills..."

"We?" Dare asked, pointedly raising his fine, dark brows.

"Mr. Spencer and I," Briar explained. "I solicited his assistance in visiting the Brewers this afternoon. I knew you would not wish me to go unaccompanied."

"Hmm." Dare's lips twitched. "Why did you not simply ask one of the footmen? And why not bring a maid along?"

"You know I do not enjoy bringing a retinue of servants when I make calls," Briar replied impatiently. "I thought I should bring a strong man along because of the nastiness with Percy this morning, or honestly, I would not have taken anyone at all."

"I see," Dare said slowly. "And? Did you? Require a strong man?"

"In fact," Briar admitted, "I did. Percy made a nuisance of himself again as we were returning home. He blocked the road with his barouche. Can you believe it, Dare? He reeked of liquor, too. Plainly, he had been imbibing all day."

"And what did Spencer do about this?" Dare asked, looking interested.

"Well, he seemed tempted to knock Percy's block off at first," Briar said. "But then, I believe he may have already done that this morning. Percy had a very bruised nose, you see, and did not seem to take kindly to Mr. Spencer's presence."

"Oh ho, one for Spencer. Good man," Dare said, leaning back against the pillar. "I wonder what prompted the knocking of the block —or nose, as you say—this morning."

"I wonder that, too," Briar said, suddenly realizing she had not even asked. "Perhaps Percy insulted Mr. Spencer when he was showing him out?"

"Hmm," Dare said shrewdly. "Perhaps. So, what then?"

"Well, Mr. Spencer was very resourceful. Since we could not take the carriage and the alternative was to retreat and go a much longer way back, he simply unhitched one of the horses, with Clifford's permission of course, and rode us off."

"He rode off with you on horseback?" Dare was looking at Briar closely.

"He did. I suppose it was a little improper, but I am home safely and that is all that matters, is it not?"

Dare stepped away from the pillar and came toward her, putting his hands on her shoulders. "It is. Welcome home, Sister." Then he smiled perceptively. "And now that you are back, I assume you will leave Mr. Spencer alone for the foreseeable future."

"Why, whatever do you mean?" Briar exclaimed. "We had a lovely afternoon. He was most helpful."

"Yes, I'm sure he was." Dare sighed. "But leave the man in peace now, Briar."

"But he is family, Dare," Briar replied hotly. "I suppose you do not like being reminded of it but—"

"Here now, that isn't fair," Dare said sharply. "You know I have nothing against the Spencers. Many men in my position would have tried to put a stop to Kat's marriage, not encourage it."

"That is true," Briar conceded. "But it is not as if you have, well, as if you have..."

"As if I have what?" Dare looked amused. "Invited them all to dinner? The gardener, the housekeeper, and... what is it that the youngest sister does?"

"I'm not quite sure," Briar replied. "Not that it matters. Why could we *not* have them all to dinner, now that you mention it?"

"Briar, really." Dare rolled his eyes. "I would help them in any way necessary. I would lend them our aid, our ear. I am making no attempt to deny the connection. But of course, we shall never be as close as say..."

"As close as we would be to the Quintrells if I were to marry Percy?" Briar snapped.

"Not at all. You see, if you were to marry Percy, I should be forced to disown you entirely," Dare said. He grimaced. "But please. Do not even say such things in jest. Are you truly tempted? Have you changed your mind about matrimony, then?"

"Certainly not." Briar tossed her head. "I am too young to marry. Look what happened to Kat. She misjudged a man so completely and wound up utterly miserable. I am only nineteen going on twenty. Mother was twenty-three when she married. And look at you—past thirty and unwed. Why are the standards so different for men? It is very unfair."

"It is," Dare agreed, putting his arm affectionately around his sister's shoulders. "As far as I am concerned, you need never marry. You may become a spinster and live here with me, forever. Of course, I am bound to wed someday, and my wife shall become the new mistress of Blakeley Manor. But I'm sure you will be able to work out some sort of amicable arrangement." He smiled sweetly.

Briar frowned. "When you put it like that, it is not particularly appealing," she complained. "You make it sound like a sure thing that I will never marry, too."

Dare laughed. "Not at all. You have only to ask for your Season in London, you know. And I will even make Kat come down with us to help see you through. You'll have all the young men eating out of your hand—if you so choose, though it does seem most unsanitary now that

I give the expression more thought—and will be married to your own charming prince within a month or two. Is that what you want? Say the word and we set out for London, posthaste."

Briar was silent for a moment. "Not... yet." She looked at her brother. "I really do want more time. To simply... be myself."

Dare returned her gaze with sympathy. "Not all men are like Percy, Sis," he said softly. "Just because Kat made an unfortunate choice in her first husband does not mean you will, too."

"But what if I do?" Briar asked, her voice becoming small. "You will not be able to save me. We could do nothing for Kat when..."

Dare's face had darkened. She knew it was not a subject he enjoyed being reminded of.

"No, the laws are clear. Clear and wrong. Though if she had come to us for sanctuary, I would not have allowed him to take her back. You know that, Briar." He alluded to Kat's first husband, the Earl of Colworth, who had been an abusive bastard to her elder sister. "No matter what the consequences were to me."

"But he would have separated her from Oliver," Briar reminded him, her voice still hushed. "She could not leave her son."

"No," Dare agreed, his expression sad. He gazed at her. "Is that truly what you are most afraid of, Briar? Being similarly trapped?"

"Men have a great deal of power over their wives, Dare," Briar said. "It is rather terrifying." She tried to smile. "Perhaps spinsterhood will not be so bad. I'm sure you will pick a very nice wife."

"Indeed, I promise I shall," Dare said lightly. "Now, come. Are you hungry? And have we come to an agreement? You will leave Mr. Spencer alone?"

"Oh, is that what you think this all has been? An agreement?" Briar elbowed him sharply. "I don't see why I should not pay attention to the Spencers. I have already had some dealings with Laurel, the eldest sister. She seems a very fine woman."

"I am sure you are correct. Very well," Dare said, heaving a long-suffering sigh. "Pay attention to them. However, do me the courtesy of leaving Wren Spencer, in particular, alone. Did you not ever stop to consider there might be a reason a retired soldier like himself might have become a solitary gardener?"

"He prefers solitude, you mean?" Briar asked slowly. "But it is not as if he were a hermit."

"No, but from what I know of the man, he prefers to keep to himself. He has family in Scotland, you know. Scottish nobility of some sort, I believe. Yet he has spurned them for some reason. He prefers to reside with his half-siblings here in England but shies away from the other servants. From what I understand, he never even frequents the village." Dare hesitated. "Yes, he is rather a hermit, I suppose. The war changed many men, Briar. He may not have always been this way. But the regiment he fought in..."

"Yes?" Briar's ears perked up with interest. "What regiment? What happened to him?"

"I don't know much about it. Only that he was a captain. He fought alongside a group of Highlanders..."

"Other Highlanders, you mean. For he is a Highlander himself, is he not?"

"He is half-Scottish, I believe. I really could not speak to his parentage. May I continue?"

"Of course," Briar said hastily. "Pray go on."

"Well, the regiment suffered considerable losses, and by the end, Spencer was one of the few to return home. I don't know the whole tale, but I presume he feels some misplaced measure of responsibility about the whole thing..."

"Why misplaced?" Briar asked sharply. "I should think it was very understandable for a man to feel guilt over the death of the men serving under him, especially his own countrymen."

"Of course," Dare said gently. "It reflects a fine sentiment, that Mr. Spencer perhaps carries the burden still. And when he returned home, I believe he suffered some further disappointments to do with the Scottish side of his family. He is a man who may very well be in considerable distress, Briar."

"Yes, indeed," Briar said reflectively. "Perhaps he needs us even more than I thought. To help him. To draw him out. To help him heal. Perhaps the visit to the Brewers was only the first step. You should have seen him today, Dare. He spoke to Mr. Brewer so confidently. So commandingly." She gave a little shiver of delight. "He smoothed everything over. Convinced Mr. Brewer to accept our help, for the sake of his family—but not in a way in which the poor man felt he had lost face."

Dare was groaning to himself. "Let us go in and have a peaceful dinner with no more talk of the Spencers. Would such a thing be possible?"

"I don't know," Briar said doubtfully, a glint in her eyes. "It is past six-thirty. Have you not eaten already? Is this simply a way for you to have a second dinner after your first?"

She giggled as Dare poked her threateningly, and they both went inside the house.

"Oh, there you are." Laurel poked her blonde head into the shed where Wren had been working on replanting some seedlings. "It's nearly pitch black in here. How can you see to work?"

"Nearly isna completely."

"*Nearly isna completely*," she mimicked back. Her dark blonde locks were braided neatly and pinned to her head, and though it was the end of the day, her blue eyes were still dancing with energy. "Is that all you're going to say? Did you have a fine time riding out with the daughter of the house today?"

Even in the darkness, he could see her white teeth as she smiled.

"I didna 'ride out' as ye put it. We took the carriage," he said crankily. "And it wasna my choice. I was conscripted."

"Conscripted, were you? By the beautiful Briar? She is an exceptionally pretty girl, isn't she? Not just pretty, of course. She's clever."

"I have absolutely no idea what she is or isna, nor do I care. Now would ye please go away and leave me alone," Wren said, putting the planter down and turning his back on her.

Instead of obeying, Laurel stubbornly folded her arms and leaned back against the rickety wooden door frame.

"Are you going to read the letter?"

"What letter?" Wren frowned into the dark. He knew the letter she spoke of, aye. He might ask how Laurel knew of it. Why she had been snooping through his things. But it had probably been Marigold. And acknowledging the letter at all would be disastrous. Better to pretend he had no idea there was one. And then deal with it as he should have when he first received it and put it on the fire as soon as he got home.

Laurel snorted. "Please, Wren. You know that I know there is a letter. From Scotland."

Dropping the planting pot with a clatter, Wren began to swear in Gaelic and whirled around to face her.

"Why did you have to be cursed with two nosy sisters?" Laurel asked helpfully. "Is that what you're saying?"

"That is a rough translation," Wren said between gritted teeth. "That letter is none of yer concern, whether I read it or no', and I'll thank ye to..."

"To just let you live your sad lonely life in the gardens, thank ye very much, Laurel, the bane of my existence," Laurel interjected. "Yes, yes, I know."

He glared.

"Let us say, for conversation's sake," Laurel said, studying her fingernails carefully. "That there was something important in the letter. Something which might change the course of your life, as it is presently."

Wren growled.

"Then do you not owe it to yourself to read it?" she continued, ignoring his bristling. "You returned from fighting the French, not to Scotland, but to us—here at Blakeley Manor. But I cannot help but wonder if it is where you truly belong. Of course, we have been very happy to have you back with us. But I cannot help but think *this* is not your true purpose, Wren. You became captain of your regiment. Why, you led men into battle. And yet afterwards, you simply gave up..."

"Stop," Wren cautioned. "I willna speak of it. Dinna make me out to be a hero, Laurel. I willna stand for such nonsense."

"Very well. What I am saying," she said hurriedly, "is that you were always meant to lead men, not..." She twirled her hands. "Well, not simply to grow green things. Not that it isn't also a worthy occupation of a sort. If you were a monk or some sort of penitent..."

Wren growled low in the back of his throat. It was a warning.

"Leave well enough alone, Laurel," he said curtly, beginning to brush past her. "Is it no' enough that I am here? That I am... home?"

Laurel's gaze softened, and she reached out a hand to touch his shoulder. "We are so glad you are here, Wren. It has been a joy, having our older brother back with us. Wherever we are, there will be a place for you. But perhaps in your case, a man may have more than one home?"

"Mayhap," he said gruffly, then sighed. "I'm tired, Laurel. Can we no' leave off with this? Please? I am tired, and I am hungry. It has been a long day."

"Well," she said, sighing her surrender. Taking his arm in hers, she began to walk with him down the path from the greenhouse in the direction of their cottage that the three siblings shared. "Very well. I suppose. Since you said 'please.'"

Chapter Four

Fate did not care if one said, "Please."

Fate swooped in like a hawk and did whatever it wanted, running amuck, marching willy-nilly all over one's hopes and dreams. "The best laid schemes o' mice an' men," said the poet Rabbie Burns. "Gang aft a-gley."

At first, Wren Spencer thought Briar Blakeley was the only "fate" he had to thwart that summer. He was successful for over a week, too, as he occupied himself with planting and hoeing and restoring one of the hothouses that had fallen into disrepair.

Anything that required working off the usual beaten path and out of sight of the big house received his immediate and devoted attention. The most recent project, the hothouse, lay on the edges of the estate gardens, off a disused path. He felt quite confident it was as secluded a place as one could hope for when hiding from a duke's debutante sister.

As the days passed peacefully, he assumed Lady Briar had forgotten all about him. She had other things to occupy her time, after all. Doing whatever rich young ladies typically did.

If she had paid any further visits to the Brewers, she must have found a footman to attend her. For certainly, she had not found Wren.

He felt quite satisfied with the dedication with which he had wiled himself away each day, hardly stopping his work to emerge for a midday break.

Satisfied, that is, until he came out of the greenhouse one afternoon carrying two large pails full of debris and ran smack into the very young lady he was trying so hard to avoid.

She was wearing a dainty, frilly white muslin dress, and the first thing he realized was that he had left a muddy print across it. He scowled, looking at the stain. Less than a minute near him and she was soiled. If that wasn't a sign, he didn't know what was.

"Oh, there you are! Finally! I have been looking everywhere for you, Mr. Spencer," Lady Briar exclaimed, seeming delighted. "You should really leave clearer information on your whereabouts with your subordinates. I had to ask half a dozen workers where to find you. None seemed to know. But they seemed quite reluctant to *admit* they did not know. Or perhaps—" She paused, her pretty eyebrows arching. "Perhaps they *did* know?" She smiled ruefully. "Well, that is all right. I thought I would simply ask. You may say 'no,' you know."

"Say no to what?" he replied curtly. "I am busy as ye can plainly see, my lady. Is it a gardening matter?"

He began to walk down the path, hoisting the heavy pails. Lady Briar trotted alongside him.

"Well no, not a gardening matter, though you are the first I would consult in any horticultural emergency, of course. You may take my word on that." She beamed up at him as if he would actually be pleased to hear this. He did not smile back.

"But in fact, no plants are involved today," she continued more haltingly. "I simply wondered if you might wish to come with me to see the Brewers again. I have some items to deliver for Bessie and thought you might enjoy further conversation with Mr. Brewer. I believe you were discussing cabbages on our last visit."

"I dinna have time to be paying social calls today, as ye can see," Wren snapped. "I have real work that needs doing."

He could hear the harshness in his tone, but it was too late. The words were out.

And as they fell upon their intended audience, Wren immediately felt a stab of regret.

Lady Briar's face fell. It may even have wobbled slightly. For a moment, he was terrified the girl was about to cry.

Then she rallied. She clenched her jaw. Her lips ceased trembling. They turned back up stubbornly, reforming into their customary sweet smile.

Wren was impressed.

"Of course. No matter. So sorry to have disturbed your work, Mr. Spencer. You were such a wonderful help the last time I simply thought... Well, it doesn't matter, as I have already said. I am repeating myself." She gave a shrill little laugh, then glanced down at the muddy mark on her frock. "Goodness, I had best go back to the house and change. I hope the rest of your day goes well. Good day."

She began to walk away, turning and marching back up the path.

"Wait," he called. He stifled a groan. "Lady Briar. My lady, please wait."

He set down the pails, cursed under his breath, and started after her.

She was still walking but had slowed her pace. Nevertheless, she did not turn around, even though she surely must have heard his footsteps.

He reached out a hand—checking it first, quickly, to make sure it was not muddy—and touched her shoulder.

Then she paused. Turned slowly. Her eyes were very bright, her smile brittle. "I understand I am making a nuisance of myself, Mr. Spencer. You need not apologize for wishing to carry on with your own work."

"I ken." He frowned. That was not right. "I ken I need no' but I wish to."

She would not meet his eyes. Her own golden-brown ones were lowered, looking down at his feet. He had done that. Broken the poor lass's spirits when she was simply trying to show enthusiasm about helping out a family in need. "Ye're no' keen to visit the Brewers alone then, I take it? Or with a footman?"

"Well of course, I may bring along a footman. However, they are unlikely to distract Mr. Brewer as well as you did the last time. I had the feeling Bessie and Mrs. Brewer quite welcomed the break, you know. The chance to talk to another woman, even one as inexperienced with such matters as myself, without the head of the family hovering over..." She hesitated.

"He can be a little oppressive, Mr. Brewer, aye," Wren agreed. "I suppose I can come along and talk cabbages and cucumbers with the mon if it will help ye. Just allow me a few moments to clean up, and I will meet ye at the carriage?"

"Truly?" Her head lifted, and he saw her eyes beginning to light up with their former enthusiasm. "But no, I could not. Really, Mr. Spencer, you have made it perfectly clear that you would prefer to carry on with your very important work. It is not as if a social call, as you put it, is more important than whatever you were doing. I should not have expected you to drop everything and simply join me again. No, you were quite right—"

"I was quite rude, was what I was," Wren interjected stubbornly. "As well ye ken."

"I ken? Do I?" Briar looked confused.

"It means 'to know,'" Wren said with a little amusement.

"Ah, I see. Well, then I don't know," she said stubbornly. "You were just being... taciturn. Your ordinary self."

"Aye, my ordinary self," Wren agreed, his lips twitching. "That's verra gracious of ye."

"Of course if you insisted upon coming, I suppose I could not stop you," Briar continued, peeking up at him. "You are much larger than me for one..."

"Aye, that would be the reason," Wren agreed, his lips continuing to twitch. Ah, the poor duke. What a younger sister to have. She was a handful, make no mistake. At least his sisters were more manageable. Most of the time. "I should certainly overpower ye with my determination to see Mr. Brewer again."

"Certainly," Briar agreed. "If you were so determined."

"Aye, and I am. I simply must visit the man. And so, I shall see ye at the carriage in a quarter of an hour," Wren said. "I hope that is enough time for ye to change yer dress. Which I am sorry for soiling."

"Oh, yes, it should be if I hurry," Briar said cheerfully, beginning to turn away again. "Thank you, Mr. Spencer. I am so glad you overpowered me, verbally speaking, I mean. You are a gentleman and so could do no other kind, of course."

Wren narrowed his eyes. They were treading on accidentally flirtatious territory, and he wondered if she had an inkling of this at all. He suspected not. She was an innocent, Lady Briar. And Wren—well, he did not flirt. So, the conversation was acceptable but best to end it here.

He turned away and marched back toward the Spencers' cottage to change his clothes.

***

Of course, they never did get to the Brewers.

The carriage ride over was rather livelier than their first. Briar seemed intent on ensuring Wren was comfortable and did not allow a lapse in conversation to occur. Rather, she ran through a list of questions, almost like she had prepared them in advance. All to do with horticulture, as if she were convinced this was the safest subject.

Wren was consulted on his favorite shape of shrubbery, the pest he believed posed the most threat to the English vegetable garden that summer, and the best and worst smelling flowers (daisies were the foulest, lilac was his choice for best).

They were nearing the Brewers' cottage and were engaged in a heated dispute over whether lilacs or roses smelled the sweetest when the carriage came to a sudden halt on a lonely country road.

"Not again," Wren said, already frowning in exasperation. "Can it be that wee pest Percy a second time? Following ye about?"

"Oh, I certainly hope not," Briar said, wrinkling her brow. "He has made himself scarce since Dare paid him a visit last week after he blocked the road. Although from what Dare says, the visit did not go at all well, and when he left, Percy was once again drunk and uttering vicious threats." She sighed and peered at the window. "Oh, someone is coming over! It must be the driver. Perhaps a farmer's cart is merely blocking the road."

"Aye, perhaps..." Wren began.

But then the door was wrenched open, and it was not the driver standing there.

"Good Gracious," Briar breathed. "Who on earth are you?"

A man stood holding the carriage door open, a pistol held casually in his hand. His face was covered by a black mask—a handkerchief tied behind his head in the style of a highwayman. He wore a black hat on his head.

Behind him, Wren caught sight of at least two other men, also with their faces covered.

"Get out," the man ordered roughly.

"I believe you are supposed to add 'or else,'" Briar said helpfully, clearly not in any danger of fainting from fear.

Instead of obliging, the man brandished the pistol higher, as if he might actually shoot. "Get out *now*."

There was something distinctive about his voice. Something vaguely familiar to Wren.

Wren had heard enough. "Get up, Briar," he said, using her Christian name for once, in the hope that familiarity would help him to stand in place of her older brother. "Do as he says. Please. I am responsible for yer safety. If anything should happen to ye, I should..."

"Very well, very well." She rose behind him, and he helped her down from the carriage.

"Now, what is the meaning of this—" Wren began, turning to face the man who had threatened them with the pistol.

But that was all he had time to say before the butt of the weapon came crashing down hard upon his face.

He saw stars. Heard Briar screaming. He felt a pang of sadness that she should see him die in such a brutal way.

And then blackness.

Wren groaned. He could not open his eyes. He was prone, his head lying pressed against something soft. Everything was moving. Everything hurt. His stomach felt awful. He believed he might be sick.

And someone was talking. Incessantly talking. The familiar voice a harsh whine that grated in his ears...

"Those fools! Those stupid fools! Devil take it, how could they have done such a thing? When I get my hands on them, I swear I'll..."

"Sit down, Percy," Briar's voice said, calmly. "You're making the carriage shake, and that can't be good for poor Mr. Spencer's head."

"As if I give a fig for Mr. Spencer's head!"

Wren groaned. "Och, God, this is hell. I am in hell with that wee *numpty* Quintrell."

"Why, Mr. Spencer, that rhymes very nicely," Briar said from somewhere above him, sounding amused. "How is your head?"

"It bloody hurts," Wren growled. He tried to open his eyes. They flickered, and Briar came partially into view. She was very close.

"Good God," he exclaimed, suddenly understanding the softness of his pillow. "Am I lyin' in yer lap?"

"Highly improper," Percy sniffed from somewhere nearby. "I tried to tell her to leave you on the floor, but she would not listen. None of the bloody Blakeleys listen."

"At least not to you, Percy," Briar said, sounding unperturbed. "Oh dear, there is still quite a bit of blood on your face. Poor Mr. Spencer."

"Where the bloody hell are we?" Wren croaked. "What is this? Why is Quintrell here?"

"We have been kidnapped," Briar explained sadly. "We are in a carriage. It is night. That is all I know."

"Kidnapped!" Wren tried to sit up. He let out a groan and put a hand to his head. Briar's hand found his shoulder and was able to, without much effort, tug him back down.

His head found her lap again. It was much more comfortable than holding his head up of his own accord. He allowed himself the indulgence of keeping it there. Just for a moment.

He closed his eyes. That was better.

He tried again. "Why are ye here, Quintrell?"

He peeked his eyes open a slit to glare at Percy who sat on the opposite bench of the carriage, looking none too happy. "Why the devil does something tell me this misery is of yer making?"

"I have been kidnapped, too. In case you hadn't noticed. I would hardly make myself miserable, now would I?" Percy said defensively. But his face was guilty.

"Ye would if ye were the complete eejit I take ye for," Wren growled and took pleasure in seeing Percy scoot a little farther away on his seat. "What the bloody hell have ye done to us, Quintrell?"

"I believe Percy had something to do with this, too," Briar agreed. "He looks awfully guilty. I suppose you paid highwaymen to kidnap me, and they've taken you along, Percy. Or perhaps you *didn't* pay them, and that's why they took you, too."

"Wouldna be a bit surprised," Wren said. "Is that the way of it? Speak up, Quintrell."

"Or you'll what? Strike me again?" Percy challenged. "You can hardly open your eyes and..."

That was all the motivation Wren needed. He opened his eyes fully and pushed himself up, ignoring Briar's heeding to lie back down.

"Aye, I'll strike ye again happily," he snarled. "Even before the lady. So, tell us now the truth of what's befallen us, or so help me..."

"Very well, very well," Percy said hastily, holding up his hands. "They're your comrades. From Scotland. Had I known they were such vindictive men, I should never have offered them my services..."

"Yer services?" Wren narrowed his eyes. "My comrades?"

"Yes, of course. They are Scots. Highlanders. Like you." Percy lifted his nose in distaste. "Basically barbarians if their behavior thus far is any indication."

"Ye sold us to Scottish mercenaries," Wren said slowly, trying to understand.

"Sold would be an overstatement as they haven't paid me yet," Percy said sulkily.

"Ye wanted revenge on the lassie, but ye wanted revenge on me just as much, is that it?"

"Oh, that's shameful, Percy," Briar exclaimed. "You are supposed to be a gentleman. What would your mother say?"

Percy did not look repentant. Only sorry for himself. "What the devil are they planning to do with me? That's what I'd like to know. And when will I get my money?"

"Ye daft doiter," Wren said in disgust. "Ye'll be lucky to get away with yer head still attached to yer neck."

He watched Percy pale and grinned, then remembered Briar and looked up guiltily. She was looking at him, her eyes wide, her face very white.

"Do you really think so?" she whispered. "Will they truly... kill us?"

Wren sighed. "I dinna see why we'd be in this carriage now if they meant to murder us. They could have done it back on the road. But I dinna ken why highwaymen would want me at all. It's ye who could bring them a large ransom." He thought quickly. "We'll have to make sure they see that. When they come back, we'll tell them who ye are. They can send to yer brother, make their demands. I'll see ye're treated well in the meantime."

Briar nodded gingerly. "Very... very well. And Dare can pay a ransom for you as well, Mr. Spencer, if that's needed. Of course, he will."

Her face suddenly flushed red, and her eyes darted to Percy. "Oh, Percy, how could you be such a fool? To get us all into such a mess! How could you? All because a girl would not marry you? How utterly pathetic!"

"Here now!" Percy exclaimed.

"Ye'd best shut up and let her speak," Wren said grimly. "She's saying nothing but the truth and more gently than ye deserve." He leaned forward threateningly. "That is, unless ye'd like me to give ye my version."

Percy cowered. "Not at all. Her insults do me no harm. I know my true worth. She has missed out on the woman she might have been had she married a Quintrell, that is all..."

"Oh, for heaven's sake, you are deluded," Briar said in disgust, shaking her head. "You would have been lucky to get Bessie Brewer to marry you, Percy. She's a better bride than you deserve."

"A farm girl!" Percy snorted. "I think not. Besides, why buy the cow when you can—"

"Oh no," Wren warned, his temper flaring. "Ye'd best no' finish that—"

"—get the milk for... Ow!" Percy let out a shriek and a wail. "What'd you do that for?"

"I told ye no' to finish that foul phrase," Wren said placidly.

"He did tell you," Briar said quietly, tossing her head. "She is the mother of your child. Perhaps you had best start talking about Miss Brewer more respectfully."

"Oh, when those men come back, I'll give them a piece of my mind," Percy groaned. "Sticking me with you two." He began to pound on the side of the carriage and shouted, "Here now! Let me out! Let me out! Do you hear?"

"Stop that," Wren commanded. "Ye'll only serve to startle the horses. And I doubt the men ye've consorted with will be pleased if they have to come back here and..."

But it was too late. The carriage was beginning to slow.

Then it stopped completely.

The three occupants of the carriage box looked at one another in silence.

Then the door opened.

"Stop that racket, do ye hear now? Ye'll spook the horses," a man said, peering angrily into the carriage.

The voice was familiar. The man who had bashed Wren's head in with a pistol butt earlier was no longer masked.

Wren stared, hardly able to believe his eyes. He knew the fellow. Of course he did. He had known him all his life.

He was a hefty man, broad-shouldered, and swarthy. His face was more grizzled than Wren recalled it; the man's once-black hair was now streaked with gray.

"Angus?" Wren asked in disbelief. "What the devil are ye doing here?"

Angus Macleod looked back at him coldly, but there was no doubt at all he knew who Wren was.

"I'll leave ye untied and yer lady. But this one—" He nodded to Percy. "Hold out yer hands."

"You must be joking," Percy said angrily. "I will not be tied like

55

cattle. I am your partner in this endeavor, though clearly you have forgotten."

"Aye, yer the Judas all right," Angus said, looking at Percy with distaste. "Do ye wish for yer thirty pieces of silver now or when we arrive?"

"Arrive?" Briar leaned forward. "Arrive where, Mr. Angus? I believe there has been some mistake. I don't see what trouble Mr. Spencer could possibly be in..."

"Spencer?" Angus snorted. "Is that what ye call yerself now, Renfrew?" He shook his head at Wren, then looked at Briar, his face stolid and impassive. "As for where, Scotland, of course."

He looked back over his shoulder and gestured for one of the other men to come forward with rope. They grabbed Percy from the bench and began to bind his hands. He said nothing, simply sat gnashing his teeth and looking daggers at Angus.

"Scotland?" Briar breathed. "So far. My brother will be very worried about me, Mr. Angus. Perhaps I might write a letter?"

"Aye, ye may write all the letters ye like. When we've arrived. In the meantime, ye have yer husband to comfort ye." He nodded at Wren.

"Husband?" Wren choked out. "What the devil are ye talking about?"

"Oh, Mr. Spencer is not my husband," Briar assured Angus. "Is that what Percy told you? Why really, Percy, you dreadful liar!"

"I didn't tell him anything of the sort," Percy protested. "That's their own bloody mistake." That earned him a belt on the mouth from the man tying him, and he quickly shut up.

Angus did not look convinced. "She was with ye, traveling in the same carriage when we took ye. Ye said ye must keep her safe."

"Because she is my employer, ye daft nitwit," Wren exploded. "Take her back! Is it me ye want? Then kill me now and be done with it."

"No!" Briar cried impassioned. "Don't you dare!"

"Never fear, mistress," Angus said, his face still stony. "That's no' his fate."

"What is my fate then, Angus?"

Angus looked at him. Was Wren imagining it, or was there real anger in those eyes? But something else, too. Pity? Nay, nothing so tawdry as pity. But regret. Aye, regret. For?

"Ye left us, Renfrew," Angus said, and his voice was hard. "What punishment befits a mon who abandons his men?"

"Abandoned ye?" Wren was near dumbstruck. "What are ye talking about?"

"Och," Angus said, his expression becoming disgusted. "I suppose ye'll try to deny it. I dinna need to hear any of this." He gestured to his man who pulled once on the rope to make sure Percy was trussed tightly. "Leave him be. Put him on the floor, so he doesn't knock his teeth out when the carriage goes over bumps."

"Thank you for not tying us, Mr. Angus," Briar said quickly. "Will we be stopping for the night? It is nearly dark now and..."

"Let the lady out to rest a moment," Wren demanded, understanding Briar's question before she could form it in a ladylike way. "See to her comforts or I'll..."

"Ye'll what?" Angus asked, grinning suddenly and showing a row of sharp teeth. "Verra well, Mrs. Renfrew. Come down and have a wee rest. But quickly, mind ye. Here, help her down," he instructed one of his men.

Wren was looking past Angus carefully. There were at least four men just outside the carriage. Not to mention the driver, who must have been replaced with one of theirs.

They could try to jump from the carriage, but from what Wren could see, there were at least four or five outriders, plus the men in front. That made nearly ten men, just that he had seen.

Wren could throw himself onto Angus now, try to free Briar by force. But he could easily foresee where that would get him. Trussed like a chicken, the same as Quintrell.

Or he could wait for nightfall. Surely, the convoy would stop to camp somewhere for the night soon. Then he and Briar could sneak away into the dark and find help. Aye, that would make the most sense.

He could sneak away into the dark—with his wife!

His wife! How could Angus have made such a mistake?

He looked over at young Quintrell, wondering if the git understood yet the full repercussions of his actions.

As the young man was staring morosely out the open carriage door, evidently feeling sorry only for himself, the answer was clearly "no."

Wren shook his head. Lady Briar had gotten more than she bargained for today. Little did she know that, when she asked Wren to go visiting her tenants, she would be binding herself to him. Not only for the span of one afternoon but quite possibly for the rest of her life.

Chapter Five

"I really don't think they mean to hurt us," Briar whispered, folding a blanket to use as a pillow. "I know you're very angry that you are... Well, that you are..."

"Tied to a bloody tree?" Wren hissed. "A bear could come across me in the night, and I'd be like a bloody feast for him."

"Oh, heavens," Briar said, blanching a little. "Do you really think there are bears?"

"Never mind that," Wren said, through gritted teeth. "Ye must get hold of a knife or something to saw the ropes with, do ye hear? This is our chance. We must escape in the night. Tomorrow we will be that much farther from Blakeley Manor. And if we are stuck together another night..." He shook his head and really did look quite mournful. Briar felt quite sorry for him. It must be wretched to be tied to a tree.

At least, Angus had tied the ropes in a rather merciful way. Wren could move a few feet in either direction and lie down.

"I suppose you are right," Briar said dutifully. She glanced over at the fire where Angus and his men sat laughing and talking. "Only... there are so many of them. And they are rather fierce looking."

"They willna hurt a wee lassie, even if they do catch ye," Wren said impatiently.

She placed the folded blanket on top of the pallet she had made up for him.

"There. I hope that will be comfortable."

Wren growled, and Briar giggled a little.

"I suppose you are more fearsome than most bears, anyway," she said, looking at him.

Then she bit her lip and wished she had not.

Even tied to a tree, he was a thing of beauty. More so, for he looked more dangerously handsome than ever before. His coat hung open, revealing a tautly muscled chest barely covered in a thin white shirt, stained with his own blood. A lock of his thick dark hair had fallen across his forehead—the only hint of softness for a face so otherwise fierce and stern. That and his mouth. Which was not soft, no, but less severe than the rest of him. There was a fullness, she allowed, which lent him just enough softness to render him, well, a rather sinful air. Dangerous, yes, and tempting, too.

Briar swallowed hard. She felt a pang in her chest and realized she had begun to breathe hard. Quickly, she tried to dissemble. "All those men," she said again, panting a little and taking a step backwards. "I am not sure I could... I mean, I..."

"Good Lord, just look at ye," Wren said, his voice suddenly much gentler. "Ye've been through hell and back today." Under his breath she heard him add, "Thanks to that young fool." More loudly, he went on, "Sit down and rest. If ye dinna think ye can get the knife... well." He was silent for a time, and she wondered what he was thinking. "Just rest now, do ye hear?"

She tried to nod but was suddenly more determined than ever to do what he had initially asked. What would happen to him back in Scotland if she did not set him free tonight? Would they hurt him? Kill him?

Why did these men want him in the first place? They seemed to know him—at least, Angus certainly did.

She shivered and glanced back at Wren Spencer with a sudden thought. What if he had committed some sort of terrible crime in Scotland? Is that why they had come for him? So that he might stand trial of some sort?

Wren had closed his eyes. There was still some dried blood caked to his forehead. The pistol butt had smashed into his cheekbone, just below his left eye. Already a nasty bruise was forming. It must hurt terribly. But he had not complained.

No, Briar reminded herself. Dare had told her that Wren had fought in the wars honorably. Her brother would not have hired such a man if he was a known criminal.

But what if he were an unknown criminal? a voice in her head whispered softly.

Well, then that was stuff and nonsense, Briar, she told herself, firmly. He was a good man. An honorable man. He just... was. She knew this, plain as the nose on her face. She believed it. And telling herself that was the truth, she suddenly realized it absolutely was. She trusted Wren Spencer implicitly. As much as she trusted herself—or Dare or Kat or yes, even their younger brother Leigh. She trusted him as much as someone of her own blood, and that was saying a great deal.

What was more, she had gotten him into this mess, and she must be the one to get him out of it.

Wren came awake immediately when Briar began to sneak through the camp.

At first, he had thought it was a bear. But a bear would not have made nearly so much noise.

She would not have made a very good scout, he thought with amusement, watching her shadow crawl from her tent—the only tent that had been erected—to the circle of stones that had been set up. Angus and his men lay stretched out on rough pallets around the fire, which had burned down nearly to ashes.

A loud snore erupted from one of the men, and Wren saw Briar freeze.

Then it stopped, and she moved forward again inch by inch.

He hoped one of the men had left a knife out in plain sight. Ideally on top of a rock right next to the fire.

Now that he thought about it more carefully, he hated to imagine what Angus or his men would do if they caught Briar with her hand reaching into their blankets or worse, the hilt of their belts. In the dead of night, they might react purely with instinct and drive that knife straight into her.

Wren swore softly. He should not have asked her to do this. What a fool he was. She could be hurt or killed. And then what would her brother say?

What would he feel? A bonny, braw lass like Briar killed because of his folly.

He was tempted to call out to her but thought that might make things even worse. He might alert the men rather than Briar. Better to be silent and simply watch.

Besides, she had reached the fire now. She was creeping up on one of the sleeping forms.

He saw her crouch beside one of the men, not Angus. A young man, hardly more than a lad.

Briar seemed to be looking him over, then she crawled over to the next man. The boy must not have had a knife. Or if he did, it was beneath him, too difficult for her to reach.

She stopped beside the next sleeping man, and Wren drew in his breath.

Then, from the corner of his eye, he saw a figure sit up in the dark, away from the fire, away from the circle of men. This figure was alone, off in the shadows, and he was tied up to a sapling tree, just like Wren.

Wren swore. Percy!

Percy was looking about. He must have heard Briar.

He sat up straighter. He glanced at the fire.

"Intruder! There! By the fire! Intruder, I say!"

"I'll strangle the wee git. I'll throttle him with his own trousers, I swear to God," Wren swore.

The men around the fire were stirring. Briar was trying to hastily crawl away, but she bumped into one of the prone shapes, who gave a shout.

And then everything happened very quickly.

Briar screeched as one of Angus's men must have grabbed for her.

All the men were roused, standing up, scanning the camp for the "intruder" Percy had shouted about.

And then Angus had Briar by the arm, holding her roughly. He was shouting at her.

This was intolerable. Wren pulled at his bonds frantically.

"Angus," he bellowed. "Stop! Let her go! Angus, do ye hear me? Get yer hands off her!"

Angus heard him. He began to drag Briar toward the tree.

"What was she doing, Renfrew? Eh? Was she to slit our throats while we slept?"

"Slit yer throats?" Wren looked at Angus in disgust. "Ye really think she would be capable of such a thing? She's a young lady, gently bred. She couldna slit a man's throat. She'd never think of such a thing."

"Hmm," was all Angus said. His face was grim. He had not let go of Briar.

Wren glanced at her. The girl's face was ashen. She said nothing, just looked at him. Why, she was crying.

"Ye've made the lass cry, ye great brute," he yelled. "Is this what the great Angus Macleod has come to now, making wee girls cry?"

"I'm not a *wee* girl," Briar said. She let out a hiccup. "And I wasn't crying." She cleared her throat, and he saw her try to stand up straighter. "But I'm sorry, Wren. I've... I've failed you." She let out another little hiccup, and his heart wrenched.

"Ye havena failed me, lass," he said, trying to keep his voice gentle. "Ye did yer best. It's this great oaf who failed me. Would ye believe he used to be my best friend in the world?"

"Angus?" Briar looked at the man holding her in amazement. "Were you really, Angus? You must be an honorable man, after all. Or at least, I suppose you used to be."

"I'm still an honorable man, thank ye verra much," Angus said, glaring at them both. "It's this one who doesna ken how to stay and face his responsibilities. Who shirks his duty. And now, it is honor that is forcing me to bring him home. Whether he likes it or no'. He will do what is required."

"What are ye talking about?" Wren asked in astonishment.

"Did ye no' read the letter at all?" Angus snarled. "I sent one to ye."

Wren was quiet. In truth, he had not. Though evidently his sisters had. "I placed it on the fire."

"The fire!" Angus shook his head. "Ye might have saved us some trouble. Come easily with me."

"Why should I come anywhere with ye at all?" Wren exploded.

Angus stared. "Because I'll be damned to hell and back if I'll let yer cousin take everything that should be yers."

Wren stared back, comprehension failing him. "My cousin? What —" he began.

But Angus was already in motion. He shoved Briar away from him, and she nearly fell. "Now," Angus barked. "See to yer wife. See that ye keep her where she belongs."

"'Twould be easier to see to her safety were I no' tied to this bloody tree," Wren growled, watching as Briar got her bearings and rubbed her arm. "You've bruised the poor lass."

"Mhmm," was all Angus said as he turned his back and marched away.

"And she's no' my wife!" Wren bellowed one last time into the darkness. "And what have ye against Alec Renfrew as laird? There was a time such talk would be considered tantamount to treason, nay?"

Angus froze.

He turned back so slowly that Wren grew impatient.

"Yer cousin, Alec, will no' be laird," Angus said, meeting Wren's eyes with his own steady brown ones.

"What nonsense is this?" Wren asked derisively. "Of course, he will. He's the heir, is he no'?"

"Alec Renfrew is dead," Angus said slowly. "He has been dead for nearly two years."

Silence.

"You're jesting," Wren said finally. "That's impossible."

"Nay, it is no jest," Angus said. He was looking at Wren as if seeing him for the first time.

"My grandfather..." Wren began.

"Dead a fortnight," Angus said. "He had been poorly all spring." He looked at Wren in disbelief. "Ye bloody fool. Ye truly didna open the letter."

He turned, shaking his head, and walked back toward his men.

Wren was silent a moment.

"Go to yer tent," he said at last, looking at Briar. She looked small and pitiful, standing there in the dark. "God, ye're shivering. Do ye no' have anything warmer to put on? Wrap a blanket around yer shoulders and lie down," he instructed.

She nodded, looking for once confused and disheartened, and went slowly to her tent. It tore at his heart to see her so forlorn, but he was also distracted by what he had just heard.

Wren leaned back slowly against his tree.

What the devil was Angus talking about? How was this possible? How could he not have known?

Tomorrow, no matter what, he planned to find out.

He was startled to hear a scuffling sound and looked up to see Angus walking slowly back toward him.

"Give me yer word," Angus said, looking down at him through the darkness. "Give me yer word if I cut ye free that ye shall no' run away nor try to escape. Then ye may go and be with yer wife. She is likely cold and frightened. There is no need for ye both to be alone."

Wren could only stare. Was Angus truly offering him a kindness? Or was this simply a way to keep him well and truly hostage for good?

He tried to think. Angus thought Briar his wife. Even though she was not, poor young Lady Briar had now spent a night alone in a camp full of men. She was unmarried, unchaperoned. There was not even a single woman about to lend some measure of propriety as they traveled.

She was compromised. Plain and simple. The only challenge would be to make her see that. Well, Wren would do so. In the bleak light of day, the next morning.

In the meantime...

"Aye, I swear it to ye," Wren agreed. "Cut me loose."

"She's a bonny lass, yer bride," Angus observed as he sawed the ropes with his knife. "I wonder what she'll make of Renfrew Castle. I wonder what the people will make of her."

"Renfrew Castle," Wren said slowly. He could still hardly fathom he was on his way back. "Ye need no' do this, Angus. Ye might still let us go. This is no way to bring a mon home, in any case."

"Aye, it might have been different," Angus agreed, scratching at his beard. "This wasna the way ye were supposed to return with me. I had my instructions. I disobeyed them."

"Ye did?" Wren raised his eyebrows. "How do ye mean?"

"Well, ye're still alive, for one," Angus said evenly. Even in the dark, Wren could see Angus's eyes, cool and steady, looking down at him.

"You mean—" Wren began.

"I wasna sent to bring ye home, mon," Angus said. "I was sent to kill ye."

Chapter Six

"**M**y goodness," Briar exclaimed, lifting the tent flap and stepping out, only to trip over the sprawling Scotsman lying across her threshold. "Have you been there all night?"

She dropped to a crouch beside him and lowered her voice, "How did you get free? Why did you not wake me? I thought you wished to... you know."

Wren sat up, rubbing the sleep from his eyes.

"Where did ye get that?" he asked sharply as she came more clearly into view.

"This?" She touched the plaid wrapped around her shoulders. "It was in the tent. Why? Should I not have used it?" She looked at him guiltily. "I must admit, I know little about Scottish traditions. Was it disrespectful to use as a blanket?"

"Nay," Wren said, still feeling a little dazed at the sight of her wrapped in his family colors. The deep forest green of the checked-cloth contrasted beautifully with the dark red copper of her hair. She looked queenly. Born to wear the plaid. "No' disrespectful. Many a Scotsman has wrapped his plaid around him on a cold night. Many a Scotswoman, too, I warrant."

"Ah, that's all right then," Briar said with satisfaction tinging her voice. "You looked rather put off at the sight of it, which is why I asked."

"Aye, well." Wren cleared his throat. "I've no' seen a woman wearing it in a verra long time, is all."

"Who was the last?" Briar asked, with interest.

"My mother."

"Oh, of course! Your mother was Scottish?"

"Aye, she and my father both. My first father." He scowled. "I hardly kent the man. He died when I was a wee boy."

"And she remarried an Englishman, I presume? Your siblings' father?" Briar asked.

Wren nodded. "William Spencer. A good man. I took his name. Really, he was the only father I ever kent. I could hardly remember my own. Tis sad, but true."

"English half-siblings, but your heritage is Scottish through and through," Briar mused. "And you returned after the war to Blakeley Manor, but before that..."

"I was sent back to Scotland as a youth, to foster with my grandfather. He insisted upon it," Wren said darkly. "My father—my stepfather, that is—had already passed. My mother had four children to care for. My grandfather offered her funds if she would agree to send me."

"Oh, I see. You must have missed your mother and siblings very much," Briar said sympathetically.

Wren was quiet a moment. "At first, I did. Then I got to ken the place. The people. I came to love it. And my cousin, Alec—my grandfather's heir—he was a good lad. He became a good friend. He and my other cousin, Loghain, were of an age with me. Angus, well, he was a little older. His family is related to the laird, and he was always close to Alec and me. We were inseparable then." He was silent, remembering.

"And then what happened? You all went off to war together?" Briar guessed.

Wren nodded. "We went off to war. And we all came back, too, more's the surprise."

"Why did you not return to Scotland with your kinsmen? Why

come to Blakeley Manor at all?" Briar asked, scrunching up her face in that way she had.

"There was a quarrel," Wren said simply. "I felt I couldna return. We... it was complicated. I dinna wish to discuss it."

Briar's eyes widened, but all she said was, "Very well."

She was quiet, clearly thinking. "Why have they kidnapped you, Wren? What is it all about?"

Wren thought of what Angus had said. He could not tell her that. No, not now. Perhaps not ever.

But he could tell her part of what he had guessed.

He rubbed his hands through his hair, trying to smooth it down.

"Here," Briar said, smiling at the sight. "Let me."

Before he could stop her, her small hands were touching his hair, busily working their way gently through the thick strands, smoothing and cajoling.

Her hands were small but strong. Her touch firm but gentle.

It felt... heavenly. He sat very still. Desperate for her to stop. Desperate for her to go on.

"There, that's better," she said, putting her hands on her hips and looking down at him with a smile of satisfaction. "Less wild bear, more..."

"Gentleman bear?" Wren quipped.

She giggled, and he felt his face breaking into a smile.

She gasped. "Your face."

Immediately he frowned. "What of it?"

"It's nothing, only that..." She shook her head. "Oh, never mind." She brushed a hand over her forehead and squinted. "I must have been mistaken," she said with great feigned dignity. "Wren Spencer never smiles, after all."

He smiled then, a broad grin as he looked up at her. "Nay, but Robert Renfrew did from time to time."

"Who on earth is Robert Renfrew?" she asked with interest. "Oh! That must be you. Is that your name? Truly?"

"Robert Renfrew Spencer is what I've always called myself, though the 'Spencer' is an honorary surname, more than anything. When Marigold was little, she thought I was brown like a bird and began calling me Wren. It seemed as fitting as anything, and it stuck within the family."

"I see," Briar said, touching a finger to her lip in a way that made Wren swallow hard. She shook her head pensively. "But no, you shan't put me off that easily. I feel certain you were about to give me an answer. Why have they kidnapped you? Surely you must have some notion? Did Angus not tell you anything?"

"Aye," Wren said, shifting to his feet. There, that was better. Standing over her, he felt more himself again. "He told me a little, but no' all. Though if it is true that Alec is dead, well... I suppose I can guess the reason."

"And the reason is?"

"Well, if my cousin Alec is dead—and my grandfather Donnell, too —then there must be a new laird."

"Yes, I suppose there must, but what does that have to do with anything?"

"Well," Wren said, awkwardly. "I believe the new laird is me."

Briar stared. "You? You are the laird?"

"Quite possibly." Wren scuffed the dirt with his foot. "Either myself or Loghain. Loghain Grant, that is. He would be next in line after myself."

"You have been second-in-line to a lairdship all this time? While working as our gardener?" Briar asked.

Wren shrugged awkwardly. "I never expected it to fall to me."

"But surely you must have... well, grown up with some expectations. At least as someone close to your cousin, Alec."

Wren was quiet. "For a time, aye, I thought I would be by Alec's side always. His right-hand mon as it were. But I suppose Loghain or Angus took that place when I didna return."

"Why did you not return?" Briar asked insistently. "What could the quarrel have been about that you allowed it to spoil your future with your family?"

"With part of my family," Wren corrected, frowning. "The Spencers are just as much my family."

"Certainly," Briar agreed. "But I am sure they wanted you to fulfill your responsibilities and obligations to your grandfather and cousin."

"Mmm," was all Wren said. He did not wish to confide what Laurel and Marigold had said about all this.

"Best get something to eat, and then it's back in the carriage for ye both," Angus interrupted, coming up to them. "I hope I willna have any trouble getting ye inside?"

A whining voice drifted across the camp behind him. "Biscuits? You call these lumps biscuits? Why they're hard as rock. I could throw one at you—see? And I bet it hurts like a rock, doesn't it? Hey! Ouch! Stop that!"

"Percy," Briar groaned. "Oh, Mr. Macleod, I should so greatly prefer to ride a horse. Perhaps you might spare one for Wren and I? Anything but sharing a closed space with Percy Quintrell for another hour."

"He's a whiny bugger, is he no'? A right milksop," Angus said, shaking his head as he watched one of his men push Percy down onto a rock and slap a plate into his hands.

"He's unbearable," Briar said, lifting her chin. "I should like to see *you* share a carriage with him for an entire day."

"Hmm," Angus said, rubbing his chin. "Well, we'll see how it goes. Perhaps at midday ye might change places for a while."

Wren did not mind sharing the carriage with Briar and Percy for the morning. In fact, he was uncomfortably aware of the fact that he required Percy Quintrell's assistance in a delicate matter.

For that morning, Lady Briar would have to be made to see just what a terrible predicament she was really in.

And once she had seen that, she would need to make a momentous decision. Perhaps the most significant decision of her entire young life.

"Are you mad?" Briar gasped. "I'm not going to marry either of you!" She shook her head frantically. "I have no plans to marry in the immediate future. I most certainly will not limit my prospects to... to... Well, I'm sorry Percy, but..."

"Me?" Percy retorted. He pointed across the carriage. "What about him? He's a gardener! You can't tell me you prefer him to me."

FENNA EDGEWOOD

"Neither of us are ideal suitors," Wren said firmly. "I am sure on that Percy and I can agree."

"Well, I certainly—" Percy began, only to be silenced by a glare from Wren. He pursed his lips.

"But yer prospects, I'm afraid, Lady Briar, are limited to the men in this carriage. Or I suppose ye could extend yer field of choice to the men riding with us. Though some are sure to be married already. Angus, for one."

"Angus!" Briar exclaimed. "I have no wish to marry Mr. Macleod, thank you very much. Not that he isn't a good man in his way, I'm sure," she added hastily.

"Oh, yes," Percy said dryly. "He has only kidnapped you and Mr. Spencer here, then gone back on his word to me. He's sure to make you a wonderful husband."

"Shut up, Percy," Briar snapped. "I am not taking a husband."

"Ye shall, and ye must," Wren said tersely. "It's no' a matter of wanting or no' wanting. Ye've been placed in a terrible position, Lady Briar. What would yer brother say?"

"He'd likely just shoot first and talk later," Briar said sweetly. "And in this case, I might not blame him. I have reached the point in our journey where I should like nothing more than to be taken back home. Preferably immediately."

She crossed her arms over her chest and turned her head to the window.

"I understand," said Wren, trying his best to. "And I am most terribly sorry. They only brought ye out of the mad belief ye were already..." He coughed delicately. "My wife already."

Percy gave a snort of laughter. "Scottish fools."

Wren's head whipped toward him. "Who is the real fool now? Says the young mon who got himself caught up in this mess. And what do ye think shall happen to ye I wonder when we reach Scotland? I suppose ye think Angus will pay ye what ye're owed and send ye back over the border?"

Percy had paled. "Why, yes. Something like that."

Wren scoffed.

"Why?" Percy scowled. "What is the alternative?" He turned paler still. "You can't think they mean to... to dispose of me?" His voice dropped to a whisper. "Me? A Quintrell? Murdered in Scotland?"

"Perhaps if ye were a bridegroom, they'd have pity on ye," Wren said dryly.

Percy's eyes lit up. "Yes, I see. And be merciful. I could say this was all a mistake. My dear fiancée and I were mixed up in their clan feud by sheer accident. All we wish is to go back to our peaceful lives in England. Perhaps we could even say my wife was with child..." He eyed Briar.

"I think not," Briar said hotly. "I am not your wife. I shall never be your wife."

Percy shot her a pleading expression. "Not even to save my poor skin?"

"Oh, please," Briar huffed. "They aren't going to kill you." She looked at Wren. "Are they?"

"I have no idea. We have gotten sadly off topic. The subject, may I remind ye both, is Lady Briar's forthcoming nuptials," Wren said firmly.

"You may as well discuss Percy's fate, for there will be no nuptials," Briar said, tossing her head. "You may pontificate all you wish, but I believe I am required to actually agree to any marriage, am I not? You cannot simply wed me to one of you."

Wren let out a frustrated growl.

"And growling will not frighten me into it either," Briar complained. "You may growl all you want to, my Scottish bear."

Wren was quiet for a while. Percy was mercifully silent as well, staring out the window, apparently contemplating his precarious future.

"When we get to Scotland, ye needs must be wed, Lady Briar," Wren said quietly, "to one of us."

He ran a hand over his face. "I may no' be able to protect ye otherwise."

Briar stared. "Protect me? Protect me from what?" She looked between the two men. "Are you saying, if I marry Percy, I will have to count on him for protection?" She rolled her eyes. "That's a laugh. He's more likely to hide behind me than protect me."

"I should do my utmost to honor my vows as your husband," Percy began loftily. "With my body, I shall worship thee..."

"Oh, shut up, Percy," Briar said, looking disgusted. "As if I could ever trust any vow you ever made. As far as I am concerned, you owe your body and your worship to one woman already—Bessie Brewer."

"Bah." Percy waved a hand.

Briar ignored him and looked at Wren. "If what you say is true, then I have no real choice at all. For you cannot truly expect me to choose Percy as my mate."

Wren gave a little shudder at the word. He had no wish to imagine Percy mating with anyone. Least of all, this copper-haired lass he was starting to become rather attached to.

"You see?" Briar shook her head. "And therefore, you are forcing yourself into a corner as much as myself. We shall be trapped together in a marriage neither of us want." She turned a doleful expression upon him. "Surely, there must be another way."

"There isna," he said stubbornly. "Angus thinks ye're my wife. The entire camp believed it. They have no idea ye're a maid. Even if we were to get them to agree to send ye back to England once we reach Renfrew Castle, what do ye suppose would happen?"

"Well," Briar said carefully. "I suppose I should explain to Dare what befell me. I expect he would be very sympathetic."

"Aye, and could ye keep it a secret from the rest of the world? That ye were off with strange men, sleeping out of doors, with no chaperone?"

"Oh, for pity's sake," Briar exclaimed. "Men do the same things all the time, and they do not have to get married because of it. The standards for young women are utterly ridiculous. This is exactly why I have had no wish to go to London for a Season. And now I suppose I never shall, for you are essentially telling me that no man in his right mind outside of this carriage would marry me."

"No man in his right mind inside this carriage either," Percy said, none too helpfully. "I don't know if your gardener is of sound mind and body. After all, he's Scottish, isn't he? Think of all they used to say about the Scots. Brutal. Barbarian-like. Is that really who you would wish to tie yourself to for all eternity, Briar? When you could marry the nice neighbor boy and settle down comfortably?"

Briar curled her lip. "The nice neighbor boy has been gone a very long time, Percy. I miss him. I really do. But I could never trust him to be a good husband. Let alone a faithful one."

She looked back at Wren, her cheeks suddenly tinged with pink. "And that is another thing... You cannot tell me you wish to be tied to me, forced to be faithful to me the rest of your life, just because of a stupid mistake! I am sure you have other women you might... wish to wed." The pink on her cheeks had deepened to a dark rose.

Wren shook his head, willing his own face not to redden. He was a man, not a boy, was he not? "I dinna. There is no one. If ye are asking, would I be faithful to ye? Aye, I would. I would mean the vows if I said them," Wren said stubbornly. "I should make ye as good a husband as I was able. Ye deserve nothing less."

"Oh," Briar said, her voice small. "I see." She was quiet a moment. "Well, thank you. That is a better offer than I am sure I deserve."

Wren shook his head in frustration. "Ye deserve yer Season in London. Ye deserve to marry a mon like yer brother. A duke or an earl or some such lord. Ye're the daughter of a duke, and yer family must have had high hopes for yer future. Now they are dashed to bits. Dinna think I dinna ken it is all my fault."

"You mean you don't think they'll be altogether thrilled to hear she's eloped with a Scottish gardener?" Percy drawled. "I daresay they won't care. Her sister married your brother, and he worked in the barn, didn't he?"

"He was a groom. And he is a good, brave man who makes my sister very happy," Briar said angrily. "I'll thank you to mind your own business, Percy. Stay out of this. The Spencer brothers are better men than you, I should say. I have not heard of them debauching village girls nor abandoning infants."

"Renfrew," Wren reminded her. "Ye wouldna be a Spencer if we wed."

"Oh yes, Renfrew." She looked at him, eyes widening. "Should I be calling you Robert, then?"

He shook his head. "Wren is fine. But when we arrive in Scotland, well, some might call me Renfrew. Some Rabbie, perhaps."

"Rabbie," Percy said in mocking delight. "What a sweet little nickname for you, Spencer."

Wren glared at the young man. "Shut yer trap, ye whelp."

"Rabbie is rather a sweet nickname, Wren," Briar said more delicately. "I have always liked the name Robert."

"I suppose you'd best pick the Scot, then," Percy said bitterly. "Never mind that Percy is a far more elegant name. And the Quintrell family has noble roots going back six generations, all the way to…"

"How would we do this? Were we to… wed?" Briar asked abruptly, ignoring Percy's listing of his lineage. "It is not as if there were a vicar traveling with us. And to wed, you would have to tell Angus that we are not wed right now."

"We dinna need a vicar or a priest," Wren replied. "That's an English requirement. In Scotland, it's different. A mon and a woman marry by mutual consent."

"What does that mean?" Briar asked, not comprehending.

"It means we are married if we say we are married—before witnesses," Wren explained. "Ye dinna need a kirk to make it official."

"How absolutely heathenish," Percy observed with fascination. "I should have expected nothing less from the Scots."

"Shut yer gob, Quintrell," Wren said, but mildly. He was growing used to Percy's annoying tendencies.

"How very free. And there are no other requirements? We simply say we are married? As Percy as the only witness? If I were to say I were your wife right now, that would be all there was to it?" Briar's eyes were wide, and she had turned rather pale.

"I should prefer Percy Quintrell no' be the only witness to our marriage," Wren said gruffly.

Not only because he didn't like the young git, but because he would not trust him as far as he could throw him. If Percy later was to deny that he and Briar had made marriage vows, things could become very awkward. No, he would prefer to inform Angus of the truth of things and do things properly. Or as properly as they could, on the road, out of doors, surrounded only by men.

"As the only party present who knows Briar's family, I should think she would wish for me to be a witness to her nuptials. I could stand in place of her brother," Percy drawled.

Briar seemed to repress a shudder. "That is very kind of you, Percy, but..." She shook herself, as if trying to wake. "I am not sure about any of this. It all seems so difficult to fathom. You say I must be married but..."

"Ye had no wish to marry, lass?" Wren asked gently. "I dinna ken what to say. I have no wish to force ye."

It was all very awkward. He realized he was not the sort of man she had likely spent her girlhood dreaming she would one day wed. And while she was a very tolerant young lady with more liberal views than Percy, the fact remained he was a Scot. To some noble English families, that would be a detriment all in itself. Scottish prejudice was at what seemed like an all-time low among the English, after the admirable performance of so many Highland regiments in the wars with Napoleon. However, Wren suspected that many English still secretly harbored views of Scotland as nothing more than a kingdom of wild barbarians.

"You are hardly an ideal suitor, Spencer... or Renfrew, whatever your name really is," Percy sniffed. "Can you really blame her reluctance? I suppose I should have been her immediate preference were it not for my slight mishap. Women are so prudish when it comes to such matters. I pity you, Briar. You must choose between the devil you know and..."

"And the Scot?" Briar finished, glaring angrily at Percy. "Mr. Spencer... Mr. Renfrew, that is, is hardly less than ideal compared to yourself. Do you know why they have kidnapped him, Percy? Did Mr. Macleod tell you that, when you were selling information to him for as much as you could get?"

"I didn't much care what they wanted with him. In fact—" Percy cleared his throat. "Well, I didn't care what they wanted." He shot a quick glance at Wren, who immediately understood. So, Percy had hoped Angus had planned something much more nefarious than mere kidnapping, had he? Well apparently, he was not so far off as he might have been.

"They are bringing him home because he is their new laird, Percy. Because his grandfather and cousin are dead, quite sadly and unexpectedly, and he is the next in line," Briar said.

"Not quite so landless and penniless after all then," Percy said, raising his brows. "Well, good for you then, Renfrew. I'm sure her brother will be happy to know he doesn't have to support your entire family."

"He should not care if Wren made me happy," Briar said quietly, looking down at her hands. "And I do not care a whit about the lairdship. I hope you know that. I care about whether my husband is a good man. A caring man. And that is why Percy is out of the running." She clenched her hands together suddenly. "Yet, I still do not wish to marry anyone. Anyone! This is all entirely unbearable. I am trapped in this carriage, and now... Trapped. Just... trapped." She shook her head, bit her lip, and looked out the window.

Wren said nothing. He did not know what else he could possibly say. Part of him longed to take her hands in his, gently separate them, hold them reassuringly. But he did not have that right. He should let her be. Let the girl think. She would decide what was best. All he could do was wait.

For she was trapped. That was all true. Thanks to he and Percy and yes, thanks to Angus Macleod.

"Very well," Briar said after a stretch of silence. Her voice sounded dull and listless to Wren. She was resigned, not ecstatic. "I suppose if you both tell me I must, then I must. Tell me what we must do to... finish this."

"Very well, lass," Wren said softly. "I shall speak to Angus when next we stop and explain matters."

Briar nodded, then tucked herself more tightly into her corner of the carriage seat and, closing her eyes, pretended to fall asleep, ignoring both the men.

At about midday, the carriage stopped and the three prisoners—guests, or whatever they were—were permitted to clamber out into the sunshine.

After a brief meal of hard bread, slices of yellow cheese, and dried meat, Wren had gone to speak to Angus.

While she waited, watching covertly, Briar strolled back and forth along the road beside the carriage.

Was this truly to be her wedding day? Here? Now? Alongside the Great North Road?

They had passed the Scottish border that morning. She was not in England any longer.

But no matter where she was, would Dare not have come for her? Or sent men after her? Yet, they had been stopped by no one.

One might think kidnapping an easy pastime based on how simple it had been for Macleod and his men to make off with her and Percy and Wren.

She spoke her thoughts aloud as Wren approached her. "Why has Dare not come for me? I understand that I am compromised. Very well. But what I do not understand is how I can have been abducted in plain view and carried away from my home without anyone making a fuss about it. Do you not think it strange?"

Wren shifted uncomfortably back and forth on his feet. "Perhaps no' so strange as ye think."

"What do you mean?" Briar frowned.

"Well, it seems Angus didna leave things to chance. Once he scooped us both up and decided to bring ye along, he sent a mon back to throw yer brother off his trail as it were."

"He did what?" Briar exclaimed.

"Aye, it seems his mon paid a few folks along the road to go and tell yer brother they had seen ye being taken. But taken in the direction of London. No' Scotland. So, he is most likely going quite mad looking for ye, but he is looking in the wrong direction."

"Poor Dare!" Briar's face was stricken. "Well, that is dreadful. And cruel. Someone must send word and tell him."

Wren took a step closer, glanced about, then lowered his voice, "I dinna disagree, lass. And when we reach Renfrew Castle, that is just what ye shall do. Ye must write to him and tell him just what has occurred. Ye may even return home to him if that is what ye wish."

Briar stared. "Even though we shall be... married by then?"

"Aye, I willna keep ye against yer will, married or no'," Wren said stubbornly. "But until we have arrived, until I have sorted out what exactly is going on, well..." How could he tell her what Angus had said? That this was not supposed to be his wedding journey but a funerary one?

If Angus was to be believed, that is. Wren still had not decided if his old friend could be entirely trusted. Oh, Angus certainly believed that Loghain wanted Wren dead. But perhaps the man had simply... misunderstood. Loghain had always gotten along with Wren. Could he really want the lairdship so badly that he would kill a man for it?

Wren would arrive at Renfrew Castle and take stock. See who was loyal and who was not.

But in the meantime, this group of men they were surrounded by? Angus could be trusted, aye, but the rest? No, he could not risk it. He would play the docile prisoner—until they reached Renfrew Castle.

"When we are back at Renfrew Castle, among people I ken and trust, ye will be safe and can send word to yer brother," he finished.

"You would really wish for me to return home? To Blakeley Manor? Rather than stay with you?" Briar was still caught up on that, it seemed.

Wren could not meet her eye. "It isna about what I wish. None of this has been my choice."

"No, I suppose not," Briar said thoughtfully. She sighed. "And I suppose you do not wish to be stuck with me."

"Do ye wish to be stuck with me?" Wren asked, surprised.

"I..." She hesitated, and he was shocked. "You are the only person here who is even slightly safe and familiar to me, Wren. And you are to become my... husband." She stumbled over the word, blushing.

"Aye, and I will continue to see ye're safe," Wren promised. "For yer brother's sake and for yers."

"You do not owe him anything," Briar said, frowning.

"Nay, that's where ye're wrong," Wren said. "I owe him a debt of honor greater than I can ever repay. He employed me. Trusted me to accompany ye on yer visits. And now he has lost ye entirely."

"He will certainly be worried," Briar agreed. "But I will not have been entirely lost to him. I am still alive. I will be a married woman, though." She looked up. "What did Angus say?"

"He understands the situation now. Properly," Wren said. "He willna apologize for taking ye, though he should."

"Well, he is a Scot, is he not?" Briar asked breezily. "They are notoriously stubborn people." And she smiled teasingly up at him, the expression transforming her face into a thing of such perfect beauty that Wren took a step back.

"What is it, Renfrew?" A hand clapped Wren on the shoulder and squeezed, none too gently. "Simply canna believe yer good luck in a bride, eh? She's a bonny lass. I'll say that frankly. Much too good for ye, I'm sure."

Wren tried to smile. "Aye, she is that."

"Which? Bonny? Or too good for ye?"

"Both," Wren said easily. He met Briar's eyes. Well, let the lass know what he truly thought. "She is a braw, breathtaking woman, and any mon would be lucky to have her take him as husband."

He watched Briar's eyes widen, then her lips part slightly.

"Well, Wren is not so bad himself," she said quickly, smiling over at Angus. She lifted her chin and tossed her copper hair over her shoulder. Somewhere along the way, it had come out of its original coiffure, with many curls and pins, and she had simply plaited it into a long, loose braid. The simple style suited her and showed off the exquisite shades of her rich red mane. "I wouldn't be taking him otherwise."

"Sure she's no' a Scottish lassie, after all?" Angus teased, elbowing Wren. "Look at that hair! Stirs the sporran, nay?" He winked teasingly at Wren who glared.

"What's a sporran?" Briar asked innocently.

"It's a sort of pouch worn over a kilt." Wren cleared his throat. "Well, shall we get on with it, then?"

"Aye, certainly. How do ye wish to do it? Have ye vows prepared?"

"Vows?" Briar shook her head wildly. "I have no vows prepared. I suppose we might recite from the Book of Common Prayer. Though I cannot say I know it well enough by heart."

"The Church of England?" Angus wrinkled his nose.

"I ken what I wish to say," Wren interrupted. "And we will keep things simple, aye?" He nodded at Briar who hesitated, then nodded back. "Are ye ready, lass?"

He saw that Percy had come up nearby and was standing, watching the proceedings along with a few of Angus's men. The observers were quiet. Good. Let one of them laugh, and it would be Wren's fist in their face. Poor Briar looked sick with nervousness already, lest she have to deal with mocking men jesting about her wedding night.

Wren nodded at Angus.

"Well, ye may as well proceed with the vows as I have nay else to say. I am merely a witness, along with these other lumps, aye?" Angus said easily. He folded his arms over his chest.

"Aye." Wren cleared his throat awkwardly and looked at Briar. "May I take yer hands in mine?"

"Certainly," she said hastily, coming a few steps closer and holding them out. She dropped her voice. "Though they are rather clammy. I am ever so sorry."

"'Tis all right," Wren reassured her, smiling a little. He cleared his throat again. "Well, then." He had been thinking of what he might say, and in the end, he went with words that were simple, yet ones he believed would be true. "Ye have chosen me as yer husband, and from this day forth, we are one no' two. I vow to give ye all that is mine to give. I vow to serve ye in every way which ye may require. Whatever ye wish, I put myself in yer hands. My body, my goods, my heart, and every part of me is yers, this I vow before God."

"What's this? Ye swearing to obey the lassie now, no' the other way around?" Angus asked, chortling a little.

"All she may require, aye?" A man standing nearby hooted. "May get tiresome, Renfrew. Who kens how much she may require and when..."

Wren shut the man down with a cold glare and turned back to Briar.

Her face was transfixed on his. There were pink spots on her cheeks. "Did you really mean all of that?" she breathed.

"Well, I shall try to mean it all, aye," Wren said a little uncomfortably. He had hesitated over the mention of his "heart" but had decided it sounded better that way. There were many ways to love another person. He had not promised to love her as a sweetheart. He had been in love once and been forsworn. He was not eager to risk that part of him again. But he was no green lad now. He would take care of his wife and cherish her. That was what it came down to, in the end.

"I have nothing nearly so grand to say," Briar said, looking even more nervous.

"Anything ye say will be fine," Wren said encouragingly.

"Aye, short and sweet, lassie. Short and sweet's the way of it," Angus said.

Briar took a deep breath and nodded.

Then she looked up, her own soft, honey-brown ones meeting his with a clash of something poignant and powerful that drew a lump into Wren's throat.

"I take you to be my husband, Robert Renfrew Spencer, from this day forward. And I shall be the best wife I can be." Here she stumbled, paused, licked her lips.

Wren gave her hands, which were still trapped between his, a little squeeze, and she continued quickly.

"I take you to be my husband, for richer or for poorer, for better and for worse, till death do us part, and thereto I plight thee my troth," she rushed out all at once. "And that is all." She looked at Wren helplessly, and he nodded.

"Very well done, lassie. And I say ye are wed," Angus said, smiling back and forth between them both. "May ye be verra happy all yer days." He turned to the crowd of men. "Now let us break bread. It's been a long day, eh?"

The men began to drift away, wandering over to where the campfire had been set up.

"I hope there is room in that tent for the both of ye," Angus said, dropping his voice and nudging Wren in the ribs as he walked past.

"Share the tent?" Briar's eyes widened as she heard what Angus had said.

"Nay, nay," Wren said quickly. He shook his head. "The men—they'll be expecting that, aye. But we dinna need to. I have no wish to..." He trailed off. How could he say he had absolutely no wish to bed his wife in a very small tent amongst strange men who would be lying there, farting and snoring and, worst of all, listening for all they were worth? No, he was in no rush. Besides, she may have no wish to consummate things at all.

He decided to tell her.

"In Scotland, a mon and a woman may be considered wed without there being... well, consummation."

She still looked puzzled.

"A wedding night," he clarified. "We need no' share a bed to be considered mon and wife, aye?"

"Oh!" Briar's eyes widened, then she blushed fiercely. "I had not even considered that part of things."

She must have been lying. Surely, she had considered it at least a little, he thought, wryly. But he would not press matters.

"We might put that off, as long as ye choose," he said delicately. "And perhaps until after ye write to yer family. Or if ye never wish to..."

"Never?" Briar's eyes widened still farther. "You are saying you would not mind? Never sharing a bed with your wife?"

Wren felt a blush begin to creep upon him and quickly brushed a hand over his face to distract himself. "None of this was by yer choice, lass. Let us simply take one day at a time. There is no need to rush. I'll set up yer tent now. There is a stream over yonder, but within sight of the camp, if ye wish to freshen up before supper."

And then he turned away from her.

How could he confess the truth? It was impossible. He could not tell Lady Briar Blakeley that part of him longed for nothing better than to throw her down right then and there amongst the tall grasses, onlookers be damned. Push up her skirts and make her his true and lawful wife in the way men and women had been making vows with their bodies for thousands of years.

He could not tell her, nay, that he longed to run his hands over her pert, soft curves, wrench the gown she wore from her shoulders, and cup her firm white breasts in his hands.

He could not tell her how he longed to devour her ripe, red lips. The ones she always was accidentally drawing his attention to with her biting and licking.

He could not say how much he desired to undo that long braid of hers and see her copper-red hair splayed loose and wanton against her fair skin with nothing but his plaid beneath her.

Nay, he couldna say any of that without scaring the poor lass senseless.

She was his to protect now, not to consume like a delicious treat.

And so, he walked away, his back straight as a rod, and ignored the other part of him that was straight and hard as a rod, too.

———

He didn't want her, Briar thought, in amazement mixed with something else. There was a pain in the vicinity of her heart, as if a fist had taken the organ and clenched up tight. He did not desire her. That much was now clear.

She felt like a fool. She had lied when she had said she had not considered that part of things. Of course, she had! Did he realize it?

Perhaps not. He likely saw her as an innocent and naïve young girl, not fit to be a man's wife at all—at least not a man such as him. A brawny, fierce man like Wren should have a wife to match. Some lovely Scottish country girl with a fiery temperament. Not a docile young English lady.

Not that she was truly docile, of course. But perhaps that was what he thought. Perhaps he believed English women did not even enjoy... marital relations. Perhaps he was trying to spare her the embarrassment of it all.

Or perhaps he simply does not find you desirable, Briar, a persistent voice in her head said. *Not all men do, you know.*

He had married her for the sake of her honor. To protect her from shame.

That meant he was a good man, not that he wished to lie with her as a... as a husband would.

As a husband should! a sulkier voice said. He should wish to. Had he not said he would do all that was required?

She felt dejected. Even more lonely than before.

But she refused to show that, not in front of the likes of Percy Quintrell. So, she stirred herself, forced herself to walk to the edge of camp, over to the little stream where she found a quiet spot. Crouching down, she splashed cold water on her face and hands.

A full bath would have been welcome, but she was not about to attempt it now, with a camp full of men a few yards away, probably watching her with interest every time her back was turned.

What would they all think when Wren did not come to her tonight, she wondered uncomfortably? It was their wedding night. And while this was not how she had envisioned it, she could not say she had any real complaints about the man she could be spending it with.

No, Wren was the perfect specimen of manhood. Even fully clothed, he took her breath away. She could not imagine how beautiful he would be naked, with moonlight illuminating his physique as he rose over her, his chest sleek, his muscles rippling as he lowered his head to hers for a passionate kiss, and his torso brushed against...

"Food is ready, lassie! I mean, Mrs. Renfrew," Angus bellowed from the fireside behind her.

There was hooting and laughter.

Briar quickly dried her hands on her skirt and rose to return.

Chapter Seven

Wren was waiting until the last possible minute to turn in for the night. Unfortunately, that meant he was stuck in the company of Percy Quintrell, who apparently had much the same idea.

The two men were sitting on opposite sides of the fire, the last of Angus's own men having turned in a few minutes before.

How long would Quintrell stay up, Wren wondered in annoyance. Could the young man not go to sleep and go back to being a nuisance tomorrow?

Instead, he saw Percy rise to his feet and come over to where he sat.

"We might as well sit closer since we're the only men still up," Percy said, sitting down much too close for comfort and giving Wren a grin that seemed meant to be friendly.

Wren glared back. "I can enjoy the quiet and my own thoughts, Quintrell. We need no' make chitchat."

"I simply wished to congratulate you on your nuptials," Percy said quickly. "After all, it isn't every day that a gardener—even one who is supposedly a secret Scottish prince—weds the daughter of a duke."

"A laird," Wren growled. "No' a prince."

"Very well, a laird. I suppose some land and money come with the position? For Briar's sake, I should certainly hope so as you promised to share all your worldly goods. That is, if you are really to inherit anyway," Percy said.

"What do ye mean?" Wren asked between gritted teeth. "Aye, the lairdship comes with the estate. Large tracts of land. And people, too. People who have been loyal to the Renfrews and lived on Renfrew land for generations. It is a clan, no' like ye English country gentlemen may be used to. The people are no' servants, but equals."

"I see, I see. Yes, it sounds very democratic. Almost American," Percy drawled. "And yet they have done very well without you all this time. Strange that they should bring you back now and in such a violent way, too." He dropped his voice secretively. "You know, when Angus first approached me to gain information about where you could be found, I almost thought he had, well, wicked motives."

"Aye, I'm sure ye hoped he had," Wren said dryly. "Looking forward to seeing me murdered on the side of the road, were ye? Must have been disappointing."

"Well, I shouldn't have liked for Briar to witness anything so horrible, of course. But it's true that I did expect there to be violence. In truth, I cooperated with Angus in part because he is such a threatening brute of a man," Percy said.

Wren snorted. "Aye, next ye'll be saying ye didna wish to cooperate but were intimidated into it. Had nothing to do with the coin ye hoped ye'd get."

"I still haven't received any of that coin, which does not predispose me to be very favorable toward your countrymen," Percy said, frowning desolately into the flames. "But no, it was something one of his men said that made me confident they did not have your best interests at heart. Certainly, I did not expect them to suddenly cart us all off together in a carriage to return you to take up a noble legacy. No, I feel certain his men were as surprised by that turn of events as I was." He gave Wren a surprisingly piercing look. "Perhaps you had best watch your back, Renfrew. If things can change so suddenly."

"Aye, I'll be on the lookout no' to be murdered," Wren said lightly, refusing to accept advice from Percy Quintrell. Nor would he admit what Angus had already confessed: The mission to Blakeley Manor had originally been one of assassination, not restoration.

"I take it you have no wish to bed her then," Percy whispered, nodding his head toward the sole tent to which Briar had retreated a few hours earlier. "Can't say I blame you."

"Pardon me?" Wren said coldly. "Are ye referring to my wife?"

"Of course, she's the only woman here you could bed, isn't she?" Percy said cheerfully. Wren resisted the urge to smack him—for now. "But I must say, the Blakeleys have always seemed like cold fish to me. Do you get my meaning? I doubt you have much to look forward to between the sheets, as it were. I suppose that's why you're out here, talking to me, instead of in Briar's tent already. Oh well, I doubt she'll complain if you seek out other ladies. Have a sweetheart back in Scotland already, I expect, no matter what lies you told her, eh?"

"I have no sweetheart back in Scotland," Wren said coldly. "I was betrothed at one time, but she married another."

"Oho! Did she now? That's interesting. What must that have done to the prideful Renfrew now! Is that why you didn't go back after the wars and took up servant life instead?" Percy asked, looking too interested.

Wren ignored him and instead rose to his feet, brushing the dust off his trousers. "Goodnight to ye, Quintrell."

Percy raised his eyebrows. "Turning in? Time for your bedroll?"

"Goodnight," was all Wren would say.

Then he marched over to Briar's tent and lifting the flap, ducked and went inside.

❧

Briar had been in the midst of a restless sleep when a burly Scotsman tripped over her foot and went down on his knees.

She let out a little yelp and sat up straight, the blankets falling to her waist.

"Wren?"

"Aye, who else would it be?"

"Well, it is dark. How should I know?"

"I'd kill any other man who tried to enter yer tent." A pause. "How is yer foot? Did I squash it?"

"It is all right," Briar said, rubbing it. "How is yours?"

"It's nothing, just a stubbed toe," Wren said dismissively. He had sat down in a corner of the tent but looked ridiculously large in such a small place.

"What are you doing here?" Briar hissed. "I thought we were not going to... you know."

"Aye, we aren't," he said quickly. He scratched his chin thoughtfully. "But that whelp, Quintrell..."

"Oh, no, you are here because of Percy?" Briar groaned.

"He has quite the mouth on him," Wren said, and she could almost hear him scowling. "He was sayin' disparaging things. I shallna repeat them."

"About me?" Briar asked with interest. "How unsurprising. And that made you come into my tent?"

"Our tent," Wren corrected. "Though I willna share it with ye if ye ask me to leave." He hesitated. "Shall I go?"

"Or else what? Are you asking if you may sleep here?"

"Aye. Just sleep, mind. If ye think there is room enough for two."

Briar looked about her. There was hardly room for one in the little tent, let alone the addition of a huge man like Wren. But she knew she would not be asking him to leave.

"Well, it will be a tight fit," she said slowly, as if hesitant.

"I'll lie over on this side, shall I?" Wren asked gruffly. He gingerly unfurled himself and put his head down nearby, where hers had recently been.

"Yes, that'll do," Briar said. She lay back down and turned on her side to look at him. "This is very..."

"Strange. Aye," he agreed. He cleared his throat. "Do ye have enough blankets? Are ye cold?"

Briar's mind raced.

"Well," she said slowly. "Now that you mention it, I am a little cold. But then I suppose the tent will warm up with the two of us in it now."

"Aye," Wren said, looking at her. She could not read the expression in his eyes. He turned onto his back and sort of crooked the arm out that was closest to her. "Or ye might lie closer if ye like." He quickly added, "Whatever ye wish. Perhaps I should go."

"No, that would be very nice," Briar said, already scooting over. She looked down at him for a moment. Clearly, he had no plans to undress. She was in her chemise, which while white muslin and quite transparent if she were standing, was modest enough in the dark of the tent.

He looked very fine, all stretched out, with one arm tucked under his head. His dark hair contrasted against the forest-green plaid she had stretched out on the ground. She gave a little shiver, then quickly made herself lie down.

"I suppose I shall put my head..."

He grunted. "Aye, that'll do."

"I'm not hurting you?"

He chortled. "A little lassie like ye? No' possible."

"Very well." Briar shifted again, making herself more comfortable. "Yes, that is much warmer."

That was an understatement. He was radiating heat like a roaring fireplace.

Her head rested in the crook of his arm. It was hard and soft at the same time. Not quite so comfortable as a pillow, but firm and warm and masculine. He smelled surprisingly nice, too. Like the outdoors, like grass and trees and smoke from the campfire, and underlying it all, that mystical scent of hot male flesh.

His arm came around her a little closer, pulling her against his body. "Is that all right?"

"Oh, yes." Briar hoped her voice did not betray just how very all right it was. It felt wonderful. He felt wonderful, her body pressed up alongside his. She resisted, just barely, the urge to wriggle against him even more closely, press her fleshy places against his hip and...

She sighed. "Goodnight, Wren."

"Goodnight... Wife."

Chapter Eight

It was a beautiful morning. The sun was shining. The birds were chirping.

Furthermore, since entering Scotland, the scenery had been growing more and more lovely by the day. The day before they had broken off from the Great North Road, which led to Edinburgh, and were making their journey along less traveled roads that followed the coastline. Renfrew Castle and the associated clan lands lay just north of Inverness, Briar had been informed.

The terrain had become more mountainous and more awe-inspiring. They began to pass over gloriously green hills and through some of the famous Scottish glens. Before reaching the coast, they passed by shimmering lakes, which Briar was informed were called "lochs," and through moors ablaze with flax and heather, thistle and gorse.

She had been told of the beauty and majesty of the Great Glen, which ran for miles and miles from Fort William to Inverness and was surrounded by some of the highest mountains in Britain. Soon, she would see it with her own eyes as they traveled farther north.

It gave her a thrill to recall that this was her new home. She was a Scottish bride now! She was eager to learn more of the culture and people of the land she found herself in. Though the prospect of the people part of things also left her feeling nervous. What would Wren's people think of her? Would they be angry he had chosen an English wife?

And yet, just now, she felt neither thrilled, eager, nor even nervous. What she felt was primarily pain.

She slipped out of the tent, leaving Wren still sleeping behind her, his large form sprawled comfortably, taking up most of the interior of the tent.

She had to smile a little, looking at him as he slept. His black hair tousled, a few thick shining pieces nearly brushing his eyes. He was in need of a haircut. And yet, she rather liked his hair this way. Longish and unruly, and so very soft looking compared to the rest of him.

They had spent two nights together in this tent now, but she had not worked up the courage to touch his hair again, as she had done so easily that morning before they were wed. How strange. Instead, she simply appreciated the strength and warmth of his body and the precious intimate hours they spent, sleeping close together. The rest of the day they were so formal, so very polite with one another that an outsider might easily be forgiven for not realizing they were married at all.

The smile had been a mistake. Briar winced, putting a hand to her temple as she stood up, and squinted in the bright morning sun.

She had hoped not to experience one of the terrible megrims she was prone to as they traveled. Since childhood, she had suffered the excruciating headaches. She could still remember the first time one had come over her. The hammering and pounding in her head had been so confusing. She had cried from the pain of it all. Her mother had tried everything, finally putting her to bed in a dark room with a cool cloth on her head, and patting her hair until she had fallen into a restless sleep.

Now as a grown woman, they came upon her a few times a year. Sometimes as often as once a month. She knew of other women who suffered the affliction much more frequently, even daily, and so she was grateful. And yet, it was awful to be so stricken. At times, the pain lasted a full day or more, became so intense she would cast up her accounts, and could do no more than lie weakly in bed.

She could not afford to do that now. Not while they were traveling as quickly as they could to get Wren back home.

She was still not sure why Angus drove them with such terrible urgency, but she had come to trust the man enough to know there was a reason, and a good one.

She took a few steps away from the tent, breathing in deeply, allowing the fresh ocean breeze to sweep over her and refresh her. She kept her eyes stubbornly closed to the bright sunlight. Opening them would renew the pain.

She knew she should find shade. Lie down again. The piercing behind her eyes was only growing.

A stabbing pain shot through her like an arrow, and she groaned, bending over as she felt the nausea whirl her stomach unpleasantly.

"What is it? What is wrong?" a deep voice said sharply from behind.

Wren had awoken. She could not even open her eyes to turn and look at him.

"A headache. A megrim. I am prone to them," she mumbled. For a moment, she felt almost like crying. She had no wish for him to see her like this. Weak and immobilized.

"A megrim? A bilious headache?" His voice was coming closer. "Aye, my mother suffered the pain of megrims. They seem to afflict women more than men, but thankfully, Laurel and Marigold have no' had them. Though at times, I have heard, childbirth can bring them on, so I suppose we shall see."

"Yes, I have heard the same," Briar said with some interest. "Childbirth can make them worse, or for some women, I have heard they cease."

She suddenly realized they were discussing a rather delicate subject and stopped.

Good Lord! She had not even considered children. Had he?

No, no, no, she could not be thinking about this right now. She could hardly think, period. The sun was rising higher, its rays becoming stronger, and she let out a mewing sound of pain.

"The sun? Bright light makes it worse, aye, I recall that," Wren was saying thoughtfully. "We must get ye to a shady grove. I will see to having the tent moved."

"I must get ready to leave," Briar mumbled. "The carriage. Angus."

"Ye canna go anywhere like this. I will talk to Angus, never fear," Wren said, sounding very firm. "Ye will come with me to that rock over there, under those tall trees, and sit in the cool shade." He paused. "I suppose ye dinna wish to open yer eyes. Here. Let me. I shall steer ye."

He gently grasped her by the arm. She heard him make a fussing noise. Then the arm moved to slip around her waist, and he took her closest hand in his. "Here, lass. Step with me this way."

His voice was so gentle. His arm so firm and strong around her. She knew she should open her eyes, in case she tripped, but she did not. She felt safe. Taken care of. He would make sure she stayed upright.

He would catch her if she stumbled. She was not alone.

"Here we are," he said. She felt the cool shade touch her face as they stepped under the trees.

She opened her eyes, took the proffered seat he was offering her on a large gray rock, and looked up at him with relief.

"Thank you," she said with feeling. "Thank you for understanding."

"Aye," he said, frowning a little. "And I shall make Angus understand. I'll bring a pallet for ye in case ye need to lie down. Once I speak to Angus, I'll move the tent. We must keep ye in a cool, dark place, aye?"

"Aye," Briar echoed. The pain came in waves. Stabbing waves. She closed her eyes again, grimacing. "I should warn you..."

"Aye?"

"It could grow... worse. I might be... sick."

"I take yer meaning. More reason we must stay put today and let ye rest."

"I am so sorry, Wren," Briar said plaintively. "I know you and Angus are in a hurry to get home. I am so sorry to delay you... Perhaps I might try to ride in the carriage. It might not be so bad." She knew it would be worse. Awful. Her stomach would roil and rile, and she would certainly be sick throughout the day thanks to the jostling and closed space. But she could try.

Wren let out a soft huffing noise that clearly conveyed any further protesting would be no use, and she should do what he said. "I'm no' in any hurry, though Angus certainly is. A day willna hurt anything. Stay here, lass. Rest."

She had closed her eyes again. She heard his footsteps fading, and then he was gone.

She lay on the pallet Wren had made up near the big rock, her eyes closed, listening to the waves of the sea. Thank heavens for the sea. The waves were so soothing. Their faithful repetition. And the cool breeze that came with being near the sea. The megrim had stayed the same, it had not gotten more severe as she had feared. Lying down and not moving helped. So did the shade.

She heard the crackling of feet upon the sandy grassy ground and opened her eyes to see Wren coming into the little grove of trees.

He came near and crouched down beside her. "How is yer head? Better or worse?"

"Not worse. Perhaps a little better," she said cautiously. She looked at the cup in his hand. "What is that?"

"Nettle tea. I picked the nettles myself. Have ye had it before?"

"No." Briar looked into the mug with interest. The water was tinged green. She sniffed. "Will it help?"

"Aye, my mother said it did. It may taste slightly bitter," he cautioned as she took a tentative sip.

"I don't care how bitter it tastes if it will help the pain to go away," she said with determination, taking another hearty swallow.

"That's the spirit," he said, and she looked up to see him smiling.

She smiled back, feeling a surge of pleasant warmth go through her. It was not from the tea. His smile—it did that to her. He did all sorts of things to her.

Suddenly she wondered about other cures for megrims. Being near him was a remedy all on its own. What would other types of closeness bring?

Wren seemed to have had a similar awkward thought, for he was clearing his throat and standing up.

"It is an ancient affliction, ye ken," he offered.

"Is it?"

"Aye, the Scots poet, William Dunbar, suffered terrible megrims. He even wrote to King James IV about them."

"He wrote to the king about a headache?"

"Aye, even wrote a poem." Wren was grinning now.

"Surely you are teasing me," Briar said, smiling back and feeling the liquid warmth. She focused on what they were talking about. "A poem? Do you know it?"

"Aye, it is called 'On His Heid-Ake,'" Wren said. Wrinkling his nose, he seemed to be trying to recall it, and quoted:

My head did ache last night,

so much that I canna write today.

So severe the megrim does wound me,

piercing my brow as an arrow,

that scarce I may look on the light.

He shrugged and looked a little chagrined. "There is more, but I canna recall the rest. It is a verra old verse."

"Pierced with an arrow is a very apt description," Briar said. "I feel much the same. I pity poor William Dunbar."

"He is hundreds of years dead, but I am sure he would appreciate it," Wren said.

"And you recalled that? From memory? Impressive," Briar commented. "Wherever did you learn it?"

"A tutor in Scotland. It was in one of the books he had us read from. A collection of the works of William Dunbar. I took special note of that one because of my mother. I copied it into a letter to her, I believe."

Briar felt an odd sense of pride. "You and Dare have more in common than you think, you know. You are—were—both very considerate sons. That is the sort of thing I could easily see him doing. Now, my other brother, Leigh." She gave a little snort. "Well, he is less considerate. And hardly home. Though," she hastened to say, "he is not a Percy Quintrell, thank heavens."

Wren nodded. "Aye, that is good. Well, I've found some lavender.

I'll bring it in a moment. If ye put it on yer forehead, near yer temples, the scent may help to soothe the pain."

"Thank you, Wren," she said. "You do not have to do any of this. You might just leave me here alone all day, you know."

"I am yer husband, nay?" He looked a little shocked at what she'd said. "It is my duty to care for ye."

"Do most husbands do this? Where you are from?" Briar asked, scrunching up her nose. Then she laughed. "I know Percy certainly would not."

"That git," Wren said dismissively. "I shouldna look to him as an exemplar of manhood."

"No, true," Briar agreed. She thought a moment. "Dare would do it for his wife. I have no doubt."

"He is a good brother to ye," Wren said.

It seemed more comment than question, but Briar nevertheless replied, "Yes, he is. A very good brother." She felt a lump in her throat. "He must be very worried about me. I miss him." She shook her head and forced herself to think of something else. "My father was thoughtful like Dare. He would try all sorts of things for my megrims. He hated to see his little girl in pain. Never nettle tea, however." She smiled up at Wren. "That one is new. Oh! I should drink the rest before it grows cold." She picked up the mug and quickly took a large sip, choked, and felt a strong hand slapping her on the back.

"Th-thank you," she managed, coughing and wiping her eyes. "I am all right now."

"Yer parents are dead, nay?" Wren asked.

"Well, we think they are," Briar said dubiously.

"Ye think they are?" Wren's eyebrows shot up.

"I suppose you know little of my family's history," Briar said, considering. "My parents were rather unusual aristocrats. Some called them eccentric, others artistic when they wished to be more complimentary. In truth, they were dedicated, passionate scholars. Egypt was their particular fascination. They were horrified by Napoleon's pillaging there. When they were younger and newlyweds, they would travel a great deal together. Their preference was to visit the places to study their history, not to cart items away for a collection like so many do. Of course," Briar said, as an afterthought, "they did take some items. But they were never ones to participate in the ghoulish. They did not practice desecration of mummies, for instance."

"What now?" Wren's eyes had widened.

"Unwrapping Egyptian mummies for entertainment," Briar explained. "Oh, I don't know which awful, entitled aristocrat began the trend, but my parents were horrified by it. Imagine, having a mummy unwrapped and despoiled in one's drawing room. Someone's mother or father or daughter or sister! Can you imagine it?"

Wren seemed to be imagining it in clear, grisly detail. "I canna, no."

"In any case, my parents did not enjoy a settled lifestyle. They rather enjoyed being vagabonds."

"But had four children," Wren pointed out.

"Indeed. And so, they put that life on hold for quite a while. They paused their adventuring and devoted themselves to research that could be completed at home. But when I was fourteen years old, they decided I was grown enough for them to leave. And so, they left." Briar paused. "And they never returned."

Wren wrinkled his brow. "And ye have no idea what happened to them?"

"Well, Dare and Kat had every possible inquiry made, of course. They even hired men to track them. But in the end, we have no idea whether they disappeared in Alexandria or Cairo or even Aswan. In fact, they had mentioned a possible extension of their journey to India. You see?" She shrugged helplessly. "Whatever happened to them, I'm sure they did not regret that it happened while they were on one of their journeys. And, at least they were together. It's comforting to tell myself those things."

"Is it?" Wren looked at her oddly. "To lose both yer parents so young..."

"Well, but I was not really so young, was I? And I had Kat and Dare and, even though he is a scallywag, Leigh, to take care of me, didn't I? It could have been much worse. At least my parents had left their affairs in order." She gave a reluctant smile. "Of course, I still dream of them reappearing one day. Coming back from the dead, like the pharaohs of ancient Egypt were supposed to. I suppose that is natural. Every child's dream." Briar's face was thoughtful.

She sighed and looked at Wren. "In any case, what I am trying to tell you is that they were unconventional in all ways. And they raised their children to be the very same. I mean, you don't really think that many families like ours would have put up so little fuss over Katherine marrying your brother, do you?

"But my parents would not have minded in the least. 'Follow your hearts,' my mother would always say. It would drive my grandmamma wild when she heard her tell us children that. She would stomp her cane and snap, 'Follow your elders, not your hearts. There is no place for hearts in a drawing room.'" Briar giggled, then her face sobered. "Dare is perhaps the most conventional and serious of us all. And yet even he is able to recognize the most important things. He wished for Kat to be happy. First and foremost. Snobbery and a false sense of superiority played no part in it."

She gave Wren a mischievous glance. "And of course, I am doing far better. For I have caught myself a lord. That is what 'laird' means, is it not?"

Wren scoffed. "Lairds have little power these days. Once they ruled almost like princes. Caring for thousands and thousands of people."

"And the English changed all that? Nothing of the old system remains?" Briar asked.

Wren scratched his chin. "Well, nay. That is no' true. The Renfrews have been more fortunate than some. My grandfather, stubborn bastard, held on to power in every way he could. And his father before him. When the English demanded the clan turn over their weapons, for instance, my ancestors did what many other Scots did and passed in rusty old things and hid the rest. Nor have the Renfrews cleared the folk from their land as other lairds have done. Ye have heard of that horrid old besom, the Countess of Sutherland, aye?"

"She married an Englishman, and together, they have evicted many of their tenants, have they not?" Briar asked, trying to remember.

"Murdered thousands of tenants more like," Wren said, his face hard. "They cleared them off the land as if they were worth no more than cattle. Nay, far less than cattle. The people had nowhere else to go. Many starved. Many died. Some came to Renfrew land."

"That's wonderful," Briar exclaimed. "How charitable of your grandfather."

Wren snorted. "Charity may have been a small part of it. If they could work, they were put to work. All must contribute, was my grandfather's motto. But aye, he was a hard man who could have been harder. He had loyalty to the people. Always did. It is hard to believe the old bugger is truly gone. I dinna think I shall believe it until we arrive, and I see for myself that he isna there."

He glanced at Briar. "How is yer head?"

"It still aches," she confessed. "Though I do think the tea helped some."

"Give me yer hand," he commanded, holding out one of his own.

"My hand?"

"Aye, give me yer hand," he said again, this time more impatiently.

"What are you going to do with it?" she asked, complying and placing one hand in his.

"I'm going to rub it."

"Rub it? Oooooh." Briar's eyes widened as Wren began to work his two large hands over her smaller one, stroking over the palm with his thumbs, slowly but firmly.

"Oh, my goodness," she said faintly, closing her eyes. "That feels..."

"My stepfather would do this for my mother. She said it was a great relief."

"Did she now?" Briar closed her eyes. Waves and waves of... something... were washing over her. All stemming from where Wren was touching her. Her hand felt limp and warm and wonderful. The gentle but strong movements were sheer ecstasy. She never wanted the feeling to stop. What was more, the pleasure was creeping up her arm, into the rest of her body. Yes, even sweeping sensations of calm pleasure up through her head, her temples, behind her eyes. Perhaps the pain was not vanishing completely, but the pleasure Wren was giving to her hand was a remarkable distraction.

"Am I hurting ye? Should I go more gently?"

"No, not at all," Briar said feebly. "It's perfect. Wonderful. Don't stop." She sounded pathetic. It was tempting to beg him not to ever stop. Or to do more. If this was how his hands felt upon her hand—such a chaste body part—how would they feel stroking her... elsewhere? Everywhere? She felt red hot heat shoot through her cheeks and put a hand to one.

"Yer cheeks have grown hot," Wren observed. "Are ye feverish?"

"No," Briar replied quickly. "At least, I don't think I am. Perhaps a little?" She blushed harder, knowing it was deceit.

Wren frowned, then reached out a hand to touch her cheek, then her forehead. "Ye are no' feverish yet, but perhaps ye will become so."

He moved his hand back to resume his massage. "Now the other," he commanded, dropping her right hand abruptly and beckoning for her left.

She complied immediately. "You can tell if I have a fever so easily?"

"Aye, battlefield skill," Wren said gruffly. "There were no' many surgeons. No' enough to go round. We had to tend one another. My men, my responsibility."

"You'll make a wonderful father someday," Briar said, without thinking. "If you are able to tell if a child has a fever simply by a brief touch."

Wren looked amused. "My mother could tell in the same way. I'm sure ye'll learn."

Their eyes met. Briar felt her face becoming pure flame as she saw understanding dawn in his eyes. Were they really talking about becoming parents one day? She and Wren?

That would mean actually producing a child. And to produce a child, they would have to...

"Oh, good heavens," Briar let out an unladylike moan of satisfaction. "That feels..."

Abruptly, Wren let go of her hand. "I suppose I should go and check on the rest of the camp. See if Angus needs anything done."

"Oh. Yes, of course." Briar looked up guiltily. "You have other duties besides tending to me. I quite understand."

"Aye, I wish for the men to stop seeing me as a prisoner. If I am truly their rightful laird, then I wish for them..."

"Of course," Briar said quickly. "They must learn to respect you. See you for who you truly are."

He nodded, stood, and turned to go.

"Thank ye, Wren," she said, hearing the humble tone in her voice. "For taking care of me today."

He turned to look down at her. "Of course, lass."

As he strode away, she replayed the words in her mind. She was his. His lass. His wife. His voice was so gentle at times when he talked to her.

And his hands... Oh, those glorious hands... She sank back onto the pallet with a groan, closing her eyes, missing those hands.

⁓

Wren strode away from his wife. Not because he wished to be away from the lass, but because if he had stayed another moment, it would not have been her hands he'd have been caressing.

Her facial expressions. Her little mews and moans of pleasure. It was enough to bring any man to his knees. Or a cock to full mast.

The girl had no idea the effect she was having upon him, of course. And likely never would if things went on like this, Wren thought, wryly.

God, but what was he to do? At night, he lay pretending to be asleep, cradling Briar's soft, warm form to his. It was the best time of his day.

Until now. Until today. Speaking with her, helping her, tending to her. Seeing her animated expression as she spoke, as she listened. She seemed genuinely interested in getting to know him and in sharing her own life with him.

With that bonny face, clever mind, and beautiful form, a man could easily fall in love with a lass like Briar Blakeley. Briar Renfrew, Wren corrected himself quickly. Renfrew was her name now.

And the question was, would she keep it? Or would her brother see this marriage as nothing more than farce? Would he demand his sister break the vows she had made out on the Scottish moors and take her home again, leaving Wren bereft—this time, not of his betrothed, but of his wife.

No matter what Briar believed about her unconventional family and her understanding older brother, the man was the bloody Duke of Dareford. And Wren was a minor Scottish lordling at best. A gardener, a servant, at worst. He had tried to spare Briar's honor, but would her brother see it that way?

He could not risk it. He could not make her his only to lose her again.

Chapter Nine

And yet the next day he came close to doing exactly that.

They were traveling along the sea again. When he woke in the morning and turned over, hoping to fill his face with one last covert whiff of his wife's scent before rising, she was already gone. He sat up, ran his hands through his hair, and looked about.

The plaid they had been sleeping on caught his eye.

They were still at least two days from Renfrew Castle. Nevertheless, it was time.

He picked up the dark green plaid, more than five yards of wide fabric, and shook the sand off it, then carefully lay it down on the ground again and lay himself upon it. Then began the wrapping. He closed his eyes, remembering with his fingers what he could not have put into words, pleating and draping, then sitting up and fishing in his satchel for the silver pin he always carried. Donning his coat, he pinned it to the front, holding plaid to jacket.

Then came his socks and his boots. And a leather belt, which generally held a dirk, at least a small one.

Two days from Renfrew Castle, were they? Two days from Loghain.

Wren fished in his satchel once more, found his pistol, and strapped that on as well.

When he was finished, he slipped through the tent flap, expecting to see his wife boiling water for tea.

But the camp was quiet, and she was nowhere to be seen.

Sudden alarm ran through him. A current of fear.

He looked down to the beach. It was deserted. Could she swim? Had she gone down to the water and been swept away?

Or perhaps bandits?

He strode through the camp, looking back and forth. Most of the men were still sleeping, though some were beginning to rouse. These he asked in a short, clipped tone if they had seen his wife. But nay was the answer each time. None had witnessed the bonny red-haired lass go through the camp that morning.

These were not Wren's men. He trusted Percy as far as he could throw him. Angus was still asleep.

And so, Wren allowed his suspicions to overpower him and counted the men. Every one was accounted for. He breathed a quick sigh of relief and continued his stride across the field in which they had camped, to the edge of the sandy bluff looking down onto the beach.

Now that he stood there, he had a better view of the water in both directions. He peered to the right. No sign of her.

He peered to the left. There! In the distance. A small dark figure.

In the waves.

It was high time for a bath, Briar had decided as soon as her eyes opened that morning.

The dust and grime from almost a week of traveling had become too much for her. The night before she had washed with a cloth as was her routine before bed, but the simple cloth and bucket of water could not refresh her.

She feared she stank.

And when one was a new wife, sleeping beside a husband who was, well, very, very handsome and very difficult to read, one did not wish to stink. One wished to smell like delicate French perfumes. At best. At worst, like lavender and wild flowers.

But Briar smelled of campfire smoke and, well, herself, and while she did not mind natural human smells, this was too much.

She needed a bath. And the sea was right there.

Therefore, she decided, she would slip out now before the camp awoke and have a sea bath.

Something told her not to ask Wren. Besides, he was her husband, not her commander. She would not consult him on when or when not to bathe! She would simply reappear in the camp shortly, clean, fresh, and sightly. He would look at her approvingly, and that would be that.

It had all worked out very well, except she had forgotten to bring anything to dry herself off with and had decided to go into the sea with her clothes and give them as good a scrubbing as she could. She had done what she supposed many a Scottish woman had done over millennia and scrubbed them as furiously as she could with sand, then carried them back to the shore and laid them out over the rocks to dry.

Oh, she had gone a long way down the beach to avoid being seen by the men at camp. Of course, now that she was standing stark naked on the shore like Botticelli's *Venus*, she certainly hoped she had gone far enough away.

She quickly waded back into the water. It was frigid but tolerable. She sluiced her hair, scrubbing her scalp as best she could and, for the first time, desperately missed her poor maid, Jane. What must Jane be doing now? Had Dare found other work for her? Or had she already packed her things and gone off to be some other young lady's maid? Perhaps in London. Jane had always wanted to live in London.

A sound caught her ear. She looked back at the beach, hoping it was simply a seagull, to see a man waving his arms and calling.

Her heart lurched. Not just any man. Her man.

What on earth did he mean to do? Stand there until she came out? Did he not see her clothes lying there, Briar thought, a little crossly.

She tried to holler back.

"Go away! I have no clothes! Go away, Wren!"

But instead, the figure crossed his arms over his chest and seemed to hunker down for the long haul.

"Oh, for heaven's sake," Briar muttered.

This was quite the pickle.

How long could she linger in the sea? When she lifted her shoulders out of the water, the cool air was even worse.

Well, she could become a mermaid and remain in the water... until Wren came out and bodily fetched her. Not an entirely unpleasant possibility, she had to confess.

Or? Or she could emerge, truly like Venus, from the waters and show her new husband his wife's full glory.

The only problem was that she was rather shy. She decided the first option might be preferable. Once he came in the water and was closer, she could explain she had no clothes on and would he please go away and leave her be.

And then, ideally, he would obey.

Or at least turn his back!

Something pushed up against her legs.

It might have been a gentle, nuzzling touch. Briar did not know, for she had already opened her mouth to scream.

Gentle or nuzzling or not, no one standing naked and vulnerable in the sea would wish for anything to suddenly brush up against one's legs. This really was the last straw. No more sea bathing for at least a week, Briar decided.

Besides, she was quite certain it was a sea monster. She had never believed in them until now, but suddenly the conviction was real.

She saw a dark shape swimming off to one side. It was a very large shadow.

Wren was shouting something from the shore. But the only word she caught was "shark."

The creature, whatever it was, was not coming closer. Nevertheless, she heard herself scream again.

She looked back to the beach.

Wren had stripped off his boots and was striding into the shallow water. His face was grim. Was that because he feared his wife was about to be eaten by a sea monster?

He need not have bothered coming in after her, however, for Briar had quite lost her head. She was scurrying back to the beach as quickly as she could go, pushing against the waters and the low waves.

Fear was a wonderful motivator.

First her shoulders popped out.

Then her, well, torso. She crossed her arms over her chest and hoped for the best.

With relief, she saw that the shape in the water seemed to be swimming away. Good! Perhaps she had frightened it with her loud screams.

She looked at the beach. Wren had stopped. He seemed to have finally comprehended his wife's state of undress.

Would it be altogether too indelicate for Briar to shout just once, "I am bloody naked. Please go away!" She decided it was not only indelicate but too late and took another step forward.

They were close enough that she could finally see him clearly.

Her eyes took in the sight of the Scot, standing tall in full Highland dress.

"Oh, delightful," she muttered to herself. She was at her worst, with seaweed hair streaming water, while Wren had apparently decided to put on his Sunday best.

And didn't he look absolutely magnificent!

If her heart had not already been doing troublesome things before, it was pounding in brazen excitement as she looked at him now.

This was her husband. Dear Lord. This was her husband.

He was always a very striking man. The cleft of his chin. His sturdy Roman nose. The softness of his dark, sooty lashes over those gorgeous blue eyes. His height, his breadth, his width. His girth? Briar almost giggled. Shush, she told herself.

But now? Gracious, he was unbearably handsome.

There was something about a man in a kilt. Especially the way Wren was wearing it. The dark green Renfrew plaid, shot through with its strands of red and white and gold, was already a lovely thing. Against Wren's form, contrasted against his dark hair, it was a god's finery. Every pleat, every fold fitting his leanly muscled physique.

She swallowed hard, then took another step.

This time when he bellowed, she heard him loud and clear.

"Stop!"

She stopped.

Wren's face was a picture of perplexity. She could not tell his thoughts.

"What are ye doing?" he called.

"I am coming out of the water. Is that not obvious? Did you not say there was a shark?" she shouted back, rather crossly.

"A shark," she heard him mutter to himself. "Afraid of a shark." He raised his voice. "What is obvious is that ye..." He paused. Cleared his throat. "Is that ye're no' wearing any clothes!"

"Of course I'm not," Briar shouted, feeling a little annoyed. "They are on the rocks behind you. Could you not see that?"

She watched him turn, inspect the rocks. When he looked back at her, his face was redder than before.

"They're no' yet dry," he informed her stiffly.

"Well, they'll bloody well have to do, won't they? I have nothing else to put on. Unless you would like me to stay in the sea all day and become a selkie?"

A selkie! Perhaps that was what she had seen. She let out a little giggle. "What was that in the water? Was it really a shark?"

"Aye, a basking shark most like," Wren said, shrugging so casually that Briar felt a little offended.

"It was very large," she reminded him.

"They wouldna eat ye," he said, his lips quirking. "They're gentle giants, nay?"

"They are giants, aye," Briar said, trying to make a joke.

Wren did not look impressed. "Basking sharks are verra large but no' interested in eating lassies. Their skin is verra rough, though. Did it brush against ye? Are ye hurt?"

Briar glanced down to where the creature had brushed her leg. "Nothing there."

"Perhaps it was a seal then and no' a shark at all," Wren guessed. Then his face darkened. "Ye shouldna..." He seemed to be trying to hold himself back.

"Yes?" Briar prodded.

"Ye shouldna have snuck off like that," he huffed. "I couldna find ye. I had no idea what had become of ye."

"Well, I knew where I was," Briar replied, tossing her head. "I had not lost myself."

He glared. Perhaps that had not been the best response, she decided.

She sighed. "Will you not go away and let me dress? I am becoming rather cold, standing half in, half out, with the breeze on my..."

Wren raised his hands abruptly, as if to shield himself from her words.

"What on earth are you doing?" she asked in amusement.

"Dinna say..." he begged. "What ye were going to say."

"What? Skin?"

He met her eyes. His lower lip twitched. "Oh. Ye may say that."

"Oh!" Briar exclaimed. "You thought I was going to say..."

Wren raised his hands again.

Briar burst out laughing. "Bosoms?"

He glared. But his glare no longer was enough to stop her. It never had been, she realized. She saw through his glare—at least, when he was with her. She was sure it was still very effective with others. She knew it was.

"Is there another word you are more afraid of, Wren?" she asked innocently.

"I'm no' afraid," he barked, narrowing his eyes.

"Not of a naked woman?" she asked, eyes twinkling.

His glare deepened. He folded his arms over his chest. "Do ye have any idea how ye look? Any idea at all?" He closed his eyes and made a sound that was suspiciously like a groan.

"Like something the sea washed up?" Briar guessed. "Like a piece of kelp? Like shark food? Perhaps you might help me with that and let me get to my clothes, dear Husband."

His eyes popped open, his face amused. "Oh, is that what ye are calling me now?"

His gaze softened as he looked at her. "Nay, no' a piece of kelp," he muttered with almost shy reluctance.

"No?"

"Nay." He kicked a rock by his foot. "Ye look... lovely. Beautiful. Verra, verra beautiful."

Although she had been paid many compliments in her young lifetime, Briar was more moved by this one than any before it.

There was a lump in her throat. She was not sure how it had gotten there.

"Well, thank you," she said finally. "So do you. *Verra, verra* beautiful."

He smiled wryly. "Thank ye."

And then, he started unfastening his plaid.

"What are you doing?" she asked.

He ignored her and continued his work of unfastening and unfolding. She had already known the plaid was large. After all, she had been sleeping on it. But now she took in the complexity of the ancient garment. The time it must have taken to fold and pleat it so elaborately. Why, there were even pockets, made out of careful folds tucked into the leather belt around Wren's waist... which he was now removing.

"What are you doing?" she asked again, more fascinated than put off.

"Ye are shivering where ye stand," he snapped gruffly, not looking up at her.

It was true. She was covered in goosebumps. The part of her that was still in the water—everything from the waist down—was actually rather warm. But she knew as soon as she continued her trek onto the beach, she would be freezing.

"There," she heard him say with satisfaction, and the plaid slipped off and into his hands.

"Oh, my," she said a little faintly.

If a broad, strong Highlander draped in his plaid was an impressive sight, an undraped Highlander standing only in his shirttails was another matter entirely.

Few men could manage to look handsome stripped down to only the long, white linen shirt reaching mid-thigh that Wren had on. Yet Wren more than managed it. His long legs were bare and muscular. She could see the shapes of his brawny thighs through the shirt, like the barrels of cannons, and gave a little shiver, imagining how hard they would feel pressed up against hers, skin against skin.

"But..." Briar tried. But it was no use. He was coming toward her with an expression of fierce determination.

"Step forward now," he commanded. "I shallna look at ye."

Briar did as she was told, more than ready to be enfolded in the warm wide swaths of cloth.

What she was not ready for was the feel of the hands that came with the cloth. Without meaning to, Wren's hands brushed against her bare back and the tops of her shoulders as he draped the plaid and held it, averting his eyes modestly as she took another step forward, then another, and finally stepped onto dry sand.

When she was fully out, he turned back to her, still with eyes carefully lifted upwards, and pulled the plaid more firmly around her.

It was all very... proper. Briar was almost disappointed. He was so very close. And he had put the cloth still warm from his own body upon her.

It should have been romantic.

And yet, he seemed so very determined for it not to be.

"You take very good care of me," Briar said softly. "But you regret being forced to marry me already, do you not, Wren?" She had lowered her head and now kept her eyes fixed firmly on the sand, but even so, she caught the movement of his head snapping toward her.

"It is all right," she went on bravely. "I quite understand. You did not wish for this. And yet you are trapped."

"If I am trapped, so are ye," he said quietly.

She did not reply.

When his hand touched her cheek, she looked up in surprise. He was looking at her closely.

"What are ye really asking?" he asked wryly.

"Don't you... want me?" Briar asked, her voice very small. Now it was she who had to avert her eyes.

But the finger on her cheek moved down to her chin and lifted it gently.

"Look at me, Wife," she heard him say. "Look at me. In my eyes."

Slowly, she complied, lifting her eyes to meet his.

She gasped. It was as if he had lowered a curtain. There was a raw, naked hunger as he looked down at her. A fire of desire burning as fierce as any flame she'd ever seen. It made her feel her own power. He thought her beautiful. Desirable. The proof was right there, written in his eyes.

"You do," she said amazed. "But then..."

"Desire. Want. Lust. Aye, I want ye. That is all verra well," Wren said, waving a hand, almost as if he were disgusted with himself. "But it will no' serve ye when ye are with child. Nor if..." He cleared his throat. "Nor if more becomes involved than merely lust, aye?"

"More?" Briar was confused. "Do you not want children, then? What do you mean if more becomes involved?" She looked at him. "Do you mean more than desire? Our hearts?"

He nodded, his face abruptly bleak. "I have felt that pain once before. I have no wish to feel it again. Ever."

Briar had no words to reply. She felt stunned. He had loved before? There had been someone before her? And his heart had been lost?

"As for bairns," Wren continued. He scratched his chin, then sighed. "Let us simply get to Renfrew land. What will be, will be."

He turned away from her. She felt a swell of loneliness but, more than that, anger, too.

She was more alone than she had even realized. So, he would care for her but not care *about* her. Was that how it was to be?

Before she could even think it through, she had reached out a hand and grasped his arm as hard as she could, yanking him to a standstill.

And then she was standing up on tip-toe, for she was considerably shorter than him, and lifting her head up to his, lifting her soft lips to his firm ones, and touching them with her own.

She clutched the plaid to her with one hand and raised her free one to his shoulder, then grasped the back of his neck, her fingers spinning into his hair.

She felt strange and hot and light-headed as their lips touched. She had seen lightning strike a tree once, and it seemed the closest thing to compare the feeling to. Something sparked. He must have sensed it too for she felt him jump, and she tightened her grasp on the back of his neck, her fingers slipping through the silky strands of his hair. It was soft, very soft. She gave a little tug and pressed her lips against his harder, wondering if she was doing this right.

She must be, she thought, for his hands had moved to grip her waist, pulling her flush against him. And as he did, she felt the pulse of his desire: his cock ramrod hard against her belly.

Perhaps most young ladies would have been put off by the sensation, but to Briar, it simply left her woozy with the knowledge of their reciprocal want. Her breathing had quickened, her heart thudding a heady, dangerous rhythm. She felt flushed and trembling. And the space between her legs pulsed with need, urging her on, desperate to be filled.

Wren's hands were caressing her waist, stroking her gently, moving over the plaid that covered her with a teasing tenderness that sent shivers down her spine. Meanwhile, his lips were responding to hers with a strength that sent her stomach somersaulting. His kiss deepened, lips warm and hard upon hers in a way that was intensely pleasurable. He pulled her more tightly against him, and she heard a groan escape. His lips slipped to the corner of her mouth, his teeth nibbling against her plush lower lip, then moving to her jaw, her nape. Briar let out a gasp as the brush of his lips on her neck sent her shivering, hot and cold with desire.

He was whispering words, too. Strange words that must have been Gaelic. She did not understand them, but oh, they sounded sweet.

Her hand slipped on the plaid fabric, first by accident. Then, a second time on purpose. She felt the plaid slide from her shoulders, nearly to her breasts, and gripped it just before it fell, holding it so that she was still mostly covered. But oh, how close it was to falling. If a hand were to give it a gentle push, she would not resist. Oh no, she would not resist at all. Her nipples strained against the fabric, already hard and rigid, desperate to receive their share of Wren's touch. Oh, what would that rough mouth feel like upon them...

She thrust herself forward a little more, rubbing her breasts—still covered in the plaid—against his chest. His lips had been doing wonderfully wicked things to her neck, but now, they froze.

He leaned back, away from her, and she felt a mournful moment of regret. She had gone too far. He would stop this now. Damn the man's self-control.

And sure enough, he pulled back, his hands on her waist holding her in place so she could not lean toward him.

His breathing was ragged, his face flushed. She had done that to him, she thought, a little triumphantly. And it was only her first time, too. She would not stop. No, not if this was how good it could be, the two of them together.

He was looking down at her, with almost a pleading expression. "I must..." He shook his head, tried again. "I must no'."

Briar decided she would not argue. She could see the battle warring within him. She had stoked it. She must be content with that for now.

"Come back to camp with me," she said gently, touching his hand. She pulled the plaid more snugly around her, over her shoulders.

"Your clothes!" His eyes lit up, and he turned back to retrieve them, happy for a distraction.

She smiled as she watched him run back, his long legs gleaming in the sun.

Another woman may have stolen her husband's heart, but one thing was certain. That woman, whoever she was, did not have it now.

Wren was Briar's. Her lawfully wedded husband.

And as it was too late for her own tender heart, there was only one thing for it. She would make her husband care for her if it was the last thing she did.

Yes, Wren, it does hurt, she thought. It hurt to look at him. Hurt to know he wanted her but would not risk the pain of heartbreak a second time.

Well, Briar Blakeley had already lost her heart to her husband. And she would be damned if she was going to be the only one in this marriage to do so.

Chapter Ten

It took almost losing her for him to finally surrender to desire.

Anywhere one traveled, there was always the danger of bandits. But a caravan made up primarily of men—who were clearly hale and strong warriors, too—was not one Wren had considered might soon be attacked.

Only cowards attacked in the dark. One or two men might sneak into a camp, steal food or goods, slit a throat or two, and then slip out again.

But this attack came at night and was a heavy one. There was planning behind it.

The men, whoever they were, had been trained and clearly well paid, for they were motivated in their intent. And their intent was not theft, but death.

Wren was nearly asleep when the first man shrieked. The man Angus had left on watch to one side of the camp. Then came a second shriek. The other watch man, across camp, near the road. Wren was bolt upright, his hand on his dirk, his other rifling through his bag for his pistol. Not that it would be much good.

Deciding quickly, he shook Briar awake and pressed the pistol into her hands.

"We're being attacked," he said, his voice low. "Ye must follow me out of the tent and crawl to the treeline. I will find ye. Dinna scream unless ye're attacked. I will come to ye. Do ye hear me?"

Her face had instantly turned fearful. He watched her nod, then pulled back the tent flap, and stepped out quickly, turning to watch her crawl out behind him.

It was a moonlit night, and her hair gleamed brightly. He cursed, then glanced around. The fight seemed to be so far focused on the spot by the wagons, horses, and carriage. There was the sound of clashing weapons, shouting men, and the cries of the wounded. No one was looking at where their tent lay, on the outskirt of the camp near the woods. No one had caught sight of Briar. Good.

"Go. Now," he commanded and watched her crawl across the camp.

He moved past the campfire, kicking Percy awake where he lay, somehow still snoring.

"Whaa—" the young man began, sounding affronted as he sat up groggily.

"Get up. Get a weapon. We're under attack," Wren shot back impatiently. "Or would ye prefer to be knifed as ye slept?"

"Bloody hell," he heard Percy mumble.

And then he was past and striding toward Angus and his men and the group of attackers.

Angus and his men were bellowing, shouting words of encouragement and instruction back and forth to one another, their voices deep and confident. No hint of fear there. Like the true Renfrew warriors they were, Wren thought with pride.

He ran into the fray, his dirk already in hand. He hefted it quickly, then slid it home into the belly of a dark-haired man who wore a scarf over the lower half of his face. The man fell, and Wren turned to face the next.

This man's face was covered, too. Not unusual for a bandit. But this was a large group for bandits.

Angus had twelve men with him. The group attacking them must have numbered twenty if not more.

At least five of their attackers had already fallen, Wren saw. Plus the one he had just brought down. Plus the one he was about to.

"Nice of ye to join us from the newlywed tent," Angus bellowed as he spotted Wren. There was a glorious grin on his face that Wren remembered well from their days of battle.

"Missed this, did ye?" Wren shouted back, then turned back just in time to see a second attacker join the first man he was fighting. He grabbed the second man by the scruff of his coat, noted his face covered in a cloth, then slammed his head into his friend's, hearing the satisfying crunch of bone against bone.

The first man, he dropped unconscious to the dirt where he lay unmoving. The second, he lifted off the ground with one hand, then delivered a powerful blow to the jaw with his other, before dropping him beside his comrade and whirling around to check on Angus.

The big Scotsman was fighting two men, his face still a picture of pure glee.

Glancing about, Wren saw that while a few of Angus's men had fallen, most were performing admirably and fighting off the invaders.

Even Percy had entered the battle. The young rooster had his scrawny fists up and was yelling his head off while pummeling a short, tubby man who looked shocked by his opponent's fierceness.

Wren felt a grin stretch across his face.

Then a scream broke through the air.

He saw Percy throw one last blow, and his man fell. He turned to Wren, his face full of recognition. "Briar!"

Wren nodded tersely, already moving toward the woods.

"Renfrew!" It was Angus. He turned back to see the older man had been cornered against the carriage. Three men were moving in on him.

"A little help!" bellowed the Macleod man. Clearly, Angus had not heard Briar's scream. Wren clenched his fists, freezing in place.

But then Percy was there, beside him. He looked up at the taller Scot, his face strangely solemn.

"Go to her," he instructed, his young face grim. "I'll see to Angus."

And so Wren did.

Cursing his choices. Praying the young cub would know what to do. Hoping it would be enough.

It had to be. For he must get to his wife.

Looking ahead into the dark shadows of the treeline, he saw two figures struggling over something.

His heart lurched. The pistol. The damned pistol. Why had he given her the pistol? He did not even know if she knew how to use one. How easily such a weapon could be turned on a woman if not.

And sure enough, he saw the gleam of silver. The man attacking her was trying to wrench it away, but Briar was holding fast.

Praying that it did not go off in her hand, Wren increased his speed and barreled into the trees.

He let out a cry of fury. A battle cry. A bone-chilling sound. It had the intended effect, for the man fighting his wife paused and looked up just in time to see Wren hurtling toward him.

"Get back, Briar," he shouted and reached out an arm to break the two apart, pushing her out of the way none too gently as he stretched his other arm out to the man who had dared to lay hands on his wife.

———※———

Briar caught a glimpse of her husband's face as he pushed her away from her attacker. It was not Wren at all. It was another man. Some medieval warrior come alive from an ancient time. His eyes were cold and brutal with fury. If his gaze had been directed at her, she would have been terrified, she had no doubt.

But Wren's eyes were not fixed on her but on the man trying to harm her. The sandy-haired young man, who had laughed cruelly when he had found her crouching in the trees, had pulled her up by her hair, shouting to his friends about finding a prize for them all to share when they were through.

Briar had felt the tears running down her face then. *That* had been fear.

Now she felt only an odd calm as she watched to see what her husband would do to the man who had treated her so callously.

She knew it would be nothing good.

"Ye dared to lay yer filthy hands on my wife, ye mongrel," Wren was shouting, his hands curled into fists as he stepped toward the other man.

The attacker had gotten the pistol away from Briar; now it hung loose in his hand. It should have given him the advantage. But this young man was a coward and stupid in the bargain. He had lost every edge he had as soon as Wren had appeared, blazing with his terrifying rage.

It was clear from the young man's frightened expression, his wide prey-like eyes, that he knew he had already lost the confrontation.

"Please," he stuttered, holding up his hands. "Please. I want no trouble with you."

Wren took another menacing step forward. He was ready to kill, and God help her, Briar knew she could not stop him. All she could do was stay still and wait.

"Ye touched the lass, did ye no'? Ye meant to harm her, did ye no'? Dinna deny it," Wren growled.

"I-I..." the young man stuttered. "Here." He tossed the pistol. "Take her. Take this. Take it all. I had no idea she was your wife. I swear it."

"Ah," Wren roared. "And ye think it would mean less were she just any lass? And no' my bride?"

"I... I don't know," the man said helplessly. He was backed up against a tree. Briar almost felt sorry for him. But he had meant to rape her. He had meant to have his friends hurt her, too. She could not find it in herself to intervene.

"English," Wren said in disgust as he heard the man's accent. "Who hired ye to do this? Speak!"

"I don't know. I swear. We didn't know there would be a woman with you. You must ask the man who brought us here." The sandy-haired man gulped. "If he is still alive."

Wren sneered. It was not a Percy-like sneer. This was born of pure anger. It was the expression of a predator looking down on a creature that was already dead to him.

"I warrant he's no'," Wren said almost civilly. "Ye chose the wrong camp tonight."

"I can see that now," the other man babbled. "And if you will be merciful. If you will let me go, I swear I..."

"Ye'll what? Never harm another man or woman or child for so long as ye have left to live? Nay." Wren shook his head. "Ye ken I canna allow it." He leaned down close to the man's face and dropped his voice, but Briar still heard his words. "Ye meant to have her, no? Ye meant to force her? Then kill her? That was the way of it?"

The man's eyes bulged, as if he had been caught in the very act itself. "Yes," he confessed. "But she is untouched. I swear. What harm has been done?"

"Aye," Wren said, nodding almost as if he agreed and raising his head. "What harm. Terrorizing a helpless woman. But what harm, says he?"

When his hand darted forward to grasp the young man by the neck, Briar let out a gasp. She could see the raw power of Wren's forearm, his shoulders, the muscles straining in his neck as he lifted the man from the forest floor, held him aloft a moment, and then... She shut her eyes just in time but could not shut out the awful bone-cracking sound.

And then Wren's hands were on her shoulders. He was turning her to face him.

His hands touched her face, her cheeks, lifting her head to look at him.

"What did he do to ye, lass? Tell me." His voice was ever so gentle. "Did he hurt ye? Before I got here, did he... did he harm ye?" She heard the hitch in his voice and lifting a hand, quickly placed it upon his chest reassuringly.

"No." She shook her head. "No, Wren. Nothing like that. He yanked me by the hair. He slapped me, pushed me. That is all. I'm not even hurt. Honestly."

"Not even hurt," he repeated, not looking convinced. "He only yanked yer hair, pushed ye, and slapped ye." He shook his head unhappily. "I shouldna have left ye."

"What else could you have done?" she demanded. "I was safe there. At first. You had to go and help the others. Angus needed you. I understand why you told me to wait there. Truly."

She hesitated, then added, "Is he... dead?" She was a coward, for she leaned her head quickly against his chest. She felt his hand come up to cover her hair, running gently over it.

"Aye, he is."

"You... you didn't have to kill him," she said very quietly. "I suppose... I suppose you might have let him go. As he'd begged."

There was silence a moment, then, "Nay, lass, I couldna have done that."

She felt his hands come onto her shoulders and push her back gently, so he might look at her face.

"The bastard dared touch ye. He tried to harm ye, Wife. It is my duty to protect ye. My duty now and always. Do ye understand?"

She could only nod. She had been safe in their tent though very afraid, but even then, she had been safe. He had been nearby. He had heard her. He had come to her. He had kept her safe. She was safe with him, she told herself, repeating the words in her head.

"I dinna think I would have to fulfill it quite so soon," he added ironically. He cleared his throat. "I must see to the body."

"Oh." Briar could not help it. She winced. "Of course."

She watched as Wren stepped toward the fallen man.

A hand touched her arm, and she jumped, whirling around.

"Are you all right, Briar?" It was Percy. His eyes were full of genuine concern. Blood trickled down his face from a nasty gash on his temple.

"Percy," she exclaimed. "What happened to you?"

"I believe I was in a fight," he said thoughtfully. He licked his lips. There was blood coating them. She saw him taste the salt. "Yes, I believe I was."

"Did you win?" she asked, eyes widening.

"I believe I did," he said, and for a moment his eyes were contemplative and far away. "In fact, I know I did." Then he focused upon her. "But you? Are you well? What happened here?"

"I was attacked," she said shakily. "But Wren arrived in time. He got the man away from me before any harm was done."

Percy looked over her shoulder at where Wren stood a few feet off. "Ah. Yes. I see." He took Briar's arm very gently. "Well, come back to the camp with me now. Come and sit down by the fire. Your husband will be along shortly, I'm sure."

"My husband. Yes." Briar let him lead her.

"Wait." Wren was there. His voice gruff. "You will see to her? I must go to Angus and the rest of the men." He looked at Briar, as if waiting for her consent, and she nodded slowly. He was the laird, was he not? She was not his only responsibility. She understood. Even more, she was proud of him for remembering that.

Percy nodded. "Angus is hurt, but I think he will be all right. He's by the wagons if you wish to see him." He sounded almost shy to Briar's ears as he reported to her husband.

"Aye, I'll go there now. Good man. Ye did yer duty gallantly," Wren said, his voice brusque. "Now see to my wife, aye?"

Percy just nodded, but before he stepped away, Briar thought she saw his cheeks tinged pink.

The men gathered around the fire spoke in hushed voices. There were injuries, of which Angus's was perhaps the worst, but no one had been lost, she soon learned. Which was a miracle in and of itself, considering the number of their attackers, the men agreed. The new laird was good luck, one man said. Aye, so was his bride, said another.

Briar could hardly follow the conversation. She felt weary and light-headed. Percy had a steadying arm on her shoulder. Somehow it was not cloying, but comforting.

Then a hot mug of steaming tea was pressed into her hands. She took a sip, then another, and by the time the mug was empty, Wren was standing before her.

He held out his hands and helped her to her feet.

"Who were they?" she asked as they began moving toward the sanctuary of the tent. She did not want to think of the dead man anymore. "Who attacked us? Where did they come from?"

"Aye, well, those are the questions, are they no'?" Wren asked dryly. "And we'll find the answers. But no' now. Ye need rest. Ye've had a shock. Come back to the tent and lie down."

"I am fine. How is Angus?" she asked, ready with a steady stream of questions. "They say he is badly injured."

Wren turned to glare at the men by the fire. "Who says?" He looked down at her, his face softening, and touched her cheek. "Aye, he is wounded, but he will recover. His arm may be broken. He is being well tended, never fear. Now come. Ye must rest."

She fumbled, found his hand, gripped it tightly. "Will you come with me? I will lie down but only if you come with me."

She looked at the tent on the edge of the woods and found she was shaking.

Wren noticed and she saw his lips tighten. He nodded. "Aye, lass, I'll come with ye. Of course, I will."

He wrapped his arm around her waist and half-carried her to the door of the tent. It was unscathed. It looked just the same, despite everything that had happened. It could still be a haven, she decided, with Wren there beside her.

She crouched, crawled inside, then turned around quickly as he came in after her.

"I don't think I can sleep," she confessed, wrapping her arms around herself.

"Hardly surprising." Wren crossed the tent, sank down beside her. "Here. Come to me." His voice was low and husky. His arms were broad and open. She slipped into them gratefully, feeling their strength as they wrapped around her.

She was used to lying against him at night, but this was different. Being fully in them, in the confines of his body, having him almost all around her, encompassing her. It felt very pleasant. Very right.

They stayed like that a few minutes, an hour. She had no idea. Time passed. It was still night.

And then, finally, when she was nearly asleep but not wanting to be so, she tilted her head back.

"Wren." Her voice was a whisper. He was not asleep. His eyes were open.

"Aye, lass?"

She swallowed. There was a lump in her throat, and it had been there for days. She was not sure it would ever go away. It had something to do with him. Something to do with wanting him, knowing he wanted her but would not take her.

But now. She needed him. So very badly.

"I feel very alone, Wren," she whispered. "I don't want to feel this way anymore."

He was quiet. She pressed on.

"I need you... Husband."

There. She had said all she could.

Would he understand? Did he even take her seriously? Or was she just a young lady to him? Not a real wife at all?

"Oh, lass." He breathed a heavy sigh.

She closed her eyes. Already feeling the disappointment in her heart.

And then, his lips brushed hers.

⁓

Damn him, but he could not resist her. Not tonight. He had known it from the moment he followed her into the tent.

Holding her had been glorious, but it was not enough.

Nay, it had not been enough from the start.

Certainly not from the day before, when he had seen his bride emerge from the water, wickedly tempting in all her bare glory. She was the loveliest thing he had ever laid eyes upon.

He looked down at her now, her hair tangled from her ordeal in the woods, leaves and other brambles twisted in among the fine red strands, a spot of soot from the campfire streaked across one freckled cheek. She was beautiful, innocent, and very much his.

He kissed her, softly at first, then more roughly, letting her feel his want in the kiss.

"Ye're beautiful, ye ken," he said hoarsely. "And I want ye, verra badly. I canna stay away from ye."

"Good. Why should you?" she whispered, kissing back with an eagerness that pleased him. "I'm your wife, am I not?"

"Ye are," he agreed, nipping lightly at her bottom lip. God, that luscious lower lip. So plush and full. He might spend all night simply suckling it and feel a happy man.

But there was more to her body than her lips, he reminded himself. Her small round hips. Her full, heavy breasts were almost too large for such a petite woman. He longed to see them, uncovered by her crossed arms. Bare to his eyes, his lips, his hands in the privacy of their tent.

As if reading his mind, she suddenly twisted in his arms and leaned back, her breasts lifting to him as her back arched. "If I am your wife," she said with false innocence, her soft hands lighting on his forearms, "then it is your duty to care for me in all ways, is it not?"

"It is," he said formally, his eyes greedily drinking in her form. He wanted to see her. All of her. "Our mutual duty, aye."

"I am very ready to do my duty, I find, Husband," she said, her voice low and throaty.

"Are ye now?" He chuckled. "Take off yer shift for me, then?"

She hesitated, then stood.

He leaned over and quickly doused the single lamp they kept in a corner. There was enough light from the moon to see what he wished to see, he decided. What they were about to do, what they were about to say... well, it wouldn't be exactly private, he thought, wryly. But it couldn't be helped. He couldn't wait for the castle. He had to have her. Here and now.

He looked at his wife and drew in his breath. She wore only a simple white shift to sleep in.

Now, as he allowed his eyes to finally roam freely over her form, he saw it concealed almost nothing. Her shape glowed through the transparent linen. He could see everything. The roundness of her hips, the flatness of her belly, the pink tips of her breasts poking against the fabric, the dark triangle of hair that lay between her legs... He groaned and reached for her, pushing the shift down and off her shoulders without another word.

She let out a soft mewling sound as his hands found her breasts, cupping them and squeezing, then lowering his mouth to pay them the devotion they deserved. They were full and lush and heavy, swaying in his hands. He tugged the sweet tips of her nipples into his mouth, one at a time, feeling her gasp at the sensation, her hips already bucking against him.

"Come to me," he commanded, and lying back on the blankets, he shucked off his shirt and pulled her down to him, her body falling heavily against him, the bareness of it a fine delight. He groaned in pleasure as her breasts draped over the muscled planes of his chest. She was trembling, he saw. Not with cold, but with desire.

"Ye want this, *mo chridhe*?" he murmured, knowing she did not know what the words meant and feeling safe in the knowledge he might say them. "I dinna ken if we'll regret it." He felt he should say more, say he could make no promises. Uncomfortably, he recalled he had just called her his sweetheart.

But she only nodded, her pretty face very serious. "All of you, Wren. All or nothing," she whispered. "I want it all."

He felt his heart skip a beat as he saw the intensity behind the words. Briar Blakeley was a braw and uncommon woman, he thought. No, not just a woman. His wife.

And then she silenced his doubts with her mouth, her burnished hair falling in silken waves around both their shoulders, her breasts rubbing up and down against his chest as they kissed, their breath quickening together.

When he reached between her legs, unable to hold back from touching her there another moment, she let out a gasp of shock. His fingers slid through the damp sweet place that held her pleasure, and she moaned, low and sweet in the back of her throat.

"Good, is it?"

"Oh, Wren. So good." Her eyes were wide and amazed. He had to smile. He kissed her lips once more as his fingers began to play, sliding through the dripping slickness, readying her for what was to come.

"Ye're so wet, Wife," he murmured. "So verra wet." Good, it would make it much easier for her, this first time. He wondered if she knew that, if she had any idea.

"Wet for you, Wren," she murmured back, her voice sweet and true. "What comes next? Please." She was shuddering against him, tremulous, desperate.

Her body was more than ready for him. And his—well, his body had reacted with quintessential maleness from almost the moment he had stepped into the tent. Now as his wife rocked her hips innocently against him, he let out a low growl and reaching a hand down, undid his trousers.

She looked down, shyly, as he slid his cock out, taking in the rigid length of it. "May I touch it?"

He was so surprised he nodded before he could think it through. But it was too late. Her small hand had already slid down, grasping his cock gently but firmly, squeezing a little. He let out a groan. She did not know how to touch it but perhaps in time might learn. Not tonight, though. He did not have the patience for it.

"I need ye," he growled. "Now, Wife." He kissed her lips, fierce and savage, to confirm the truth of his words, working his tongue between her lips and thrusting into her mouth. A preview of what was to come. She gasped, moaned, let go of his cock, and it found its home, straight between her thighs, nestled in the warm, wetness there.

"Ooooh," he heard her say, and he felt her shifting. He took his hand away from where he had been stroking her, let her feel his cock in its place instead. Not entering her, simply letting her grow accustomed to him.

"And now?" she asked tentatively, shifting again, not knowing how wild it drove him.

He closed his eyes, took a breath, willed himself to be patient.

"Now," he said carefully, "I make ye mine. If it please ye."

He saw her smile. A wide, sassy grin. "Oh, it pleases me, Wren. It pleases me *verra, verra* much."

"Verra, eh?" He narrowed his eyes playfully, then flicked his tongue against her nipple. She gasped. "Verra, verra?" He moved his hips up against hers. "Verra, verra, verra?"

"Oh my, Wren, do that again, please," she gasped.

"Like this?" He moved, letting the tip of his shaft seek out the heat of her center and lifted his hips.

She let out a shuddering sigh of pleasure. "Yes, just like that."

She was very sweet and uncommonly pretty, and she was his wife. He yearned for her. He had hungered for her body all along; that was no surprise. But her sweetness, her strength, her gentle heart, her cleverness—he had almost lost those tonight. He leaned his head against her forehead and kissed her lightly, then deeply, then deepest of all. He tried to shove the thoughts away, to think only of the pleasure he would give her, but it was too late. He was afraid he was very close to loving his wife.

And then she moved her thighs, spreading them farther apart, opening herself to him, and he was lost. He moved against her, sinking into her heat, desire mounting within him and taking over all thought. Their bodies were bare and wrapped together.

Just as they should be, he thought dimly. He wanted her, like this, all of her, taking him into her fully.

"Wren," she mewed, and he heard the fear in her voice mixed with pleasure and understood it. He took her face in his hands and kissed her, holding her gently as he thrust, first carefully, then more quickly, then harder as she let out gasp after gasp of delight.

And then he slid true, filling her almost completely, feeling the muscles in her thighs tense as the pain caught her off guard, feeling how close he was to breaking her maidenhead.

"Should we stop?" he asked huskily. He wasn't sure he could, but he would damned well try if she told him to.

She hesitated, then slid her hands around the back of his neck, running them into his hair. It was to calm her, he realized, not for him. "No, keep going. Please," she whispered. "It's mostly good. So good."

He complied, driving into her with a powerful thrust, hearing her cry out in a low voice and wincing at the pain he worried he was causing her.

And then he felt her body relax. He was fully in her now. Her legs had slid to wrap against his waist. She was utterly impaled, clutching his back, his shoulders, clinging to him like a beautiful vine against a hothouse wall.

He found himself crooning sweet words to her in Gaelic again. "That's it," he murmured. "That's it, my love, my darling." She could not understand, but the thought was there. She must feel treasured. Cared for. His wife. He was determined she have all that. Everything she deserved.

He reached a hand between her legs as he thrust, slow and deep, and touched the tip of her pleasure, rubbing gently with his thumb and forefinger, bringing her closer to the edge of her crest, until finally, he felt her clutch him hard. Her fingernails dug sharply into his back, and she cried out loudly, not caring who heard. She arched, she writhed, and she cried his name.

It was that which sent him over the edge—his name on her lovely lips—and he felt the rapture overtake him. He thrust inside her with a final groan, spilling his seed into his wife and finding the ecstasy of release in her arms.

Chapter Eleven

Briar woke and her cheeks blazed like wildfire. Not for Wren, not for what he might think. But with the knowledge the entire camp had likely heard everything that had transpired between them last night.

Including blasted Percy Quintrell!

She lay back against the bedding with a groan.

"Does it hurt?" Wren was there, stepping through the tent flap, his face full of concern and his hands full of bowls of steaming hot food. Immediately, her embarrassment was forgotten as the aroma reached her nose.

"Bannock!" Briar sat back up, pushing her tangled hair from her eyes. "And what's with it?" She sniffed. "Fish?"

"Aye," Wren said, looking amused. "Fried herring."

"Fried with butter? And butter on the bannock?" She took the bowl eagerly. Too eagerly. Then looked up, almost shamefaced. "You're trying to hide me, aren't you?"

Wren's expression of amusement deepened. "Hide ye?"

"From the men." Briar let out another groan. "Did they hear... you know? Last night?"

"I didna ask them," Wren said. "Would ye like me to go back now and do just that?"

"No, I certainly wouldn't," Briar hissed, hitting him on the arm. She sat up and took a bite of bannock, then moaned.

Wren was watching with an interested expression. "Of course, if ye repeat the noises, they might just be reminded, ye ken."

Briar glared. "The noises?"

"Och, never mind," he said hastily but didn't bother to hide his grin.

"What are things like out there? Are the men all right? How is Angus?" Briar asked, suddenly remembering there was much more to be concerned with than the events that had transpired in their tent last night. Even though those were the events which admittedly concerned her the most.

Wren's face turned sober. "He's hurt worse than we thought, but he can stand. I'm trying to convince the mon he must ride the rest of the way in the carriage."

"I'm sure that will be a difficult battle," Briar said between mouthfuls of herring. The fried fish was dripping with butter. She closed her eyes. Bliss. She felt as if she had run a hundred miles last night and, with that thought, blushed.

"Worked up an appetite, did ye?" Wren said, his expression amused once more. "Shall I give ye my bowl as well?" He held it out, his eyes twinkling.

"It would serve you right if I said yes," Briar complained. "I easily could finish it."

"It's for ye, in fact," Wren said, the grin spreading across his face. "Angus insisted upon it."

Briar groaned and covered her face with her hands. "I don't even want to know what that implies."

"He simply wants to make sure ye are well nourished," Wren said innocently. "But if ye dinna have room..."

"Oh, I have room," Briar said, snatching the bowl. "Who made the bannock today? Doesn't Angus usually make it?" The hot plain bread seemed especially delicious. Was it the bannock itself, or the wonderful night that had whetted her appetite for it?

"Aye, but his arm is in no condition for cooking." Wren looked even more roguish. "Ye must guess."

Briar narrowed his eyes. "Surely not Percy?"

"Aye, the young whelp. Might make something of him after all," Wren said, considering.

Briar studied the bannock. "It looks all right. It tastes all right." She shook her head. "Percy Quintrell, cooking over an open fire. Like a..." She closed her mouth quickly.

"Like a servant?" Wren only looked amused. "Like a Scotsman?"

"There is no shame in either one," Briar said decisively. "Why, my husband was a gardener before he married me, after all." She winked saucily, and Wren let out a deep rumbling laugh.

"He saved Angus, ye ken," he said, once the laugh had subsided. "I was torn between going to ye or running to Angus. Percy went in my stead. He's a wiry one but surprisingly feisty."

"I suppose we should have known that already," Briar said, popping a piece of bannock into her mouth. "The feisty part, I mean."

"Perhaps he'll stay on at Renfrew Castle," Wren said, considering. "He might do well with honest work, instead of a life of dull leisure."

"That's very generous of you." Briar stared. "I'm sure the Quintrell land agent would thank you were Percy to stay away for a time. Dare says there is nothing wrong with the Quintrell estates that good stewardship cannot remedy, but with the way Percy has been running through money, it is an impossible task at the moment. Who knows, perhaps he might even learn something..." She stopped and nibbled her lip, looking at Wren.

"I suppose ye dinna wish me to forgive him?" Wren looked uncomfortable.

Briar shook her head. "That is entirely up to you. I was simply thinking of how impressively gracious you are being." She smiled impishly. "And I suppose I'm simply glad you don't plan to murder him once we reach your lands."

"Och, I'd rather put him to work in the fields with the sheep. Or have him mucking out the stables," Wren said, waving a hand.

"Of course," Briar murmured. "I'm sure he'd go easily to stable mucking."

Well, wonders would never cease!

Percy had saved his captor *and* made breakfast. Briar decided she would write his mother a letter when they arrived. Mrs. Quintrell would likely be very pleased to hear that her oldest son was finally doing some growing up. Not to mention the money the household must be saving by having him temporarily away!

No other woman had ever made him feel this way. No other woman had ever induced this heady combination in him—white-hot desire mixed with fierce tenderness.

He wanted to protect her, always. He wanted to hold her in his arms, wrap her in his plaid, comfort her, shelter her.

And, he had to confess, he wanted to take her as he had last night, again and again. Lose himself in the splendor of her touch and in touching her. That, too.

He had once felt something for a woman. He had believed it was love. He had offered her marriage. She had accepted.

He had been happy for a while, looking forward to a future with her. Imagining their life together. Their bairns.

Then? She had betrayed him. Given herself to another.

Wren had done his best to forget her. He had not become one of those bitter men who blamed all womankind. That was idiocy.

But neither had he been able to find a woman to take her place. Nor had he wished to.

Until now. Quite by accident. Briar Blakeley had stolen into his head with her persistence. And he feared she was stealing her way straight into his heart.

He had promised both her and himself that he would be a good husband, and he meant to keep the promise.

But love?

Love was a dangerous thing.

He had not promised love. He did not know if he had any love to give, and that was the truth of it.

He watched his beautiful wife devouring her bannock and felt an urge to laugh. She was as pure and sweet as a child as she munched on her meal. And yet in the night, with him, she had been all woman.

Every time she had moved in her sleep, her hips brushing his, he had wanted her again. Longed to grasp the swell of her curves and pull her to him.

But it was too soon. She needed time for her body to heal, especially while traveling.

So instead, he had watched her sleep, smoothed her tangled mass of copper hair back, feeling its softness, and waited.

He would not soon forget that he had almost lost her. If he had gone to aid Angus first and become distracted, he might not have heard her scream. If he had been a little slower, if the other man had been a little quicker, if his opponent had been less panicked and had used the pistol he had snatched to his advantage... Well, things might have turned out very differently.

As it was, she was safe. She had not been hurt. Or violated. His stomach twisted at the thought. Why did men believe they had the right to do such things to women? For they did believe it was their right, that minority of foul, vile-minded men. A plague upon the earth, such men were.

"Wren? Angus is here." Briar was looking up at him with concern. She nodded toward the tent flap where Angus Macleod stood, peering in with an expression of amusement.

"She's a bonny lassie, but ye must keep yer head about ye, mon," Angus cautioned, his eyes twinkling.

Wren only nodded shortly, then stepped out to follow his friend. He held the tent flap back a moment and looked back at his wife. "Dinna leave the camp. Stay near the men." He hesitated, then added, "Please, Wife."

"Yes, Wren." She said it so meekly and obediently that Wren's eyes narrowed.

"Submissive in all things, is she?" Angus chortled from where he stood, watching. His left arm was bandaged, and he held it at an awkward angle, but other than that, his face was clear. He would not easily show his pain, even if he did feel it. "Walk with me, mon."

They strode through the camp side by side, in silence at first.

Angus's men and Percy were still gathered around the fire, sipping their tea and slowly packing up the cooking supplies.

Wren glanced over to the treeline where the pile of bodies lay.

"How are the injured?" he asked Angus.

"Most are healing well," Angus replied, his voice low. "We were uncommonly lucky not to lose even one. The men I brought are well-trained fighters." He spat disdainfully. "The attackers underestimated us. As did whoever hired them."

They were far enough away from the men not to be heard, but Wren waited another few moments as they reached the sandy bluff and stood, looking out over the waves. The wind was blowing away from them, out to sea. Good. Their voices would not carry back in the direction of camp.

"Who were they? Where did they come from?" he asked bluntly. "Did ye ken we were being followed?"

Angus shook his head, his face solemn. "Nay. If I had kent, I would have warned ye, would I no'?"

Wren certainly hoped so. He wanted to trust Angus, but the closer they drew to Renfrew Castle, the more questions were on his mind.

"We must talk," Angus said, watching him carefully. "We have waited too long as it is."

"Aye," Wren said, not disagreeing.

"They were English, the men. But they had been hired. They were no common bandits."

"No," Wren agreed. "They were well dressed and well equipped. Well trained, for the most part." He thought of the ineptitude of the man who had attacked Briar. "The man who attacked my wife said they had been paid to find us."

"Now who, I wonder, would do such a thing?" Angus asked quietly. "Have ye any ideas?"

Wren looked at him wryly. "Did ye no' claim Loghain wanted me dead?" He shook his head. "I still canna believe it, though."

"After all he did to ye, why is it so hard to believe?" Angus asked quietly.

Wren's eyes widened. "After all *he* did? He did nothing to me, before now."

Now it was Angus's turn to look confused. "How can ye say that, mon? Were ye no' betrothed?"

Wren stared. "We are talking in circles."

Angus looked impatient. "When we came back from France, Esme Grant was to have married ye, nay?"

Wren nodded.

"And she had waited. Like a good lass," Angus said dryly. "Or so we all thought. But then, ye found out she was to marry Loghain. He told ye so himself. And so ye stayed behind in England, went back to yer Spencer siblings. I returned with Alec and Loghain."

"Wait," Wren interrupted. "Stop. What nonsense is this? Loghain didna marry Esme. Alec did."

Angus shook his head. "Nay, mon. Alec hated Esme. He didna even want *ye* to marry her. Never trusted the girl, never liked her. Nor did I," he added more quietly. "Nay, it was Loghain who pilfered her. Who turned her heart so easily. He told us he went to ye and told ye the truth, and when ye learned of it, ye were so broken up over it that ye wouldna return with us." His face tightened. "Made many jests about it, he did."

"He told me Alec would marry Esme," Wren said slowly, hardly able to believe what Angus was saying. "And that Alec didna wish for me to return with them. That it would make things too awkward for everyone if I did. And so... I went home to England."

"Home is Scotland. Home is Renfrew land. Ye're a Renfrew, no' a Spencer," Angus said stubbornly. "Though I ken ye love yer sisters and brother, of course. But ye're headed the right direction now. Thank God for it."

"Loghain married Esme," Wren repeated. "The bastard lied. I dinna understand..."

"Aye, he is a bastard. Always was," Angus said cheerfully. "Well, it makes more sense now that I ken the truth of it. The great bloody liar. He's no' going to like seeing yer face. Oh ho, no, no' at all. He'll be verra displeased with me, no doubt."

Wren sank down on a nearby rock and looked up at Angus. "All this time, I thought Alec had married her. We had been so close. As close as brothers. I couldna credit it. Loghain was so sorrowful when he told me. The sly trickster."

"Aye, now ye have it. He is a sly one. Always has been, always was. He and Alec were yer cousins, so I couldna say nothing to ye then. But now ye must ken the truth of it, before ye return home. He hates ye. Always has." Angus shook his head. "I thought ye were such a fool for no' coming home. Loghain made it sound like ye were simply weakhearted."

When Wren glared, he held up his hands. "Aye, more fool are we for believing him, then. But it seemed like the truth. Ye didna write to us or speak with us. Simply slipped away in the night like a ghost. All for that woman who hadna even been true."

"I thought I loved her," Wren said quietly, looking out at the water. "She was my sweetheart, from childhood."

"You might have been a child, but she was always canny. Too canny. Perfect for Loghain. No' that the pair of them have made each other happy." Angus snorted in disgust.

"What do ye mean?"

"Och, ye'll see for yerself soon enough." Angus waved a hand dismissively. "Esme isna what I wish to speak of. It is Loghain who ye must face. In yer absence and with Alec's death, he wormed his way into yer grandfather's good graces. Convinced most of the men that he was meant to inherit once Donnell passed. Donnell did no' set them straight. Ye hurt him, lad. Hurt him badly by no' coming home."

"He never wrote to me," Wren said quietly. "Not once."

"Bah." Angus looked disgusted again. "Were ye a maiden to be wooed or a man to ken yer place? Ye should have come home from the start. Ye shouldna have listened to bloody Loghain. But he did write to ye at least once. I ken that, for I saw the letter with my own hand."

When Wren shook his head firmly, Angus sighed. "I suppose we ken what became of it, then. Easy for it to be made to disappear."

"Ye must ken, Angus," Wren said almost beseechingly. "That I would have come home if I had kent it was Loghain who had wanted me gone and no' Alec. But Alec was to be the laird. His word was my law. Loghain claimed Alec wished for me to be banished. For make no mistake, that was how I saw it at the time. Who was I to challenge that? And aye, I was sorely hurt by Esme's loss. I willna deny it. But..." Wren punched the rock with one fist, his face twisting in anger. "If I had kent... Goddamn, if I had but kent. The bloody bastard."

"Good. That feeling toward him—ye keep feeling it," Angus advised. "For I tell ye now, I have no doubt at all it was he who sent those men last night. He must have had watchers on us all the way from England, and when he learned ye still lived, he put a second plan into motion."

They had not precisely been making good time, with the slowness of the carriage and the extra days they had taken so that Briar might rest. Wren considered Angus's words. It made sense. Though Loghain must have had men paid and waiting, just for this eventuality.

"He doesna trust ye," he observed, looking at Angus.

Angus grinned. "Stupid bastard for sending me in the first place. Did he really think I'd do his bidding and slit yer throat?" He kicked at a stone. "Nay, the men I brought are loyal to the Renfrew family. No' to Loghain, though he'd like to believe we're all wrapped around his finger. Nay, it was a test. And I meant to fail from the start. I chose my men, though. He was a fool to let me do that much."

"We would have died last night if ye hadna had loyal men with ye," Wren said quietly.

"Aye. But we did. And they aim to be loyal to ye, mark me. Now the true laird is coming home, to put things to rights," Angus said, sounding remarkably unconcerned about his near death and his treacherous leader.

"Are things really so bad as that? Or is it just a matter of Loghain having become overly ambitious?"

Angus eyed him sardonically. "How much do ye wish to ken in advance? As for overly ambitious, he is the laird now in yer stead in everything but right. He willna accept ye easily. Does it no bother ye?"

"I can hardly believe that my grandfather is dead, that Alec is gone, and that I am laird at all," Wren replied.

Angus seemed to understand. He gripped Wren's shoulder briefly. "Aye, a great loss. Two good men. Alec would have made a fine laird. He was ready. Damn the fever that took him."

"Had he married?" Wren asked curiously. All this time, he had been imagining his cousin with Esme. And a flock of children around them. Though he could not picture Esme as a mother. She had grown up in a house with many siblings and had always claimed to dislike small children.

He tried to picture Briar with a baby, and the image came easily. He smiled at the thought.

"Dreaming of his bride again, instead of thinking of his future," Angus observed, but he did not seem too annoyed. "Think of how to keep her safe. For she willna be for long if Loghain sees ye dead."

That, too, was difficult to believe. That his cousin would plot his murder so easily. When they arrived at Renfrew Castle, surely Loghain would see that his plan had failed and admit defeat. What sort of man plotted murder in cold blood against his kin?

But then, what sort of man stole another man's betrothed—a girl who had promised herself—and lied about it?

Wren frowned. He was not a vindictive man. But Loghain had taken much from him. Esme, he could easily get over and forgive. At least, he could now, he thought ruefully, with the gift of Briar.

But the years he might have spent with Alec and his grandfather? Those years were his birthright. And he would never get them back.

"I still canna wrap my mind around a man doing such a thing," he said.

To his relief, Angus did not scold him for his naivety. "Aye," the older man said slowly. "Taking yer lass. Lying through his teeth. Lying to yer cousin. Lying to his grandda, his own laird. He has no honor." Wren saw Angus's jaw clench. "Ye've heard of the happenings back home? Of the clearances?"

Wren nodded. "Moving men, women, and children from their homes. To new crofts by the coast mainly? Aye."

Angus made a scoffing sound. "It sounds verra reasonable when ye describe it that way. 'Moving.' What do ye call it when men are moved no better than flocks of sheep, with no more say than sheep either? When their homes are burned out from under them so they canna return, even if they wished it? When the new crofts are bleak, and they canna make a living from them? Ye canna turn men who were farmers into fishermen overnight. And yet, that is what many of these rich lairds, rich land-owners, believe they may do."

He leaned forward, his face blazing. "Ye've heard of the Sutherlands? Have ye heard of the burning of homes? Have ye heard of how an old woman was still in one as they burned it?"

"No." Wren was shocked. "No' truly!"

"Aye, truly. I dinna ken if they did it on purpose. They claim it was an accident. But the burning of the homes is no accident. And the starving of the children." His lips twisted in disdain. "And I give ye one guess as to who wishes to follow in the Sutherland's path and clear Renfrew lands just the same?"

"Loghain," Wren said, his stomach sinking.

Angus nodded. "I'm sure it's why the man wishes ye gone. He kens ye wouldna approve of such a plan. He thinks he'll get rich putting sheep where there were farmers and moving his farmers to crofts by the sea to reap fish for him. He has no mind for such things. But his men, the ones he's gathered around him, his true supporters. The ones whose pockets he lines. They will do as he commands."

"Are there many such men?" Wren asked.

"Not so many as there could be," Angus said, beginning to look cheerful again. "I've made sure of that, dinna fret. I've been looking forward to this day for a long time, Renfrew."

He called Wren by the name that was the title of the old laird. Wren supposed he would have to get used to it now. He was the new Renfrew.

"What do they call Loghain? His men, I mean?" Wren asked, frowning.

"The Renfrew, of course." Angus scowled, then spat on the ground. "That'll change."

Wren hoped so. But would it change without bloodshed? He doubted that, very much.

"A few fists to the face, and they'll be calling the rightful laird by the rightful name," Angus promised, looking cheered at the prospect.

"And ye'll provide the fists?" Wren asked, unable to help but grin at the optimism of the loyal man.

"Aye, gladly," Angus vowed. "As I said, I've been waiting for this day a long time."

He gave Wren a steady look, nodded, then started walking back to the camp.

Angus Macleod was a good man and a true friend, Wren realized. Better than he likely deserved.

And what of Loghain Grant and what he deserved? The man's name was not even Renfrew, for he was Renfrew through his mother's side.

Wren had no wish to kill a kinsman. And yet from all Angus said, Loghain had become a dangerous man, intent on achieving his own ends and using whatever means he wished to get there.

When Wren arrived back on Renfrew lands with his wife beside him, would she find a warm welcome? Or snakes in her bed?

Chapter Twelve

Briar was digging for clams.

More properly, she was digging for *spoots*. Or *spooting* as Percy insisted on calling it. Apparently one of the men had called it that, and it was the proper "Scots" way.

Percy was suddenly very interested in doing things the proper Scottish way, Briar had noticed. He had gone from sourly ignoring Angus's men to shyly sitting beside them in camp at night. Now an even greater shift had occurred. After the battle the night before, Percy had achieved something close to acceptance. The men were treating him almost as if he were one of them.

His excellent bannock-making skills had probably not hurt, Briar reflected.

And now, she thought, watching him a little glumly, his spooting skills would soon have them eating out of his hand.

"Caught another one!" he was crying, holding up a long, narrow mollusk in his hand with an expression resembling *The Ecstasy of Saint Theresa*. "It's easier this way. You must give it a try!"

Briar looked down at the knife she had been digging in the sand with.

Spoots, or razor shell clams as they were more widely known, were tricky creatures to catch. They burrowed down into the sand and could move quickly once disturbed. The trick, Briar and Percy had been told, was to walk backwards, creeping up on where they lay burrowed. Then when one caught sight of their *spoots*—the spouts of water they ejected while moving more deeply into the sand—one slid a long-bladed knife through the sand with speed and precision to root them out. But if one didn't gauge the angle correctly, the spoot simply slipped away, as Briar was finding with great frustration.

She had caught precisely zero spoots so far, while Percy's basket was full to the brim.

At least it was a lovely evening. The sun was setting as she crouched on her heels on the tidal flat, enjoying the feeling of the wet sand between her toes and the peaceful sound of the shallow waves nearby. She had hiked her skirts up, tying her dress higher around her waist so she could dig in the sand without having to worry about soaking. Now she stood and waded a little way into the water, enjoying the cool sea around her ankles.

"Absolutely shameless," Percy called teasingly from where he worked a few yards away.

"Oh, pishposh," Briar said, waving a hand. "I'm a married woman now, aren't I?"

But Percy had already lost interest in her ankles. He was too busy wrestling with another spoot. She watched in fascination as he spotted a spout of water and enthusiastically launched his fingers into the sand.

"Ah, we have a fighter!" he crowed, digging about with his fingers.

She watched as he seemed to engage in a true wrestle with the creature, finally pulling it out and holding it aloft.

"They call it 'taking them by the eye,'" Percy explained, panting a little after his vigorous battle with the razor clam. "Angus told me."

"How do you do that?" Briar demanded, looking down into her empty bucket a little mournfully. So much for impressing Wren with her clam-digging skills. "You might as well put it in here. Yours is overflowing."

"It is, isn't it?" Percy said, grinning as he looked back at his own bucket. "I hope they won't escape. Perhaps I should carry them up."

"I'll do it for you," Briar offered. "It seems I am only fit to be your assistant in this endeavor."

"You'll get the way of it soon enough if you keep trying," Percy said encouragingly.

Briar stared, then shook her head slowly.

"What? What is it?" Percy demanded.

"That sounded almost exactly like a boy I once knew," Briar replied. "His name was Percy Quintrell. Perhaps you remember him?"

Percy smiled wryly. "I've been a beast to you, haven't I?"

"To me, yes. To Bessie Brewer?" She raised her eyebrows significantly. "Rather more than a beast, I think."

"Bessie... yes." Percy sighed, then dropped the clam into her bucket and stepped back to look out at the sea.

"You aren't going to argue?" Briar asked, amazed.

Percy shrugged. "It's the truth, isn't it?"

"What on earth has happened to you?" Briar demanded. She shook her head. "Never mind. You need not answer. I don't want to know. But please, do not go back. I like you much better this way."

Percy's lips quirked. "I like myself better this way, too."

He looked at her. "Do you like being married? To Wren?"

Briar couldn't help it. He had caught her off guard. She blushed.

"I wasn't trying to imply anything," Percy said quickly. "I wasn't trying to tease..."

She studied his face. He seemed sincere. Perhaps he had not even heard her last night. One could hope.

"Yes," she said simply. "I like it quite well. So far. After all, we have only been married a few days."

"I still cannot believe you are married," Percy mused. "And to a man like that. That is to say, I think he is a good man," he added hastily. "I was not implying he is not."

"Thank you," Briar said, a little amused. "I think he is, too."

"He certainly seems to think the world of you," Percy said quietly. "When he saw you in danger the other night, he could not go to your aid fast enough. And what he did to that man for touching you..."

"Yes." Briar did not wish to think of the exact details. "He is very... protective."

"I'll say." Percy grinned. "You have your very own Scottish wolf."

"He is more civilized than a wolf, thank you very much," Briar said a little stiffly, not sure whether Percy was trying to say something about the perceived superiority of English gentlemen to Scots. "He quotes poetry. Medieval poetry. He knows how to brew tea."

"Impressive." Percy was smiling.

"Of course, you have your own fine qualities," Briar acknowledged. "Shockingly. Such as making bannock. Hunting spoots."

Percy shrugged nonchalantly. "I'm trying to contribute a little. That's all."

"You saved Angus," she said quietly. "The men know that. I don't think they expected you to fight at all."

Percy laughed. "I'm sure that's true. I surprised myself, actually. But I couldn't just lie on my bedroll and snore, could I?"

"It was very frightening, though. It must have been tempting to," Briar said carefully. "But you didn't. You were very brave, Percy."

He looked at her. "Not brave enough. Not soon enough."

"Oh, Percy." She felt a little sad. "What do you mean?" She hoped he was not going to try to speak of feelings for her or any of that nonsense again.

"We might have married, Briar," he said. He held up a hand when she started to protest. "Don't worry, I am not going to spew love poetry or beg you to take me as your lover. I'm not that much of an idiot. And I was never in love with you, in any case. But... I was thinking about it and... well, we might have married. We might even have been happy. If I wasn't such an arse. But I made sure that couldn't happen. Didn't I?" He looked down at the sand. "I would probably not wish for my daughter to marry someone like me, either. Or my sister."

"Hmm," Briar said. "What's done is done, Percy. The question is, what are you going to do about the mess you've made now?"

"I've been thinking about that, too," Percy said in a low voice. "My father had just died, you see. I know that's no excuse, but... I was very unhappy. And suddenly, I had all this freedom. Bessie was there and... well, you know the rest. I was drinking too much, of course."

"I haven't seen you drink since we were taken," Briar said, considering.

Percy shook his head. "Not a drop. And I feel much better this way. Not that there is anything wrong with the stuff. But perhaps for me there is. I can't seem to handle myself when I drink. I drink more than I should. I say stupid things. I do stupid things."

He looked very glum. Briar shocked herself by reaching out a hand and gently touching his arm. "At least you are trying now, thinking about your mistakes, I mean."

"I shall provide for Bessie and the child. I swear I will. When we reach this place we're going, I'll write to my solicitors and make the arrangements," Percy said, his face determined. "Our estate is not in a good financial situation. My father saw to that. I did not improve things. But there is certainly enough to make sure the child has a good life and a good education when it comes time."

"Oh, excellent, Percy," Briar said softly. "Bessie will be so relieved."

"I can't marry her, Briar," Percy said quietly. "Even if I wanted to. Not only because I doubt I'd make her a very good husband, but..." He hesitated.

"You must marry money?" Briar guessed.

Percy nodded slowly. "I should at least try."

"It's as bad as that?" Briar wondered if Dare might help the Quintrells in any way.

"It will be worse if I don't find my path. For my mother and brothers' sake," Percy said, staring out to sea again.

Briar looked alongside him. The sky was turning beautiful shades of red, orange, and violet as the sun sank below the horizon.

"I want to say," Percy began, turning to look at her, "that I'm very sorry about what I did to you and to your husband."

"What you did," Briar echoed. "Goodness, I had almost forgotten." The strange thing was that she really had. Percy had been so different the last few days.

"I did it for the money, certainly. But mostly because... well, because you refused me, and I was angry and stupid. But I could have gotten Wren killed. I could have gotten you killed. Or other terrible things." Percy looked very uncomfortable.

"You could have gotten yourself killed, too," Briar pointed out.

"I still could, I suppose," Percy said, grinning. "Perhaps they'll string me up from the castle wall when we get there, as a warning to Englishmen to stay away."

"I doubt it," Briar said, amused. "I think Wren is starting to like you."

Percy's eyes widened. "That is... good to hear. Though I'm sure I don't deserve it."

"He even mentioned you might wish to stay in Scotland a while," Briar said. She did not think Wren would mind, and the look on Percy's face as she said the words was worth it, anyway.

"Really?" Percy's eyes had lit up. "I might consider that. Once I make arrangements for Bessie and my mother, I mean. I wonder if there is any useful work I might do."

"Useful work? I'm sorry, I think I've been speaking to a stranger after all," Briar said, putting a finger to her lips, and smirking.

"Speaking of which," Percy said very seriously. "I must get back to the spoots."

"The spoots, yes, of course. The spoots," Briar murmured. "They won't wait forever."

"No," Percy said, evidently not noticing her tone. "And I promised the men we'd have enough for supper. I'm making bannock, too."

"Very well. Go on then." Briar waved a hand. "Gather your spoots. You may use my bucket. I'll go and empty yours and bring it back. One can never be too optimistic."

"Bring two buckets," Percy declared, looking determined.

"Two buckets!" Briar grinned and picked up the full one. "Very well."

She started walking across the sand toward the bluff. There was someone approaching. It was Wren. Her heart gave a wonderful little kick, and she waved a hand.

"Wren!"

"What are ye and Percy up to?" he asked, looking curious.

"Digging for spoots, of course," she said, giggling a little. It was such a funny word and enjoyable to say.

"Spoots?" His mirthful expression deepened. Then he caught sight of the bucket, and his eyes widened. "And ye caught all these, did ye?"

"Well, no," Briar confessed. "These are all Percy's. I didn't catch any. But Percy has quite the knack for it." She nodded back to where Percy was shouting at a spoot in the sand. "I left my bucket for him, as it was empty, and have promised to bring back two more."

"Two more? What a cocky whelp," Wren said. "Here. Let me carry it." He took the bucket of clams from her.

"Oh, it's not heavy," she protested, though it was too late. "Well, thank you."

His other arm was free. She eyed it covertly, wondering if he would balk if she slipped her arm through it.

And then he caught her off-guard by sliding it around her waist and pulling her close. She leaned against his body, drinking in his scent, closing her eyes a moment. Bliss. This was bliss. The ocean. The warm sun. And Wren.

"I've missed ye, Wife," he murmured, touching his lips briefly to her hair.

"Mmm. I've missed you, too. Where have you been?"

"Setting up our tent. Did ye think the pixies did it every night?" He sounded entertained.

"Oh!" She was taken aback. She had not really been giving it much thought. She supposed she was still quite spoiled. Used to servants doing everything, without thinking about the fact that now she had none. It was good for her, however, she thought. She could get used to doing more for herself. Wren spoiled her now. She would need to find more ways of spoiling him.

With that thought, she had another and felt her cheeks grow a little hot as she imagined it.

"What are ye thinking of, Wife? Ye're blushing." Wren sounded interested.

"Hmm? Oh, nothing," Briar said innocently. "How do you eat these, anyway?" She gestured to the bucket.

"With butter, fried in a skillet, of course," Wren replied.

"With butter. Of course." Briar gave a satisfied little sigh. Everything good was made with butter.

Wren was looking down at her, smiling. "Looking forward to supper, are we?"

Briar nodded. It had been a long day of travel. Surely, they would arrive soon. She would make no word of protest, but if she had to wear this dress another day, she would scream—to herself at least. Not in Wren's hearing.

"Are we nearly there?" she asked tentatively.

"Aye, we'll arrive tomorrow. By midday, I'd say."

"Tomorrow!" Suddenly it seemed too soon. "And there will be real beds?"

"Aye, it's a castle. There are beds."

"And a bit of privacy?" Briar fished. "Perhaps... our own room?"

"As they tell me I'm laird, I'm sure we can arrange for at least one or two rooms."

"Oh, just one, please," Briar said quickly. She did not think she would like to sleep all alone in a completely strange place. Besides, she was becoming quite used to sleeping beside Wren.

And she could become quite used to doing more than just sleeping, too. She thought again of last night. Of her legs wrapping around his waist as he thrust inside of her...

She caught Wren looking at her, met his eyes, and blushed. Could he read her thoughts? Most likely.

"And do you garden in Scotland?" she asked blithely. "Who taught you to do all that? All that you did at Blakeley, I mean?"

"Nay, I dinna garden at Renfrew Castle," he said, but there was a twinkle in his eye as if he knew what she'd really been thinking. "My mother taught me all I ken. She was a rare healer. She kent herbs, plants, flowers. She could use them for many things."

He paused suddenly and let go of Briar, then reached a hand out to pluck at something. When he raised it again, he was holding a handful of flowers with tiny white buds and green leaves.

"Ransoms. Wild garlic," he explained. "They'll be good with the spoots."

He stooped to pick some more, then put the bundle into one of the pockets of his plaid.

"What else do you have in there?" she teased. "Are they full of herbs?"

He grinned. "Mayhap."

"Did your mother teach you to forage like that?" she asked.

He nodded, his face more serious. "When my stepfather passed, things were... scarce for a time."

"Until your grandfather sent for you?"

"Aye, until he paid for me to come," Wren said darkly. He sighed. "No' that I blame him or my mother. He had the right idea, most like. And my mother, she didna want to part from me, but she had to care for the others. It was the wise thing to do, to take the money."

"And yet, your siblings... they all wound up in service," Briar said curiously.

"Aye, I might have offered them better, but once they were grown, my mother wouldna take anything further from my grandda." He grimaced. "The Spencers are as stubborn as the Renfrews."

"Goodness," Briar murmured. "And you have no idea how stubborn the Blakeleys are."

Wren shot her a knowing look. "I have come to have some idea," he said with dignity.

Briar laughed.

<hr />

He wanted badly to kiss her then. Even with Percy down on the beach. Even with the men looking on from the camp.

Damn the spoots, he thought, crossly. Damn dinner, too. He wanted to pick her up in his arms, feel her soft lightness, and carry her back to the tent now, in front of everyone.

Peel the dress from her body, touch her, take her, have her in every way there was until they were both spent and too weary to do anything but fall asleep, naked and damp in each other's arms. He wanted to untie her braid and see her hair fall gleaming in the moonlight again, watch her beautiful eyes light up in awe and shock as he entered her. He wanted to plunge into her lush softness and heat and stay there, forevermore.

And never return. Not even for dinner.

But his wife was clearly famished. Would she prefer spoots or him, he wondered? Should he pose the question? Or would the answer be damaging to his masculinity?

She was looking at him curiously, her head tilted at an angle.

"What are *you* thinking of now, Husband? It's my turn to ask."

"Do ye really want to ken?" His voice was low and husky. Could she hear the pent-up desire there? He took a step toward her and watched her eyes widen a little.

He bent his head down next to her ear. He wasn't kissing her, he told himself. Just saying words. Let the men in the camp watch if they wanted.

"Do ye ken what I wish to do to ye?" he murmured.

She shook her head almost imperceptibly.

"I want to pick ye up, toss ye over my shoulder, and carry ye to the tent right now. And then..." He paused.

"And then?" she prompted, her voice soft.

"And then," he continued, "I would lay ye down on the blankets, strip yer dress from yer beautiful body"—he sensed her shiver—"and turn my tongue upon ye." He lowered his mouth even closer to her ear. "All upon ye. Everywhere."

"Everywhere?" He watched her gulp.

"I would start with yer lips, of course. Pay them the devotion they deserve. Then the corner of yer jaw, yer neck. Then lower. To yer breasts..." She was shivering now. It was all he could do to resist putting his lips to her neck right there. "I would pay them homage. Oh, for quite a while, aye. Before moving down."

"Down?" she whimpered.

"Aye, down, down, down. Down to yer navel. Down to yer hips, the soft swells of yer curving hips. Beautiful."

"They're too wide, I always thought," she murmured self-consciously.

"They're perfect," he growled. "Dinna insult them. They're mine."

"V-very well," she gasped.

"Aye. Now where was I? Ah, yer hips. And then... the place between yer thighs. Where ye'll be wet and hot for me."

"You would... taste me? There?"

Wren pulled back a little to see her face more fully. "Aye. Have ye never heard of such things?"

Her eyes were even wider, golden pools of brown. She shook her head.

"And ye think spoots will be tasty," he said, amused. "A woman tastes the best of all." He lowered his head again, his lips brushing against her ear. "And my wife, my wife will taste best of all. I look forward to devouring her tonight. In our tent."

"Oh, my," she whispered, her face bright red. "I am not sure I..."

"Aye?"

"I am not sure I am hungry after all," she said, nibbling at her lower lip in a way that made Wren's cock harden instantly. "Perhaps we should go back to our tent now."

"And have the men hear us? Before the sun has even finished setting? Ye wanton," Wren teased.

Briar huffed and hit his arm. "Oh, you!"

"Nay, my wife must be fed first," he said, taking her arm again and resuming his steps. "I ken ye have a hunger for these spoots."

"With butter and garlic, don't forget," Briar reminded him.

"With butter and garlic. And then, the tent."

Chapter Thirteen

He went slowly. Teasing her with his tongue. Savoring the taste of her. The saltiness of her skin. And then, the saltiness of her slit, the sea-salt tang of her wetness as he parted her legs gently and slid his tongue between them.

Her responsiveness was everything. Her sweet little cries. Her whimpers of pleasure. Then of desperation.

When she began to twist her hands in the blankets, he gently untwisted them, lifted them to his hair instead.

"Tell me where ye want me, mo chridhe," he urged. She moaned, her hips bucking, but quickly did as he asked, her hands tangling in his hair, urging his mouth higher.

"There?" he teased, dipping and stroking his tongue.

"Or there?" He touched his tongue to the little bud that held the crux of her pleasure and flicked it, once, twice.

She yanked his hair, almost roughly, and moaned.

"Ah, I thought so," he said with satisfaction. He reached beneath her then, cupping the soft roundness of her bottom in his hands, holding her just the way he wanted her, bringing her more fully against his mouth.

He captured her bud in his mouth, sucking slowly, and she bucked against him.

"Wren..." she whimpered. "Please..."

"Aye, lovely," he promised. "Ye're almost there."

"Don't stop, Wren. Please, don't stop."

"Ye couldna make me stop," he vowed. "No mon could."

He sucked harder, and she cried out. "Oh, my God, Wren." Her fingers tangled in his hair, clutching him, trapping him just the way he wanted to be trapped.

He gave a low chuckle, letting the vibration rumble through him, and she groaned in appreciation.

He released one soft, sweet buttock and moved his hand to slip a finger inside her, hearing her gasp in shock, then delight as he thrust with the thick, rough finger, stroked her clit with his tongue, kissing greedily, sucking as hard as he dared, driving her mad with her lust.

Her hips were lifting off the makeshift bed now, and she was urging him on. "Yes, Wren, please, Wren. Oh, God, please."

And then she was jerking, gasping with pleasure, the mounting climax overpowering her, exploding deep within her, carrying her like an ocean wave, and then dropping her listless, silent, and exhausted.

He gathered her into his arms, caressing her as the trembling ceased, making soft hushing noises.

She raised a hand to touch his face. "That was..." She shook her head, bit her lip. He wanted her badly but could wait a little longer. "Marvelous. Exquisite. Superb."

"Superb, eh?" Wren lifted his eyebrows.

"You are marvelous," she said shyly. "My husband."

He looked down at her, the hair spread like a rich red fan of flames, her lovely lips, her bright intelligent eyes. "Ye're the superb one, mo chridhe."

"What does that mean?" she murmured sleepily. "You've said it before."

"Ye remember?" he asked a little uncomfortably. He shifted his weight so as not to squash her. "It means 'sweetheart.' Or something close."

"Gaelic, is it? It sounds very pretty." She yawned. "I like being your sweetheart, Wren."

"Do ye now? Yet ye think it's time for sleeping?" He leaned down and nibbled her lip, growling playfully, and she giggled.

"Oh? Isn't it? I thought we were done."

"I'll show ye done," he growled again.

"Oh, yes," she murmured, languidly stretching out her legs against him. "Please, show me."

That was all he needed to hear. He lowered himself over her, feeling the incredible warm flush of skin against skin, and she writhed, already moving to wrap her legs around him.

"I want you, Wren," she was whispering. "I have wanted you all day. Very badly."

The words sent him spinning, and he entered her with a single thrust, hearing her moan, hoping he was not hurting her, almost unable to bring himself to care, so badly did he want her. He made sure to lower his hand between her thighs, fingertips expertly rubbing her swollen bud, hearing her gasp. And then he felt the hot spill of his own release, his breathing grew ragged, his body convulsed, and he fell over that infinite cliff. Beneath him, Briar trembled, joining him as he fell into the overwhelming pleasure, both losing all control, primal sounds of animal satisfaction escaping them both.

And then it was over, and they were themselves, together again, in one another's arms.

They might have made a child just then, Wren thought, the idea of it filling him with amazement but also joy at the prospect.

He rolled off, then pulled her close to him, her head tucked just below his. He kissed her hair. It smelled of the sun and the sea. And quite possibly of spoots. He smiled to himself. He wouldn't tell her that. Not tonight.

She was murmuring against his chest. Some words he could not catch. He was too sleepy to ask what she was saying. He wanted to. He meant to. But sleep overcame him.

He wanted her. He desired her. He was tender and kind toward her.

But did he love her?

Briar had never wished to know the answer to a question so badly. She supposed the logical thing to do would be to pose it aloud. But she knew she would not be doing that.

As for herself, she had whispered the answer in her heart against Wren's chest as she fell asleep. Now, in the dead of night with the camp asleep and still, she had awoken and lay next to Wren, enjoying the quiet peacefulness of their tent, the rise and fall of his chest with her hand upon it.

This was it. This was love.

She loved him. She loved her husband. She did not even feel the need to blush when she thought about the sentiment. It was too matter-of-fact now for that. She had surrendered to the feeling, and she refused to regret it.

Besides, it was too sweet a thing to regret. Unpredictable and pervasive. Like trying to avoid breathing. Impossible! So too was it impossible for Briar to have avoided falling in love.

She needed him. She wanted him. She loved him.

She had not expected to marry this man, but if she was to be very honest with herself, she had been drawn to him, right from the very start, in the gardens of Blakeley Manor.

She had never felt more like a real wife than she had last night after their love-making. He was hers, and she was his.

If he did not love her yet, surely he would in time.

She yawned, smiled as she watched Wren scratch his chest in his sleep, then snuggled in closer in that space between his arm and his chest, and tried to fall back asleep.

Chapter Fourteen

They reached Renfrew lands the next afternoon.

After days of traveling and nights of sleeping in a tent, one might have expected Briar to be eager to reach the shelter of stone walls and warm beds again. Yet nothing was further from the truth. As she had helped Wren pack up their tent for the last time that morning, she had nearly cried.

As far as she was concerned, that tent was their first home. The makeshift bed of Wren's plaid and various wool blankets donated by Angus and his men was her bridal bed.

She loved Blakeley Manor. Yet no home could ever be sweeter, she thought, than the tent she had shared with Wren. No bed more comfortable or warmer than the one in which her husband's arms had come around her to protect and shelter her for the very first time.

The caravan stopped to lunch beneath a grove of yew trees. After eating the surprisingly excellent leftovers cooked up by Percy of refried spoots in butter and a salad of fresh greens, Briar lay back on a mossy bank, drinking deeply of the rich leafy scents. At first, she gazed up at the lush green foliage, the canopy of branches swaying gently against the bright blue sky. Eventually she closed her eyes, her mind a tumult.

She would reach her new home in a few hours, they said. What would it be like?

She peeked her eyes open and stole a glance to where Percy stood, briskly cleaning up the remains of lunch, for all the world looking like an industrious housewife tidying a cottage. He looked calm and content, remarkably at home for someone who had been kidnapped.

Of course, Briar was not exactly suffering, either. She felt a guilty pang as she thought of how worried Dare and Kat must be. And Leigh? Her rakish younger brother might be a rapscallion, but he loved his family dearly. Yes, even Leigh must be worried by now. As soon as they arrived, writing a letter would be her very first task, she decided with determination. Angus Macleod would put her off no longer!

How strange it would be for Dare to learn she was a married woman...

She must have closed her eyes again because the next thing she knew Wren was gently shaking her awake and helping her onto the horse. No longer were they relegated to the confines of the carriage. For several days they had mostly ridden, separately and together. Even Percy had been finally granted use of a small mare.

Something had changed the last few days, especially since the attack. Wren was an honored guest amongst Angus and his men, a prisoner no longer. No, more than a guest, he was slowly taking a place of precedence—one Angus was giving up with grace. Angus's men had begun to speak to Wren with respect and admiration. Briar suspected both had been there all along and simply hidden beneath Angus's desperate need to take Wren back with them, no matter what it took.

But in the end, Robert Renfrew was their laird. And while the tradition of lairdships may have lost power over the last century, clearly to these men, in this part of Scotland at least, it still meant a great deal.

They were coming over a ridge. Briar could see a plume of smoke in the distance, then a second, and another. Then abruptly, they reached the peak of the ridge, and Renfrew Castle came into view.

Resting on a rocky outcrop surrounded on three sides by the North Sea, the castle was an impressive sight. For one thing, it was huge. The sheer cliffs it rested upon looked as if they might slide into the sea at any moment, adding to the impression of a construction of vast size and dangerous majesty.

Briar felt quite daunted as she stared at the imposing red sandstone walls of Renfrew Castle. This was her new home? How could anyone ever call this massive place a home? Furthermore, it was not even a single building but, in keeping with its medieval nature, was more a castle with an entire village attached. There were numerous outbuildings already within view—stables, towers, guard houses, a kirk, and other structures—in addition to at least ten more dwellings and cottages.

And that was just on the headland itself. They had already ridden past what felt to Briar like hundreds of cottages, in small clusters leading up to the castle itself. The Renfrews were evidently responsible for hundreds of tenants. Thousands of people under their care.

Not the Renfrews, she corrected herself. *The Renfrew.* Her husband.

And what was she? What was her role in all this? She shifted nervously on the saddle behind Wren.

"What do ye think of yer new home, Wife?" he asked, looking over his shoulder.

"It is... unforgettable," she said truthfully. "A most impressive sight."

"Aye, it is impregnable," he boasted. She could hear the swell of pride in his voice. "Centuries old. The oldest parts are said to be more than seven hundred years old. Can ye imagine?"

Blakeley Manor was close to two hundred years old, and as a child, Briar had thought that was ancient. She tried to imagine living somewhere that contained close to a thousand years of Scottish history.

"Very impressive," she said, hoping Wren would not notice how small her voice was.

"Pudding stone," Wren said abruptly.

"What was that?" Briar leaned closer, not sure she had heard him right. "Pudding what?"

"Pudding stone," Wren repeated. "The rocky cliffs below the castle." He nodded toward them, and Briar followed his gaze. "They call them pudding stone because the rocks and pebbles jutting out look like..."

"A fruitcake! Yes, I see it," Briar exclaimed, bouncing a little. "Pudding Stone Castle." She smiled to herself. That was slightly less intimidating. Much better.

"Well, it's Renfrew Castle," Wren said. She could almost hear the frown of disapproval in his voice and hid a grin against his back.

"Yes, of course," she said hastily. "Renfrew Castle, not Pudding Stone Castle. I shall remember."

"*Mmph*."

They were drawing near to the spectacular cliff-top stronghold. The portcullis had already been opened, and a small group of people were awaiting their approach.

Briar felt her husband stiffen at the sight of the group.

"What is it?" she whispered.

"My cousin," he said finally. "Loghain and his wife."

They rode closer. Briar saw a man and a woman front and center in the group. They would have stood out from a crowd almost anywhere, not just because the man bore an uncanny resemblance to Wren.

But where Wren was dark-haired with stormy blue eyes, this man was golden-haired with eyes as calm as the summer sky. His hair was so light, in fact, as to almost be white. It curled in what looked like quite natural ringlets, reminding Briar of painted cherubs. But there was nothing childish or emasculate about this man. He was the fair-haired Greek Adonis to Wren's Pict warrior. His physique was a little shorter and on a less broad scale, but undoubtedly full of masculine vitality just like Wren. He wore a cloak of Renfrew plaid that billowed in the wind behind him, but his arms were bare and crossed over his chest, showing off rippling strength.

As Briar stared, the fair man's lips curved up in a warm and welcoming smile. To Briar, he seemed to radiate charm and grace. She had not been expecting a cousin such as this. This man was quite opposite from Angus and Wren.

The woman standing beside him must be Loghain's wife, she thought. While her glorious husband outshone her, he did so just barely. Loghain's wife was a Viking goddess in her own right, her flaxen-colored hair braided in a crown around her head. She wore a simple blue dress, and her hands were clasped in front of her like a humble maiden. She did not smile, however. In fact, Briar thought her face rather stony, though exceptionally lovely. Wide red lips and bright, wide blue eyes. She was tall and slender, too. Much taller than Briar, who had always wished to have greater height.

"What is his wife's name?" Briar whispered, wishing to make a note of it.

There was an even longer pause this time.

"Esme," came the answer eventually. "Esme Ross. Now Esme Grant."

They were reaching the gate. Briar swung down from the saddle before Wren could stop her and smiled over at the welcoming committee.

"Welcome, Cousin!" Loghain stepped forward, his arms outstretched to them both. "Welcome home. It has been too long."

Briar looked up at her husband and saw a conflicting mix of emotions passing over his face. Affection, relief, suspicion, and perhaps even anger.

Then they were gone, and his face had relaxed into an unreadable expression with the hint of a smile.

He clasped his cousin by the arm and squeezed tight. So hard that Briar saw Loghain hide a wince.

"Thank ye, Loghain. I agree with ye. Too long indeed. Much too long."

"You already know my wife, Esme," Loghain said smoothly, gesturing to the beautiful lady behind him with a smile.

"I do," Wren said. And this time Briar caught the anger in his face as he looked Loghain fully in the eyes.

She was shocked. Clearly, she was missing something crucial in this moment. But what?

She glanced at Esme, but the woman was looking down at the ground.

"Come meet our guests, Esme," Loghain called to her impatiently. "She is just as shy as ever, you see," he joked to Wren.

"Was she? Ever shy? I dinna recall that," Briar heard her husband say.

Her heart began to sink a little. So, Wren knew this beautiful woman from his life before. Was that the missing piece here? Esme Grant?

"But wait," Loghain interjected, looking at Briar and smiling even more warmly. "We are all old friends here, but who is this? You have not yet introduced the bonny lady beside you, Cousin."

Was it Briar's imagination or did Wren go very still?

He looked down at her, his face inscrutable, then placed a hand gently on her shoulder.

"This is my wife. Formerly the Lady Briar Blakeley of Blakeley Manor. Now Briar Renfrew."

"You have taken a wife!" Loghain's face was pure delight. "Welcome, welcome."

"Verra pleased to meet ye, I'm sure," Esme said quietly, coming over to her.

"As am I. Very pleased to meet you," Briar said politely, trying to smile at the other woman. "Renfrew Castle is very... impressive. Have you lived here long?"

"I grew up here," Esme said simply. "Though I didna always live in the castle."

"Oh, of course," Briar replied quickly. "Did you know Wren growing up? Robert, that is. I am sorry, but I cannot quite get used to that name. He has always been Wren to me."

Esme bit her lip. "The Renfrew now."

"Yes, yes," Loghain interrupted, overhearing them. He took Esme's arm, then linked his other arm in Briar's. "The long-lost laird has returned, and we are all thankful. In fact, we have a homecoming celebration planned for all of you. A feast in my cousin's honor. That is tonight. But first, come into the castle. Rooms have been prepared for you."

"For me as well?" Briar came to a halt. "Did you know I was coming, then?"

She happened to catch sight of Wren's face. He had been walking a few steps in front of them but now turned sharply to look at Loghain. He seemed very interested in what his cousin's reply would be.

Loghain laughed lightly. "Well, I knew you were returning with my cousin, of course. Though I did not know he was bringing a bride!"

"Have ye been married long?" Esme asked, her voice low.

"No, not long at all," Briar confessed. "It was very... sudden."

"But that's the way of it, isn't it?" Briar jumped as Angus Macleod swept past her. He went up to Wren, a broad grin on his cheerful face and slapped him on the back briskly. "The heart wants what the heart wants. And there was no doubt the Renfrew wanted this little English lassie. No doubt at all."

He winked at Briar, who tried to smile back.

"I hope ye've a large suite of rooms prepared for the newlyweds," Angus said, still smiling as he looked at Loghain. Yet there was something hard and sharp behind the smile. "If ye take my meaning. They need their space, ye see. Having been confined to a tent out of doors these past few days. No' that they were much troubled by it."

Angus burst into a hearty guffaw that left Briar blushing wildly and avoiding Esme's eyes.

"Ah, yes," Loghain said, pretending not to understand. He shot Briar a sympathetic look and, taking her arm again, resumed leading her up to the castle. "More than even the most spacious suite of rooms, I would venture to guess that you would appreciate a hot bath, Lady Briar?"

"Oh, yes, that would be heavenly," Briar breathed. She beamed at Loghain, who beamed back.

When she turned away, she caught Wren scowling at her.

"What?" she mouthed. "What is it?" But he simply shook his head.

She rolled her eyes and felt a pang of annoyance. She did not understand. If Wren had wanted her to act a certain way, behave a certain way, he could have done her the courtesy of explaining that beforehand. As it was, she felt very out of place, and Loghain was the only one who seemed to be trying to make everyone comfortable.

"You are Esme and my guests, and so you must not hesitate to ask for anything you require. Anything at all," Loghain was saying. "Renfrew Castle is your home now."

"Are we guests or is it our home?" Wren interjected, his voice gruff. "Ye canna have it both ways."

Loghain seemed taken aback. He thought for a moment, then smiled gently at Briar. "Well, I think that you can, Cousin. You are returning home. Therefore, we must treat you as honored guests. At least until you both settle in and get your bearings. Is that not right, Esme?" He looked to his wife who nodded silently. "Esme would be happy to show you around the castle and the grounds when you wish."

"That would be very nice," Briar said automatically. She glanced at Esme. She was not sure the other woman would be quite as enthusiastic, but she suddenly was determined to take up the offer, regardless. She would get to know Esme Grant and befriend her, whether she liked it or not.

"What's all this about..." Loghain began, then trailed off. For the first time, Briar noticed his smile slip into what looked suspiciously like a frown. Then the smile returned quickly. He glanced at Wren, then down at Briar. "The prodigal son must be welcomed by all it seems. Your husband is a popular man."

Briar looked ahead to the courtyard surrounding the keep, which she took as their destination. The courtyard must have been a vast space, but right now, it was difficult to tell its dimensions for it was nearly completely full of people. Most of them fierce-looking Highland men.

They were tall—giants compared to Percy—just as Wren and Angus were. Many were clad in the plaid of their clan, while others wore simple flax or linen shirts with trousers.

There were women and children, too, though not as many as the men.

Every last person in the crowd seemed to be staring at Wren, many with broad smiles on their faces. No, Briar took that back. Many were staring at her as well, ogling her openly and whispering.

She tried to smile as warmly as she could and lifted a hand to wave at some of the children.

"Well, look at this, would ye?" Angus hooted, elbowing Wren. "Looks as if everyone for miles turned up to welcome the laird home. Did ye arrange this Loghain? Verra sporting of ye."

"No, I..." Loghain began. He must have realized Angus was teasing him, for he glared just a moment, then turned back to Briar, a sweet smile returning to his handsome face. "Angus Macleod has always been a jester. I'm sure you've already learned that about him." He winked conspiratorially at her.

"Indeed, I have," Briar replied. It was easy to smile back at Wren's cousin. He had such a pleasant demeanor. She made sure to turn to smile at Esme, too. Or try to. The woman was staring off in the distance, ignoring her husband's chatter.

"Prodigal son, indeed," Angus was scoffing, evidently having overheard Loghain. "He's the returning lord. Their laird. Their leader. Nothing prodigal about a man who..." He was cut off abruptly.

Briar looked over to see Angus coughing and holding his stomach, while Wren glared at him.

"I wonder what that was about," Loghain murmured. He led her gracefully through the throng of people and up the stairs of the keep. "Well, here we are. Shall we step in?"

"Just a moment," Briar said. Wren had paused in the middle of the courtyard. He was looking about at the people who had gathered, meeting eyes with some of the men, nodding courteously at the women, smiling at the children.

She watched as he suddenly held his hands in the air above his head. It was a gesture of triumph, but she also saw his face contort with strong emotion. For a moment, his eyes shone so brightly she thought there might be tears.

"My clansmen," he bellowed, turning slowly in a circle. "It is good to see yer faces. And it is good to be home."

He lowered his arms as the people around burst into a roar of approval, then strode quickly toward the keep and, breaking between Loghain and Briar, took Briar's hand in his and swept her into the dark interior.

Briar was standing in one of the turrets, looking out of the narrow, arrow-slit window at the turbulent sea below. The wind had picked up, and the waves had turned rough and choppy. Even from way up here, on the third floor of the castle, high up the cliff, they could be heard crashing loudly onto the rocks below.

This would be a wonderful bedroom. The sound of the wind and the waves. Fresh sea air. Large and spacious, with a sitting room adjoining, and another room which could be used as a dressing room or even a small study. Not to mention it was private. There would be no loud snorts and chuckles or other unmentionable sounds from sleeping men in the night.

And yet Briar thought wistfully of the tent.

"I should have told ye about Esme and Loghain before we arrived," Wren said, rubbing a hand over his face.

He stole a glance at Briar. She did not look at him but kept her eyes on the water below.

"Yes, you should have," she replied.

She was not about to scream or shout, to play the jealous wife. That was not who she was.

Nevertheless, Wren's words had greatly unsettled her.

"So, you believe Loghain wishes you had not returned?" she asked slowly, scrunching up her nose and trying once more to understand. "That he may even wish you ill? Angus told you this?"

"Aye," Wren nodded, then shook his head. "Well, nay. Aye, Angus told me. But I still canna believe it." He scowled and muttered, almost to himself. "Loghain is family. I still canna see family doing such things."

"Doing what such things?" Briar demanded. "What aren't you telling me?"

Wren shook his head. "Ye dinna need to ken every bit of gossip or rumor. I've told ye the gist of it."

"And yet I feel you've left most of it out. Especially the most important parts," Briar muttered out the window.

So, Wren had once been betrothed to Esme. Before he went off to fight in France, they had been promised to one another. But when he returned, she had wed another, and he had chosen to remain in England with his half-siblings.

Loghain had botched a message from Wren's cousin, and so Wren had also believed that his family wished him to stay away when really they had not. He might have returned much sooner.

Of course, that would have meant she would likely never have met him. And certainly, they would not be married right now.

"You are truly all right with Esme and Loghain? You... forgive your cousin so easily?" she asked, turning to look at Wren closely.

Her husband's face was stony. "Aye. It was a long time ago. What does it matter now? He is kin. She is my kin, by marriage. They are husband and wife."

That wasn't quite what Briar had hoped he would say. Though she was not exactly sure what she wished he would have said instead.

Perhaps something more along the lines of, "What need have I to pine over the beautiful Esme, when I am married to the loveliest woman in the world, who I adore?"

Perhaps in less flowery language. But something along those lines would have been rather nice, Briar thought morosely.

"Besides, I'm a married mon now myself," Wren added stoutly. "I have my own woman."

Briar snorted. "Your own woman? I have a name, thank you very much."

She leaned her head against the cool stone wall and sighed.

"Aye, and I like it. Verra much. Lovely name and verra fitting, too, eh?" Wren was coming closer. He reached her and gingerly put a hand on her shoulder, then touched her cheek.

Briar blew out her lips. "They should have called you Thistle."

Wren laughed. "Scotch Thistle and a Scots Rose? Aye, that would do."

"I believe I will call you Thistle. In private at least," Briar said, tossing her head.

Wren leaned down and nibbled at her ear, then pressed his lips to her neck. She shivered. "Aye," he said. "That ye may. Ye may call me whatever ye like. Tonight."

He straightened up. "But first. The feast."

Chapter Fifteen

B riar was seated at the head table, right next to Loghain. Esme
had been placed between Wren and her husband. Briar could
see Wren did not like that she had been seated so far away
from him, but he said nothing, simply nodded to her as they took their
seats. A small gesture of solidarity. They were the laird and lady now,
even if Loghain had not formally recognized them as such.

In fact, Loghain and Esme seemed very much the laird and lady of
Renfrew Castle that night. Briar felt uncomfortable, a guest and not
quite a guest, uncertain of her role.

But soon dinner began to be served, and she forced herself to stop
thinking about it. Of course, Esme and Loghain were settled into their
roles. They had had to take up these weighty responsibilities when
Wren's grandfather and cousin had died. They had no other choice
when they had been unable to reach Wren, finally resorting to
kidnapping.

Someday it would all be a funny story they told their children.
Wouldn't it?

A dizzying array of dishes were being served, and soon Briar's plate
was full. From French dishes which looked surprisingly authentic, as
good as one would find in London, to simpler traditional Scottish fare,

the sideboards were soon heaped, and servants were bringing more and more dishes to add. Fish, game, soups, meat, pickles, jellies, custards, cakes, and puddings. There was something for everyone, and soon the great hall was roaring with noise and the clanging of silverware and goblets.

Briar nibbled a bite of broiled cod, then took a sip of wine from her goblet. She cast a glance down the table.

Loghain had risen with an apology, having to see to some matter outside. He had been a gregarious and charming dinner companion thus far, devoting all his attention to Briar and none whatsoever to his wife.

While Esme was as quiet and serene as she had been outside earlier, Loghain seemed determined to play the part of a merry host. He also appeared intent on winning Briar over, even to the point of carrying on a completely one-sided but light flirtation.

He was careful; she would give him that. And so, she was striving to be polite to Wren's nearest kin. Warm but not too warm, cool but not too cool. Yet, she wondered if Wren had noticed his cousin's lingering touches upon her arm. His lips very close to her ear. Those enticing smiles just for her.

And then she wondered what the rest of the room must be thinking, for sitting up on the dais at the head table, they were all very much on display. Perhaps that was exactly how Loghain liked it.

"Did you miss me?" Loghain sank back into the tall wooden chair and shot Briar a playful smile. "I told you I would return as soon as I could. Were you bereft?"

"Very." Briar spoke her line obediently and gave a smile in return. A very small one for she was becoming tired. Tired of the feast, tired of flirting even politely with a man who was not her husband. She wanted nothing better than to go back up to that turret room and lie down on the bed with Wren.

Perhaps tonight they would even do nothing more than sleep. Perhaps. Though she doubted it.

She smiled a genuine smile at that thought, and Loghain immediately caught it.

"What a lovely smile you have, my lady. I can see why my cousin sought your hand. He is a lucky man indeed to have won it."

"Well, he did not really need to seek it," Briar said, without thinking. "It was either him or Percy, you see."

Loghain raised his meticulously shaped eyebrows. "Percy?"

"Oh yes, Percy. He helped you kidnap us." Briar put a hand to her mouth to cover the impulse to snicker. "I'm sorry, there is no good way to put that, is there? I understand why you needed to have Wren abducted, but then Percy and I were rather caught up in it all. In my case, quite by accident."

"Yes, Angus rather muddled his instructions," Loghain said, and this time his smile slipped off completely, and he glanced out into the crowd of tables as if looking for Angus Macleod.

"You don't sound Scottish," Briar noted curiously.

Loghain looked put off. "I was educated at Cambridge. I made it a point to dispel my Scottish dialect. The language of peasants, as I saw it. Of course, I have mellowed in that view. Somewhat." He smiled pleasantly, but now it was Briar's turn to be put off.

"I love Wren's way of speaking," she said slowly. "It is so unique and... well, beautiful."

Loghain smiled winningly. "Would you think that if you could hardly understand what he said, and if he had the face of... oh, say, of Macleod over there?" He gestured to where Angus sat, talking boisterously with a table crowded with men and women and taking large swallows from a tankard.

Briar giggled. "I can understand him perfectly. And Angus is a nice-looking man. There is nothing wrong with him."

"That's very generous of you," Loghain said seriously. He winked. "But now back to what you were saying. Who is this Percy?"

"Percy Quintrell," Briar explained. "An English gentleman and my neighbor." She decided to phrase things tactfully. "He helped Angus to find Wren. And then Angus took Percy along with us."

"He was not supposed to take you at all," Loghain said, wagging a finger, teasingly. But his face was interested. "I had no idea my cousin was married. Nor to such a stunning lady."

"Well, he wasn't. Not before Angus snatched us," Briar acknowledged. "Angus thought that I was Wren's wife and so he took us both, you see. But we weren't married. Not then."

Loghain's eyebrows went up. "I see. And so you, a young English lady of good birth, were abducted by my fool of a servant."

Briar was not sure what Angus would say to being called Loghain's servant but decided not to broach it.

"And wound up married to a laird." Loghain clapped his hands gleefully. "And Percy was your other choice? You had no desire to marry an Englishman, I see? The Scot won your heart?"

"Well, no," Briar said, deciding not to explain all her reasons for not wishing to select Percy as her husband at the time. Nor to explain how Percy had since improved. Best not to muddle things. "Wren seemed the best choice. And yes, he did win my heart," she added firmly. "Very much so."

"What a lucky, lucky fellow to have done so," Loghain murmured, a gleam in his eye. He leaned in closer, as if about to whisper in her ear, but just then a hand clapped down on his shoulder.

"And ye're a lucky one, too, are ye no', Loghain?" Wren's booming voice startled Briar. She looked up at her husband, wondering if he had heard her last words or just Loghain's. "After all, Esme is sitting right here beside ye, is she no'? Though sadly neglected."

"Well, I was paying all my attention to our lady guest," Loghain said, smiling and showing beautiful white teeth.

"How long is it now since ye were married?" Wren pressed. He was looking at Esme, Briar noticed. And Esme was looking down at her plate, eating small steady bites.

The flaxen-haired woman finally looked up at the question. "Two years," she replied quietly.

"And are there bairns about, somewhere in this castle? Running amuck?" Wren asked.

"We have not yet been blessed," Loghain replied. "But soon, we hope. Any day now."

"Yes," Esme murmured.

Briar was ready to go. She wondered if Wren was. She stood up from her chair. "What a wonderful meal."

"And now for the dancing and drinking part of the evening,"

Loghain said, smiling dazzlingly at them both. "My cousin must surely remember that part. Our feasts go well into the next morning. Why, I remember you and Esme dancing one night..." He trailed off, as if he had mentioned the memory quite by accident, but Briar got the distinct impression the reference had been quite deliberate.

Esme was looking at Wren now, her placid expression temporarily vanished. In its place was stark longing. When she turned her wide beautiful blue eyes upon Briar, the longing disappeared and was instantly replaced with something very different.

Not the hate that Briar expected to see, but despair.

Then Esme's face cleared. She looked back at her plate, her face serene once more.

"Aye, we had many nights of revelry. With Alec, too. Many good nights," Wren said quietly.

"Ah, yes. Alec." Loghain sighed.

"We will bid ye both good evening now. My wife is tired. We will retire to our room," Wren announced. Briar nodded gratefully and caught his hand in hers, squeezing it tightly.

Loghain began to protest, but Wren would not let him speak. "It was a good feast," he continued stiffly. "I appreciate the welcome, Cousin. But tomorrow, we will speak of other matters. Alone. Of our lands and of the people, aye? I wish to be caught up. On everything." His tone was serious.

There was nothing for Loghain to do but nod his compliance.

Wren had been very gracious in his use of "our" Briar thought to herself.

And then her husband was clasping his hand over hers, helping her down from the dais, and leading her out of the great hall and into the corridor and back to the steps that would take them to their turret room.

Chapter Sixteen

Briar was up and out of the castle early the next morning by Blakeley standards. She had bathed, dressed, and snatched a still-warm biscuit from the great hall all by the time the bells of the little stone kirk in the outer bailey were chiming nine o'clock.

But she was late compared to her husband. Wren was already gone when she awoke.

They had made love upon returning to their room after the feast, and then Briar had sat down at the little desk overlooking the sea. She wrote to Dare while Wren lay in the bed, watching her scribble until his eyes had drooped and grown heavy, and he had finally fallen asleep.

"Dear Brother," she had begun the letter, then had paused just as quickly. She had been about to write *I am a married woman. Can you believe it?* But something stopped her. While she longed to pour out the happiness of her heart, to do so would be to disregard the pain her family had likely been left in, not knowing her fate this last month.

Dear Brother,

I can only imagine the pain you have been in, not knowing what had become of me these past weeks. How I have longed each day to write to you since then and put your mind at ease. But circumstances did not permit the sending of a letter until now. Today I arrived in Scotland, Dare. I am well and happy. Much happier than I deserve to be after what you have been through in my absence! What is the reason for my happiness, you will wonder? Was I not plucked from the road and taken away from my home and my family? Should I not have been terrified and miserable and longing only to return to you and Blakeley Manor?

All reasonable questions. And surely that would have been the case, were I not swept away on an adventure with a man such as my husband. Yes, your eyes have not deceived you. My husband. I am married, Dare, and happier than you can imagine. Let me start at the beginning and tell you everything...

It was more than an hour before she finally lay down beside Wren and fell into a heavy sleep. She had a vague memory of him kissing her goodbye that morning as she snuggled farther under the blankets a few hours earlier. Presumably, he had gone to do what he had said he would do the day before and was meeting with Loghain and getting an account of the Renfrew estate.

She meandered down the stone stairs of the keep and through the courtyard, then out into the great bailey where the kirk and various buildings lay, including some small crofter cottages. She was walking with no real purpose, having a vague idea of wanting to get closer to the sea but not entirely sure how to navigate the steep cliffs surrounding the castle. She supposed she could walk back across the headland, then find an easier path down to a beach, but it might take some doing.

She had just passed the little stone kirk, which looked quaint and medieval, when she heard the sharp cries of a woman in distress. A woman in pain might be more accurate, she decided, as she quickly honed in on the source of the cries. A small cottage, with the typical thatched roof and single-story stone walls. The door of the cottage was partially open.

Stepping quickly, Briar went across and over to the door.

Another sharp cry, then a much longer one. The sound of a woman coming close to the end of her endurance.

Was the poor woman being murdered?

"The pain is bad, aye, but ye must push now for me," a voice murmured.

Briar could not resist. She peeked in through the open door.

The single room of the cottage was at first too dark to see into.

Then Briar's eyes became accustomed to the dim, and she began to make out the shapes within.

A woman lay panting like a wild creature in a rickety wooden bed, her nightdress pulled up to her knees. Her face was sweat-soaked, and she was shaking her head tiredly.

Below her, kneeling at her feet on the flagstone floor was Esme Grant.

"I canna, I canna," the woman in the bed cried. "I canna do it." She put a hand to her face, covering her mouth and closed her eyes. "Oh, Dougal, Dougal, help me." The cries she was making were so pitiful that Briar felt her own heart wrench.

"Dougal is gone, Maisie," she heard Esme say softly to the woman. "He is dead and gone, but ye are here. Ye must push when I tell ye. Soon ye will have a bonny bairn in yer arms to comfort ye."

"I canna do it without Dougal," the woman cried, and Briar could see Esme's face becoming impatient.

"Ye must, Maisie. Ye have no choice. Ye canna stop a bairn from being born, but if ye hinder it, ye both may die. Now are ye ready to listen? Are ye?" Esme's voice was impassioned, and Briar saw Maisie's face tremble as she took in the seriousness of her situation.

So fascinated by the situation unfolding, when Esme's head suddenly snapped around, Briar did not even think to step back from the door frame.

"Are ye going to watch from the doorway, milady, or do ye have plans to help us?" Esme demanded, her eyes finding Briar's like a hawk's. She wiped a hand over her brow. Evidently Esme had been at this for quite some time, perhaps many hours.

"Tell me what to do and I will do it," Briar said quickly, pushing the door open and stepping into the little house. There was no point in denying she had been watching. "Though I must tell you, I have never seen a birth before." She licked her lips and tried to smile reassuringly at the bed. "I am sure you are doing very well though, Maisie."

"A fine young lady like yerself has never seen a woman brought to bed before. Aye, it is surprising," Esme muttered. "Well, ye can at least hold her hand and help me that way." She shook her head as she looked Briar up and down. "At least ye have no fine clothes to muss up. Childbirth is a messy business. There will be blood." She seemed to take great delight in stressing this last part.

"I don't mind," Briar said firmly. "And no, I have no fine clothes to ruin, but even if I did, I should like to help."

The dress she wore had been provided to her the afternoon before when the castle housekeeper took in her worn traveling dress. She had been instructed to remove it at once, which she did only too happily. Presumably, it had been taken away for cleaning. Briar did not care if she ever saw it again. Now, she was dressed plainly in a simple, red homespun gown with a leather-braided sash. It was nothing fashionable. Indeed, she would probably be laughed off the streets of London if she wore it there. But she was not in London, thank goodness. She was in Scotland, and here at Renfrew Castle, she rather liked the dark red simple gown.

"*Mmph*," was all Esme said. She had opened her mouth, perhaps to say something else, when they were both startled by Maisie's cry of pain.

"It's starting again. She's close now," Esme muttered, peering between the other woman's legs. To Maisie, she added more loudly, "Come now, Maisie. The bairn is close, ye hear? Push now!"

She glanced at Briar, who was still standing nervously at the door. "Take her hands, let her squeeze them."

Maisie was a very hard squeezer. She had an impressive grip for a woman, perhaps intensified by the pain she was in, and soon Briar was gritting her teeth and clenching her jaw.

But she would not let Esme see her discomfort. She squeezed Maisie's hands back as best she could and murmured every comforting thing she could think of to say.

Time passed and wave after wave of painful cries came, closer and closer together, more intense each time, until finally, the small cries of a newborn joined the mother's. Briar watched Esme's face transform as she caught the baby in a clean white cloth and gently patted it clean.

Esme's arms were streaked with blood, and there was a dab of it on her nose, but for the first time since Briar had met the woman, she could see something like happiness on her face.

"Ye have a beautiful daughter, Maisie," Esme crowed, carefully passing the small bundle to the poor exhausted Maisie. Briar was relieved when Maisie finally released her hands and took her baby in her arms. The woman's eyes were wide.

"A baby. And no' a boy," Maisie murmured. "I had thought to name it Dougal."

Esme glanced at Briar. "Dougal Mackay was her husband," she explained in a low voice. "He died. Fighting the men who came to pull down their house."

"Pull down their house," Briar exclaimed. "What do you mean? On Renfrew land?"

Esme shook her head, a scowl darkening her face. "Nay, no' Renfrew. Maisie is a Ross, like me before my marriage. They lived on Ross lands. Their laird is clearing many of his crofters, making them move from their ancient lands to near the sea."

"Dougal had nay wish to live near the sea," Maisie said mournfully. "He wouldna go."

"Aye, stubborn lout, for ye wound up by the sea nonetheless," Esme muttered. She shook her head. "Maisie came here, seeking shelter. She has been here ever since."

"How good of you to take her in," Briar murmured, her eyes wide.

"Aye, well, Loghain doesna want to, but I say we must." Esme looked down at the flagstone floor almost bashfully. "The Renfrew will decide, now that he is here."

"There are no girl names for Dougal," Maisie lamented, looking down at her tiny daughter.

"Did Dougal have any other names?" Briar inquired tentatively. "A middle name, perhaps?"

"His middle name was Lorne," Maisie said, sniffling. "Dougal Lorne Mackay."

"What a fine name," Briar said, smiling. She came over to the bed and looked down at the baby. Little Baby Mackay was already suckling on her mother's breast. "What about Lorna, then?"

"Lorna Mackay," Maisie said, turning the name over in her mouth.

"Aye, Lorna is a pretty name for a bairn," Esme agreed. She was puttering about at a table across the room, which Briar now noticed held a large wicker basket. Beside the basket were bottles of what looked like various herbs.

Esme noticed Briar's gaze. "Tinctures and salves and so on."

"Esme is a fine healer," Maisie said proudly, finally raising her head from her baby. "A white witch."

"Bah," Esme wrinkled her nose, holding a bottle aloft to read the label, then peered inside sniffing. "Such stupidity. I ken the wild things, that's all. Anyone who cared to, could learn." Briar watched as she began to shake out some of the leaves from the bottle into a teapot. She added leaves from a second small jar, then a third, and filled the pot with boiling water from the cauldron over the hearth. The scent of herbal tea filled the cottage, but it was a mild, pleasant aroma.

Briar sniffed appreciatively. "What is it?"

"Lady's mantle. Nettle. White oak bark. And raspberry leaves," Esme said, coming over with a cup of the steaming tea in her hand. She put it down on a little table next to the bed. "Drink this, Maisie. I'll leave a mixture for ye, so ye can make more. Drink plenty, for it will help ye heal."

Maisie looked up at her, an impish look on her tired face. "I hear the leaves of the lady's mantle can be put over a woman's breasts to restore their youth."

Briar giggled.

Esme scoffed. "Such nonsense. Ye've youth enough. Besides, I thought ye didna care about such things now."

Maisie looked chagrined. "I dinna, but perhaps someday..." She trailed off, looked down at her sucking babe.

"Yer breasts are fine," Esme said authoritatively and with absolutely no embarrassment. A clear sign of a woman who was familiar with natural life events, Briar thought. "Ye're more likely to get a rash than restore yer bosoms. Keep the lady's mantle for the tea."

"Aye, Esme," Maisie said meekly.

"Lady's mantle is such a lovely name," Briar said quickly, trying to change the subject and hiding a smile.

"Aye, for the Virgin," Esme said, her voice still authoritative. "The leaves resemble her cloak, tis said." She shot Briar a quick glance. "Perhaps I'll show ye where they grow, sometime. The tea is verra whole-some for new mothers. It helps to stop the bleeding, ye see."

"How fascinating and how useful," Briar said with genuine apprecia-tion. "Have you helped many women brought to bed, Esme?"

Esme looked considering. "Aye, mayhap fifty or more."

"Fifty!" Briar's eyes widened.

"And yet she has no bairns of her own," Maisie said sadly. "At least, no' yet."

Esme shrugged. She did not look concerned, but she did seem uncomfortable. "I've never wanted them. But Loghain's heart is set on many sons."

"He must be hoping every day for a child then," Maisie said cheerily.

"Well, I'm sure they'll come with time," Briar said, trying to be more tactful. "I know it took my parents years to have me, their fourth child."

Esme simply shrugged. She was rinsing her hands from a basin she had filled.

Briar wandered over to where the wicker basket lay on the table and peered in. "You have so many things in here. A veritable treasure trove of remedies!"

She picked up one bottle and squinted. "Pudding grass. Like pudding stone!"

"Except pudding stone wouldna kill ye. Put it down," Esme commanded sharply, looking up from the basin.

"Kill me?" Briar carefully set down the little bottle.

Esme stepped over, drying her hands on a clean apron she had just tied on. "Aye. Pudding grass. Pennyroyal."

"It's a poison, then?" Briar asked with interest.

Esme cleared her throat awkwardly. "Aye. A helpful one."

When Briar's eyebrows went up, she continued, "Taken sparingly, pennyroyal may be useful. When a maid doesna wish to have a child, say."

"Oh!" Briar understood. "Yes, I see."

"Now, aconite," Esme said, picking up an even smaller bottle filled halfway with a crushed powdery substance, "was what Medea used to kill Theseus. Also kent as wolfsbane. Verra, verra deadly."

"Why would you keep such a thing?" Briar asked, peering at the powder.

Esme shrugged. "To get rid of varmint and small pests." She tucked the little bottle back in her basket. "Athena used aconite to transform Arachne into a spider. Didna like the girl much. I admit, I've no' tried it for that yet."

She looked up down at Briar and winked.

"I should hope not," Briar said with false seriousness and then smiled at the pretty woman. "Thank you for letting me help you this morning, Esme. I wanted to speak with you more last night but..." She did not know how to politely say that Esme's husband had completely monopolized her. "But I did not find an opportunity. I wished to say that I hope we can be friends. I can already see you have much to teach me, not only about healing herbs but about the history of Renfrew Castle and..." She hesitated, but then decided to add it. "And about my husband. You share a long history, and I should love to know more of it."

She snuck a glance at Esme's face. It was impassive. "If it is not too painful, that is, of course."

Esme studied her in silence. "Well, ye did no' scream or faint with Maisie," she said eventually, nodding briskly. "That is a good sign."

"Esme!"

A man's voice was calling loudly from outside in the bailey.

"Esme! Goddamnit, Esme, where are you?"

The door of the small cottage burst open, and Loghain stood there. His face was transformed into an ugly, angry thing as he glared at his wife. "Where were you? I have been looking for you."

Then he noticed Briar. Immediately, his face cleared. He smiled and suddenly was radiant once more.

He ran a hand over his golden hair, smoothing back the curls. "Lady Renfrew," he said with a small bow. "Good day to you. I did not expect to see you here."

"I have just been helping your wife," Briar explained. She frowned, put off by the way he had spoken to Esme. "She was kind enough to allow me to help her with the birth of Maisie's daughter. Your wife is quite the wise woman."

Loghain smiled more broadly. "Indeed, she is that. Such a blessing to women in need." He looked past Briar at Esme. "If only she could use such skills to help herself when it came to bearing me a child."

Briar did not know what to say or where to look. Loghain was still smiling, but what he had said was so awkward. He made Esme sound like livestock and not a wife with tender feelings of her own.

"Come and look at baby Lorna, Laird," Maisie called from the bed. "Isn't she a wee beauty of a thing?"

"She's a braw lassie," Loghain said heartily, doing as she requested and going over to the bed. "But you must not call me 'laird' now, Maisie. Not when the true laird has finally seen fit to return to us all. He is the Renfrew now."

"Aye, Loghain," Maisie said obediently. "Aye, of course."

Briar's hackles had been raised instantly. Finally seen fit to return? That was not at all how she would have put it. Was that truly how Loghain saw things? Was that how the people viewed it?

Then she thought of the courtyard full of men and women yesterday, all there to welcome Wren home. Loghain had not seemed to anticipate the crowd, nor had he seemed pleased by it.

The man was simply used to leading, and giving up the position he had evidently expected would be his indefinitely might be hard for a while. But Wren was his kin, his laird. He would do his duty, of course.

Nevertheless, she could not deny there was something about Loghain she did not like. An insincerity beneath the gilding. All the golden honey he poured from his lips would not dissuade her of that.

"If you are back, then my husband must have returned as well. I believe I shall go and find him," Briar said lightly. "Good day to you all. Congratulations again, Maisie. I will come and visit you and little Lorna soon if that is all right. And if there is anything you need, please let Wren—I mean the Renfrew—or I know."

She slipped out of the cottage with a little nod of farewell to Esme.

As soon as she took a few steps away from the house, she heard Loghain's voice raise again. Was he simply excited? Or shouting at Esme? And if so, why?

Loghain and Esme's marriage did not seem particularly happy thus far, Briar thought. Esme might have married Wren instead, and yet she had given him up—thrown him over would be more accurate—for Loghain. Was it because she had been seduced by Loghain's appearance? He was very attractive for a man. His fair features were certainly unusual.

But he also seemed hollow, as if he were entirely used to charming his way through any situation. What was beneath the handsome veneer? A man worth knowing? A kinsman worth having? For Wren's sake, Briar certainly hoped so.

Chapter Seventeen

Wren had felt as if ants were crawling all over his skin as he watched Loghain try to butter up his wife at the feast the night before.

Then he'd had to spend all morning with the man. With his cousin, his kin, he corrected himself. And while he had hoped they might be able to move past Loghain's betrayal and start anew, the morning had shown him that this was not to be.

For one, Loghain seemed to have absolutely no intention of apologizing or even acknowledging his past deceit.

And then there was the matter of the way he had sent Angus to abduct Wren in the first place. Or to kill him, if Wren accepted that as the truth.

Then there was the bandit attack. Except there was no way Wren would ever accept that bandits had been what they were. Someone had sent those men. Loghain was the obvious answer as to who.

Unless there was some other kinsman lying in wait to have Wren murdered and steal the lairdship.

Wren rubbed his forehead tiredly. Why anyone would want the Renfrew lands was the question. The accounts were a muddle, but it was clear that more money was going out than was coming in. Even a quick glance had already given Wren many ideas for things which could be changed and improved to stop the flow of debts.

They would not be solving things Loghain's way, however, and that was final. There would be no clearances. No moving of clansmen by gentle request, force, or otherwise. Loghain had heralded the clearances as a solution to all their problems and a way to get rich quickly besides. He had been furious when Wren had put a damper on his plan and laid down the law.

Esme had the right idea. Loghain had complained about his wife's tender heart and the way she had encouraged him to take in refugees from other Highland clans. People who had lost their homes and saw no way to make a living on the new crofts that they had been directed to. Some too old to even try. Others, widows with children.

Loghain had not allowed any of them to stay out of the goodness of his heart, that much was clear to Wren. His cousin evidently had some plan in mind for putting them to work and making a profit. Loghain had mentioned the possibility of a coal mine on nearby land, which he'd had surveyed. Was that the end goal? Would he have had refugees working in the new mine? Women and children and the elderly, too?

Wren shook his head in disgust and stepped into the stables. He had no horse of his own yet to ride, but just being in the place brought a feeling of calm. It was the next best thing to being alone in a greenhouse, he thought wryly, suddenly missing the peace and tranquility of the gardens and greenhouses at Blakeley Manor for the first time.

Well, the refugee crofter families would stay, and that was that. Dwellings would be found. Money would be found. The Renfrews would make do and care for the people who had put their trust in them. As they always had.

"Enjoy yer morning with yer cousin, did ye?" Angus Macleod stepped out of the shadows, a bridle in hand. "Make some happy family memories?"

Wren cocked his head. "Were ye waiting for me, Angus? Ye shouldna have. They'll say we're sweethearts."

Angus gave a great belly laugh. "I've been waiting for ye to return, aye, so I might show ye something. Alec's stallion." He nodded toward a stall behind him, and Wren stepped forward with interest.

A great big beauty of a horse stood in the stall, pawing gently. A rich black velvet stallion, at least seventeen hands high.

"My God, he's a beast," Wren said in awe. "Pure black?"

"Och, there's a spot of white on his back left fetlock," Angus said. "But he's a braw creature, nonetheless."

"He was Alec's?" Wren asked, stepping around the horse to look at him carefully. Yes, there was a small white star on one of the stallion's rear fetlocks.

"Aye, Alec loved to ride him. But when he passed, Loghain didna want him. Afraid of him more like is what I always thought." Angus snorted, then looked at Wren. "I've been riding him, tending to him. Waiting for ye to take him off my hands. He's been well cared for. Take him out for a run now, if ye like."

"Very tempting," Wren admitted, grinning.

"Did Loghain win ye over? Or do ye believe me fully now?" Angus asked, looking at Wren closely. "He's a bastard. Dinna ye turn yer back on him, Renfrew."

Wren met his friend's eyes and nodded slowly. "There's something amiss. I could never trust him, that's the truth. He'll never acknowledge the wrong he did. The lies he told. I tried this morning. Spoke as gently to him as to a newborn colt. But it was no use. The mon thinks he's as pure as the driven snow, or that I'll believe he is." He shook his head and sighed with frustration. "He's kin, Angus."

Angus nodded his understanding. "He's kin, aye. Kin that would kill ye. Do ye understand that? I dinna want to lose another." He stared into Wren's eyes intently.

"What do ye mean?" Wren frowned. "Another? Another what? Another Renfrew ye mean?"

Angus said nothing, simply looked.

"My grandfather died from natural causes," Wren said slowly. "A fever, ye said. And Alec, too..."

"Aye, Alec died from a fever, that is true. Yer grandfather..." Angus scratched his head. "He had been poorly, that is also true. But then his decline... it was so rapid. Loghain wouldna let anyone in to see him. Only he and Esme could tend him. She is a healer, ye see."

"So, what are ye saying?" Wren asked harshly. "Ye suspect they killed Alec? My grandfather? Both?"

"Nay, no' both," Angus said, his voice calm. "But yer grandda, mayhap. Aye, mayhap. Esme is a fine healer. She also kens her way around the poisons, ye see."

"Esme Grant may be many things. But she is no murderess," Wren said hotly, before wondering how he could defend the woman. Seeing her had been a great surprise to him. He had taken note of her beauty; she was mostly unchanged. But she had no effect on him now. None whatsoever. He had feared he would feel... something. When he had not, it had been a great relief.

The only woman on his mind was his wife. She tormented his mind, his body, plagued his thoughts, his imagination. And it was a welcome torment, one he relished.

He shook his head and tried to focus.

"She's changed," Angus was saying. "Loghain has changed her. Well, ye will see. That's all I'll say about the matter. But yer meeting with Loghain today. It went well?"

"Loghain wasna happy about anything we discussed by the end, no, if that is what ye mean. State yer point, mon," Wren said grumpily. "He is being supplanted and doesna much like it. Who would?"

"Aye, who would? Well, I wouldna much like it, but I tell ye what, I would no' kill ye over it," Angus said cheerfully. "Nor send men to do it for me. Twice."

"All right, all right," Wren complained. "Point taken. I shall watch myself."

"Watch yer wife, and ye'll do better," Angus advised. He pointed down the row of stalls. "And here she is. Take this black beauty out. His name is Cerberus, by and by. Take Cerberus out. Give yer wife a peek at her new home. Take her for a ride."

"Aye, a ride," Wren repeated, watching Briar walk down the row toward him.

She looked tired already for so early in the day, but happy. Her bright hair was braided and hung over her shoulder. She wore a simple dress of dark red that should have clashed with her copper hair, but instead simply brought out the rich rosiness of her lips and cheeks.

"She glows like a rose. Her namesake," Angus said admiringly, and Wren elbowed him sharply. "Take her out, mon. Show yer bride the moors." Angus elbowed him back in the chest, hard, then walked off laughing.

"Where is Angus going? What is he laughing about?" Briar asked curiously, smiling up at Wren as she reached him. She reached out a small hand and touched his arm, and he felt a warm current flow through him. He had been so wrapped up in the doings at Renfrew Castle and concerns over Loghain that he had almost forgotten the pleasure of simply being in his wife's company.

"He wants me to take ye out riding," Wren said a little stupidly. "Would ye like that?"

"Oh, yes," Briar said happily. She looked into the stall. "On this fellow? He is rather large."

"They tell me he is my horse," Wren said. "We'll have to find ye one of yer own. A mare, perhaps. One ye like, of course. But for now, would ye like to ride Cerberus with me?"

"And get away from the castle? Ride out? Oh yes, please." Briar nodded her head vigorously.

"Already tired of Renfrew Castle, are ye?" Wren asked, amused.

"I miss traveling with you, though it is strange to say," Briar admitted. "I don't miss the crowd of men. But I miss our tent. I miss the peace, the sense of adventure."

"Aye, bandit attacks at night are quite the adventure," Wren remarked, quirking his lips. "Well, come then. Let us see what we shall see."

Briar had told him all about her morning adventures. Watching Maisie be brought to bed and the arrival of the little bairn. She had hastened over Loghain's arrival. He could tell she was put off by the man, too, though she was too polite to say anything disparaging about his kin. She was a loyal woman, and Loghain was part of her new family as far as she was concerned, he realized sadly.

But Loghain could not stay at Renfrew Castle. Angus had made that clear without putting it into so many words.

Even though they had not a shred of proof to accuse Loghain of the attack on the caravan. There was Angus's own word, which Wren knew he would swear to, that Loghain had sent him on a secret mission to kill Wren in England. There was always that.

Wren had dismissed it long enough. He must face it and decide what to do with it. Before someone else got hurt.

Loghain would not be happy at Renfrew Castle in any case. He was not the sort of man happy to be in second place.

"Stop thinking and look at me," Briar instructed, gently putting her fingers under his chin and turning it. "Look at all this." She stretched out an arm and gestured to the wide-open green moors and the sea in the distance. "I never knew until now how much I wanted to live by the sea. Now you could not drag me away from it."

"I'm verra happy to hear that," Wren murmured, leaning down to kiss her lips. "So, it's the sea ye would miss if yer brother came to take ye away, and no' me?"

"I would miss you both," Briar said playfully. "But the sea, especially."

She wriggled away from him and stood up. "And after all, we are all alone out here, are we not? There is no one for miles and miles?"

Wren nodded with amusement. "There are crofter cottages a few miles to the west, but this is grazing land. I doubt there is anyone within shouting distance."

"Or looking distance?" she asked innocently.

He had just opened his mouth to ask what she meant, when she began to shuck off her dress, unfastening the side ties and shrugging it from her shoulders until the tops of her breasts were exposed.

"What are ye doing?" he asked hoarsely, already wetting his lips and imagining taking the small buds of her nipples in his mouth.

"I am undressing," she said primly. "Do you wish me to stop or to go on?"

"Go on, go on," he urged, swallowing hard. "Dinna stop."

"Very well," she said smoothly, pulling her dress down to her waist and eliciting a tormented groan from him. "After all, we are man and wife. It is not as if a wife may not undress for her husband. And in such a private place."

"Absolutely. Ye'll hear no argument from me," he said encouragingly, drinking in the sight of the high firm white breasts, the little pink tips. "God, ye have such beautiful nipples. Like little rosebuds. Perfectly formed."

"Do I?" Briar looked down at herself curiously.

"Aye," Wren said, deciding this tantalizing spectacle had gone on uninterrupted long enough, rising to his feet, and coming to her in two long strides. "Ye do."

He pulled her flush against him, rejoicing in the feel of her soft body alongside his, and in the knowledge she was naked from the waist up. He took her mouth in a sweet, fervent kiss, then moved his lips down to her neck, murmuring her name, down her fine white chest, over the tops of her breasts, and then cupped her breasts in his hands possessively and lifted one pert nipple to his mouth to suck.

Only when it was flushed and red, and Briar was panting and tugging at his hair, did he release it and move to the other, giving each one its due.

"Too slow," Briar moaned. "Too slow. Take this off me. I can hardly breathe."

He released the nipple and looked up, grinning. "I dinna want ye breathing. Much. Just panting."

His cock was already stiff and hard under his kilt. Now he quickly stripped it off, unknotting and untying, then throwing the plaid down on the ground behind him as a makeshift bed.

"Oh, you're more than ready for me, too, I see," Briar murmured playfully.

He turned back to her, unashamed of his nakedness. Men were nude around one another all the time, especially in army life. It was having a woman see him that was the new and strange thing.

"Aye, I want ye," he said directly. He tugged at her dress, not wishing to rip the new gown but impatient, sliding it down her smooth soft hips.

She stepped out onto the grass, her slippers already long discarded, like a lovely creature out of a fairy tale.

"Will ye take me back to fairyland with ye, my lady?" he murmured, brushing his lips against her ear.

He slid his hands over her body, stroking and caressing, as his cock bobbed against her mound eagerly. He ran his fingers lightly over her breasts, brushing her nipples, plucking them gently like harp strings, teasing and squeezing until she moaned.

"Mo chridhe," he whispered reverently, looking down at her flushed face. "How are ye so lovely? And mine?"

He saw something flicker in her face. "Are you glad I'm yours, Wren?" she asked, almost hopefully. "You wouldn't trade me?"

He smiled. "Not for anything in the world. I love ye, ye silly lass. Ye ken that." The words had spilled out so easily. He had not even said them as anything romantic. Simply as a statement of fact. Surely, she already knew. Didn't she?

But she was looking up at him, eyes wide, lips half-parted. She had not known.

"I didna want to," he admitted. "I thought I could be a good husband to ye, without love." He kissed her cheek, as much to quiet the pounding of his heart as anything. Then her throat. His voice had dropped almost to a whisper. "But when that mon nearly hurt ye. When I could have lost ye. Just when I had found ye. Just when we were..." He wanted to say it properly but found he could not go on.

"When we were each other's?" she finished. "Yes." She stroked his cheek, the most tender touch. "I love you, too, Wren. So very much. I wasn't sure you... did." She looked down at the ground quickly. "And with Esme..."

"Esme?" He was amazed. He suddenly shook his head and laughed. Here they were standing naked out on the moors and speaking of Esme Grant. "I feel nothing for the woman. Nothing. She hurt me, aye. I thought I loved her once, aye. But now, with ye..." He shook his head. "I didna ken what love was, Briar. It is tender and sweet, never jealous, never cruel. It doesna betray. I would never betray ye. Never."

"Nor would I, Wren," Briar promised fervently. "I could never hurt you."

"I ken that," he said softly, taking her hand and pressing it to his lips. "I ken ye. I ken yer heart. Yer tender, kind heart. Brave and true. I never kent Esme's. Can ye understand that? We were children when we thought we were in love, when we promised ourselves. With ye, Briar, I am a mon."

Briar nodded shyly, then licked her lips. "I want..." She stopped, but he understood.

"Aye," he said, picking her up and lifting her off the ground easily, then gently placing her naked on his plaid. "We'll make love. Out under the sky. Out on the moor. With no one for miles. We need no one but ourselves."

She nodded, looking up at him, her eyes so full of love, so beautiful and starry that his heart clenched with something close to pain.

He parted her legs with one hand, easily separating the soft curls of her sex and slipping his fingers into her wetness as his mouth found hers again. She gasped against his lips as his hand spread her wide, and he drew one finger languidly across her bud.

***

And then he took his mouth away from hers, and for a moment, she was bereft.

Then his tongue slipped over her sex, tracing the folds, exploring every slick wet curve, and she was gasping, moaning, her body straining against him. He licked and stroked and traced his way across her most private place, and her body was aflame. She was making sounds she had never made before in her life. Moaning and twisting, pleading and begging. His tongue slipped inside her, thrusting like a pale imitation of his cock, and she moaned in frustration.

"Please, Wren, you're torturing me."

His head popped up. "Torture, is it?"

"Well, pleasant torture, but yes," she admitted hazily.

He grinned, then dropped his head back, his wicked mouth landing right on the place where she needed it most. She felt a shock of pleasure reach through her from head to toe, her legs turning to jellyfish and parting even farther, feeling brazen and wanton.

"Aye, open for me, mo chridhe," he was murmuring, and then she was coming, coming, and he was sliding up her body, his mouth removed, his flesh pressed against hers, and she was in heaven, the climax finishing just as he entered her. She cried out loudly, not bothering to silence herself as she would have in the tent or even the turret room. She cried out as he thrust inside of her, her husband's hardness stretching her muscles, opening her in exquisite pleasure. He began to thrust, pumping in a rhythmic steady motion, as his hands found her breasts and flicked her nipples, cupped the soft mounds, then lowered his mouth and tugged sweetly as he pushed inside her.

He was going frustratingly slow on purpose, she realized. Determined to satisfy her first. And it was working. The climax was rising once more. Soon she was trembling with the force of it working through her, her hips bucking against him as she cried out.

"You, too, Wren," she panted. "Please. Don't leave me alone in this."

And she saw him nod once, and then he thrust hard, plunging into her as if he could not stop if he wanted to, three times, four, five, followed by a shudder and a harsh guttural growl.

He fell atop her as she felt his release. A pleasure all in itself. One she would never have expected to find so satisfying—having his seed spill into her. Her arms went around him, and she held him tight, her head nestling in the crook of his neck just above his shoulder, and she looked up at the blue sky feeling immense peace.

He was part of her. She was part of him. This was as close to oneness as they could get, and it was enough.

Their connection was strong. She was reassured of that now. He loved her.

Together, they were unbreakable.

Chapter Eighteen

T he next day, Briar realized she had missed her monthly
courses.

While they had been traveling, she had registered that
she was a day or two late. Rather than being bothered, she rejoiced at
the time because having one's courses while traveling in a group of
men, without the adequate materials to deal with such things properly, would have been vastly inconvenient. Especially for a newlywed
bride.

Once they had arrived at the castle, she had spoken to the housekeeper, who had provided her with the necessities.

And then... they had not been required.

Today she woke with the realization that she was no longer simply
"late." Her courses had not come... and she was not sure they would.

Ever since she had reached womanhood, she had taken special note
of her courses. They were highly regular, which was almost a pity, for
like clockwork she could count on a painful megrim occurring a few
days before they arrived. That was the reason her mother had
suggested she keep track of them in the first place. There was a
soothing predictability, if not of a dismal sort, in knowing when the
next prolonged megrim would manifest. She knew some women were

prone to missing a month here and there. But not Briar. She never had, ever, to the best of her personal recollection.

Until now.

And of course, now was very different from before. Now missed courses did not mean the potential relief from a month of megrims but rather heralded something quite different.

A child.

Hers and Wren's.

Could it be? So soon?

She thought of who she might ask. If she were at Blakeley Manor, she would immediately write to her older sister, Katherine. Or better yet, pay her a visit.

But she was hundreds of miles away in a strange land where she knew no one, save her own husband.

And Percy. And Angus.

Hardly useful acquaintances in the circumstances.

Then she thought of the perfect person she might consult. A woman. A healer. Esme Grant.

But was Esme the sort of person she could trust to keep such matters quiet? She did not wish to worry Wren, not until she knew more.

She recalled what Esme had said about the pennyroyal. If Esme included such herbs in her supplies, then evidently she was experienced in using them to help women in need. Such women would obviously not wish for their circumstances to be known, and thus, Esme must be a trustworthy woman, the kind other women went to in times of distress, taking her into their confidence.

Well, Briar decided, she would do the same. Had she not said she wished for Esme and her to become better friends? Perhaps this would be the perfect way to develop that friendship.

After all, there was nothing like sharing secrets to test the mettle of a potential friend, was there?

Esme and Loghain resided in Renfrew Castle. They had the largest suite of rooms, as the housekeeper had not so subtly made sure to inform Briar.

Briar did not care. They could keep them as far as she was

concerned. Though she supposed Loghain would have to give them up, for the housekeeper had made it plain that only the Renfrew himself could retain the suite, which was, in her view, evidently as prestigious a residence as Buckingham Palace itself.

But when she checked with a passing servant in the great hall, Esme had been seen leaving the castle already that morning to visit one of the crofter cottages outside the castle. The servant was apologetic but could not tell her which family Esme had gone out to see.

No matter, Briar decided to take a walk through the castle grounds in the hope she would spy Esme upon her return and be able to speak with her in private then.

But of course, she had the bad luck to run into Percy along the way.

"Where are you off to so early in the morning?" he asked, jogging up alongside her as she crossed the courtyard, looking remarkably jovial.

"I might ask the same of you," Briar replied. "It is not even ten o'clock, and yet you have risen from your bed. I thought young gentlemen of ill-repute did not rise before noon."

"That was the old life," Percy said cheerfully. "I became used to early rising while we were... traveling."

Briar shot him a look. "You almost said 'kidnapped,' didn't you?"

"I did," he admitted. "But the word no longer seems apt. Truly, I am tempted to describe our experience as a 'rescue' instead."

Briar quirked her eyebrows. "Indeed. Have you written to Bessie?"

"I knew you would ask that," Percy said with a wry chuckle. "And so, of course, the answer is yes. I would not have dared to approach you otherwise."

Briar's eyebrows went higher. "Indeed! Very well done, Percy." She bit her lip. She had almost said, "I am proud of you."

Percy seemed to read her expression accurately. "Thank you," he said seriously. "I feel quite relieved, actually. Like a weight has been lifted."

Briar impulsively reached her hand out and touched his arm. "Because you are a good man at heart, I think, Percy," she said quietly. "Who wants to do the right thing. You knew, in your deepest heart, that it was not right to leave your child unprovided for." Nor Bessie unwed, she thought sadly. But she knew that would be going too far. Besides, with money coming in for the child, hopefully Bessie would be able to make a decent match with some other good man. Perhaps one more mature than Percy.

"I think I will visit the babe when I return," Percy said thoughtfully. "Though I am not sure when that will be. Your husband has offered me some training in estate management, and I must say, I am rather inclined to take it. God knows, my mother and steward would appreciate my returning, knowing more than when I left. I should rather enjoy impressing them."

Briar found herself happily surprised. She found she would not mind Percy staying at Renfrew Castle a little longer. How strange that things could change so rapidly. It would be nice to have someone from home about the place. Someone familiar.

"That's wonderful news, Percy," she said.

They entered the outer bailey, and she looked around, drinking in the atmosphere. The hustle and bustle of people going about their day in such a medieval place, surrounded by ancient stone walls that must have been besieged countless times. She never failed to feel appreciative of the remarkable place Wren had brought her to.

"In some ways, it feels as if we have stepped back in time, doesn't it?" Percy remarked, following her gaze. "The stone walls. The arrow slits. That medieval little kirk. One might easily imagine we could still be attacked by Viking invaders at any moment."

"Yes, I feel the same way. Precisely. And I quite enjoy the sensation," Briar said.

"Oh, I do as well," Percy agreed. "Not to mention, there is something refreshing about being in such a different place, where no one knows your childhood history or all your past mistakes." He gave her a significant look. "At least, not many people."

"I am not about to share what I know with anyone if that is your concern," Briar promised.

"As you have seen me at my absolute worst and most pathetic, thank you. I appreciate that," he said, grinning sheepishly.

"Oh, look," Briar cried suddenly. "There is Esme!"

Percy gave her a surprised look. "So it is. Esme Grant. Loghain's wife. She is not a particularly chatty lady, is she? At least, she has not seemed interested in speaking with me. Why? Were you looking for her?"

"Well, yes, I was hoping to ask her something. She is a healer, you know," Briar explained, searching for an appropriate excuse. "And my megrims..."

"Ah," Percy exclaimed, nodding. "Yes, of course. Perhaps she has a remedy you have not already tried. They seem like dreadful things. Well, go. I will not keep talking your ear off."

Briar smiled appreciatively and quickly stepped away, walking toward where Esme had just strolled through the portcullis. She was walking absently until Briar called out to her. Then she paused her walk, looking at Briar with an uncertain expression.

"I have been looking for you, Esme," Briar said, unable to hide her excitement entirely as she came up to the woman. "I was hoping to speak with you. In private if possible."

She took in Esme's tired expression, her listless demeanor.

"If you are not too tired, that is," she stuttered. "Are you quite all right?"

"Oh, aye," Esme said distractedly. She did not meet Briar's eyes. "Just weary is all." She resumed her walk, though more slowly, and Briar took up a place beside her.

"Is the family you went to visit this morning doing well?" she asked cautiously. "Were they very ill?"

"Oh, aye," Esme answered. "'Tis an elderly lady. Her son asked me to look in on her for she has been feeling poorly."

"And was there anything you were able to do?"

Esme shook her head. "No' for simple old age. I left her an infusion of lavender and poppy, for she has trouble sleeping. But I've no' cure for getting old. There isna one, so far as I ken." She gave a small wry smile, and Briar smiled back.

"Nay," Esme continued. "'Twas no' the visit which troubled me. I... had a disagreement with someone." She looked uncomfortable.

Briar was quiet a moment, then ventured to guess. "With Loghain?"

Esme hesitated, then nodded. "Aye. With my husband."

"I'm sorry to hear that," Briar said quietly.

"He isna an easy man to get along with," Esme said. "I try. But... we quarrel."

Briar found herself longing to ask a bevy of questions. *Why did you choose him over Wren then, Esme?* But she held her tongue.

"I'm sorry," she said again, trying to keep her tone mild. "That must be very frustrating."

"Aye," Esme agreed. "He demands I give him a child. But it isna so easy, now is it?" She sounded angry. "Men always seem to believe it is something we women can control. But there are two involved in the making of a child. He blames me. Says I am barren. And yet he hasna had any success producing one elsewhere, now has he?"

"Elsewhere?" Briar was shocked. "You mean he..."

Esme waved a hand dismissively. "Men will be men."

"Still, he is your husband. Do you not wish him to be faithful to you?"

Esme shot Briar a wry look. "If he is gone from my bed, I sleep much better." She shrugged and looked a little pensive. "The older I get, the less I find I care about such stupid matters."

"Such matters as love?" Briar's eyes widened. "But..."

Esme burst into laughter.

It was the first time Briar had heard her laugh. It transformed her face to a thing of beauty, and the peals were bell-like in their prettiness. She stared.

"I forgot," Esme choked out, trying to stop laughing, "who I am talking to."

"What do you mean?" Briar was confused.

"I mean," Esme wheezed. "Ye are clearly smitten with him. Are ye not?" She stopped laughing and looked at Briar with a sad smile.

"With Wren?" Briar blushed.

"Aye, ye are a new bride. And ye love yer husband." The sadness on Esme's face seemed to deepen. "Well, good for ye. At least ye picked a good one."

Esme resumed walking, and Briar fell in beside her. They walked silently for a few steps.

"I am smitten," Briar admitted. "And Wren is a good one. At least, I truly believe he is."

"Aye, he is." Esme sighed.

"Why did you..." Briar began. She stopped herself, just in time.

Esme glanced at her. She seemed to know what Briar had been about to ask. "Why did I throw him over for Loghain Grant?"

Briar nodded cautiously.

Esme shook her head. "There is always more to the story than gets told," she said in a low voice. "No matter what Angus Macleod may believe."

"Wren believed you had married his cousin Alec," Briar said, quietly. "That is what Loghain told him. Did you know that, Esme?"

Esme's head snapped up. "Alec?"

"Wren did not even know you had married Loghain..." Briar began. "Not until Angus told him."

Esme looked angry. "Loghain couldna even do him the decency of telling him the truth. Of course no'. The bastard." She bit her lip so hard that Briar could see the blood draining. Then abruptly, she changed the subject. "What was it ye wished to speak with me about?"

"Oh!" Briar wondered about the appropriateness of the question, after all Esme had just told her, but decided to press ahead. "You know a great deal about childbirth, do you not, Esme? I mean, it is obvious that you do..."

"Ye need something to get yerself with child? Is that it?" Esme asked impatiently. "Aye, I have things ye may try."

"No," Briar replied. "I mean, yes, that would be very helpful. And perhaps I shall need them. I certainly would not turn them down. But..."

"Ah!" Esme paused her step. "Ye think ye may be already?"

"Aye. I mean, yes. I mean..." Briar lowered her voice and looked around furtively. "I have missed my courses."

"Once? Or more than once?" Esme demanded.

"Oh, just the once. Wren and I... We were only married..."

"Aye, on the road. So, it has no' been long. Ye're certain?" Esme looked at her astutely.

Briar nodded.

"Aye, it may be then. I dinna say it will remain, however. It is still too early. But aye, it seems likely. I assume ye have been—" She made a gesture Briar had only ever seen used rudely, and she blushed harder. Esme looked amused. "Aye, ye likely are. But wait and see. Many women begin to bleed. They lose the child early on, ye see. If that happens," she cautioned, "do no' fret. It is natural. It happens to many. It doesna mean ye willna carry a child to completion."

"Very well, I will bear that in mind. Thank you, Esme," Briar said, her face still hot. She was suddenly desperate to be gone. "Please. Don't tell anyone yet. I haven't told Wren. And if I may lose this child, as you say, then perhaps I will wait. Until I am sure."

"Aye, that is a wise decision," Esme said nodding. "Many women regret telling their menfolk, only to have to disappoint them again. I willna say a word."

"Thank you," Briar said. She clasped Esme's hand in hers quickly. "Thank you, Esme. I had no one else I could ask…"

"Ye may come to me whenever ye like. All the women do."

That did not make Briar feel particularly special, but she tried to look grateful. "Thank you. I had best be going now."

She walked away quickly, thinking about what Esme had said. Not about losing the child. But rather about there being more to the story than anyone was ever told.

What was the full story of Esme and Loghain, she wondered? How had they come to be?

⁓

She had an opportunity to ask sooner than she expected.

The very next afternoon, the door to her sitting room was pushed open (no knock) and Loghain entered. Smiling, of course.

"Would you like to come and see a broch?" he asked with no formal greeting. He gestured to the window behind her. "It is a beautiful day."

"You call a stormy, overcast day 'beautiful'?" Briar asked doubtfully.

"I call it bracing," Loghain replied, grinning. "And your husband is out, isn't he?"

"He is," Briar replied cautiously. Wren had ridden out with Angus to visit some nearby villages. She did not expect him back until the next morning. "I suppose there is something thrilling about a nice, windy day."

"Exactly. The perfect day for exploration. Why not come along?" Loghain encouraged. "You'll be bored to tears if you stay here knitting all day. Or whatever it is women do."

"I was writing letters," Briar replied a little affronted, but Loghain had already strode to a window and was looking down at the sea. He did not seem to hear her. Nor did he seem prepared to take "no" for an answer. "Very well. Let me get a cloak." She put down the letter she had begun writing to Mrs. Quintrell. The story of Percy's incredible transformation from wastrel to bannock-baker, spoot-digger, and savior of Scots would have to wait, she supposed.

A few minutes later, they were walking out the portcullis gate and over the headland.

"What exactly is a broch, anyhow?" Briar asked.

Loghain hooted arrogantly. "You came even though you did not know?"

"Well, I assumed it had to be something interesting, or you would not want to show it to me," Briar said, smiling and trying not to take offense.

"A broch is a round, stone tower. Very old. This one is ancient. Built by the Picts," Loghain explained. "It's crumbling, of course. But still interesting."

"I see," Briar said. "And is it very far? We do not need horses?"

Loghain laughed again. "No, it is not a far walk." He gestured. "You cannot see it from the castle, but it is only over that hill. The hill is so high, it blocks your view, or you might have observed it from your tower room. Here, you should be able to catch a glimpse from atop this next cliff. Let me help you over this rough bit, my lady. We are not far now."

He took her hand firmly in his before she could politely decline.

"You must call me 'Briar'," she said a little awkwardly. She did not particularly wish to encourage Loghain to be more familiar and yet she did not wish for him to call her by a formal title. "After all, we are family now. And I call your wife 'Esme.' Though perhaps I should not have done so. Perhaps she does not appreciate such familiarity..."

Loghain smiled dismissively. "I'm sure she does not mind. She must be honored to be singled out by the new Lady Renfrew."

"Well, I am not sure about that," Briar said with surprise. "She is an exceptional woman in her own right. With her healing skills and..."

"Bah!" Loghain snorted in derision and waved a hand. "Healing skills. Yet she cannot bring her own child into the world. Not a single one. Yet others call on her for all sorts of help. It boggles the mind."

Briar said nothing. She was not about to join Loghain in his dismissal of his wife's worth. She thought of what Esme had said about Loghain enjoying the beds of other women and felt her stomach turn. She frowned and pulled her hand away from his.

"Ah, yes," she said, squinting off into the distance, eager to change the subject. "That stone construction over there on the cliff? But it has no windows, does it?" Why did Scots build so many things on cliffs overlooking the sea, she wondered. Was everything built with warfare in mind? Loghain seemed to confirm this.

"They were often built windowless. They were built for defense, you see. Many people would crowd into them when an area was under attack," Loghain explained.

Briar tried to imagine it. A stifling windowless tower full of frightened people.

"They would bring their livestock, too, sometimes," Loghain added.

"Frightened children and frightened cows," Briar muttered. "However did they all fit?"

"They had no choice," Loghain said. "Things were harsh. People made do. They were stronger, then." He frowned toward the broch. "We need to be more like our ancient kin. Too soft nowadays."

Briar suppressed a sigh. Loghain sounded like some of the older gentlemen she knew back home. And yet he was no more than thirty-five. Every generation criticized the young and believed they were softer, weaker in some way than the one before.

When the reality was, Briar thought, they were probably all very much the same. No better and no worse.

They had made their way down the hill overlooking the broch and were approaching the ancient stone tower, which was on a rocky cliff, though lower than the one Renfrew Castle sat upon.

"This broch is unusual," Loghain said, pointing at the crumbling keep. "For it has stone stairs leading up. There is a wonderful view from the top. Come, I'll show you."

Somehow, Briar wound up going first. The stairs were ancient, and crumbling was an understatement for their condition.

"Surely no one goes up these," Briar protested, staring at the steps. Some were missing. She would have to pick up her skirts to leap across and did not particularly like the idea. "They look dangerous."

"Oh, nonsense," Loghain said breezily. "Consider it your initiation. Everyone visits the broch, and everyone climbs to the top at least once, from the smallest child up. Think of it as a challenge." He smiled insolently at her. "You wouldn't wish for the clanspeople to say the new Lady Renfrew was cowardly, would you?"

Briar stared, unsure of whether he was teasing.

"No, I should not," she said slowly, feeling like a fool for risking her life for what was essentially no more than a dare. And one made by a man she did not like, nonetheless.

She sighed. "Very well. Would you like to go first?"

"Oh no, you go ahead. I have climbed them countless times," Loghain said, gesturing for her to go forward. "You know, I remember climbing these stairs with your husband when we were children. Many is the time we would race to the top. Ah, fond memories."

He shook his head as if lost in his reminiscence as Briar eyed the flagstone stairs nervously.

"Very well then," she said, lifting her chin and her skirt and taking the first step.

"Ho there! Wait up!" Another voice called out.

"Who is that?" Loghain was looking behind them and frowning. "Go ahead. Go up the stairs. I'll see who it is."

Briar ignored him and decided to wait. Besides, she thought she already knew.

"Percy," she called. "Is that you?"

There was a clatter of stones from the winding path leading up to the broch.

"Oh, dear, I hope he hasn't fallen," she exclaimed.

Loghain snorted. She observed he did not budge an inch to go and see.

A moment later, a head popped through the stone doorframe of the broch.

"I thought it was you," Percy said with a triumphant smile. "I was just in here, exploring, seeing what there was to see, then decided to walk along the shore." His eyes popped open. "Goodness, you aren't going up those steps, are you, Briar? I thought they were for appearances only. They look quite unstable."

"Loghain said they are quite safe," she began just as Loghain interjected.

"Of course, she is. They're safe as houses. What would you know about it?" He sneered at Percy in a way Briar found quite rude.

"Well, they don't look safe," Percy observed, his eyes looking upwards over the circular stairs. Then he perked up. "But if Loghain says they're all right, then I suppose he would know. I believe I shall join you. Must be a bloody good view from the top."

"An exceptional view, I promise you. Very well. You may follow behind her," Loghain assented, sounding so haughty and imperious that Briar had to hide a laugh. "I will wait below for you both, or it will become too crowded at the top."

Briar sighed and started slowly up the steps. They were quite wide, so that was not the problem. The flagstone and earth steps must have been very well constructed to have lasted more than a thousand years. But here and now, after decades or centuries without any maintenance, they were in poor condition.

Small stones came away under her feet with every step she took, some no more than pebbles, others as large as eggs.

She let out a little shriek as one flagstone faltered under her foot and leaned against the wall, steadying herself before she could lose her bearings.

She continued upwards, looking inwards at the immense, thick stone wall curving upwards on her left, rather than at the earthen floor below to her right which was becoming farther and farther away.

There was a clatter of stone. Percy yelped, and she froze. "Percy?"

"It's all right," he called cheerfully from behind and below her.

"Thought I was a goner for a moment there, though. Are you well, Briar?"

"Yes, very well," she said, determined not to reveal her fears and taking another step up. She could not wait to see the view and then speedily make her way back down.

Brochs were highly overrated monuments, she decided, crossly.

Or perhaps this one would have been enjoyable to visit in the right company. But as the right company was undeniably Wren and he was miles away, this was one sightseeing expedition she could have done without.

She was not looking forward to spending a night alone in their bed. She was unaccustomed to sleeping alone. Funny how quickly that had happened. She had just had this thought when two things happened in quick succession. She reached the top of the broch, found there were no handholds of any kind, and had taken a tentative step toward the edge to drink in this view Loghain had so lauded, when the parapet beneath her feet gave way, and she found herself sliding out of control.

"Help! Percy, help me! Loghain! I'm falling!"

"Briar! What's going on? I'm coming, Briar, hold on!" Percy was shouting. "Loghain, get up here, man! Loghain!"

And then Briar stopped paying attention.

She could hear herself screaming, and still she was sliding, slipping.

Her hands were grasping, grasping, grasping for anything to stop her slide, and she was taking great gasping breaths as if she were choking on nothing, so great was her panic.

This was how she was going to die.

Sliding off the top of a thousand-year-old broch. Her body would hit the rocks on the seashore below, and a wave would come and sweep her away.

And then, miraculously, her hands caught on a solid flagstone, gripped it, and somehow, that one, ancient stone held where all the others had fallen away.

But her situation was precarious in the extreme.

She was dangling from the waist down, over the edge of the broch.

"Percy. Loghain," she sobbed. "Help me. Please."

She saw Percy emerge at the top of the steps.

Wren had been unduly annoyed to find Briar was not at Renfrew Castle upon his return. Of course, he did not expect her to sit in her room writing letters all day and pining for him.

Though perhaps a small amount of pining would have been acceptable.

For had he not missed her desperately?

He had returned unexpectedly, however, and so could not blame her for wishing to go out. At first, he had assumed she must be out walking with one of the women. Perhaps even Esme.

But when Angus returned to find him brushing down Cerberus in the stables, he informed Wren that Briar had gone out with Loghain to see the broch. Wren immediately felt a cold, unsettled feeling in the pit of his stomach.

Angus was watching him carefully.

"Shall we go and see if the lass is enjoying her stroll?" Angus asked casually.

"I'm sure Loghain is an adequate guide," Wren said shortly. Then he nodded. There was no point in hiding his unease. Not from Angus. "Aye, let me saddle Cerberus again."

Angus did not make the mistake of suggesting Wren call a groom to complete the task for him. He was already striding down the row of stalls to do the same for his own mount.

A quarter of an hour later, they were cantering across the hills toward the broch. No one had suggested they ride at such a breakneck pace over the rocky moors. Angus had simply known and followed Wren's lead.

They had nearly crested the hill overlooking the broch. From the top, they would be able to see down to the ancient tower. Wren felt his heart speed up. Would she be there? Or had Loghain taken her someplace else?

They rode over the peak, and his heart lurched.

"Bloody hell," he heard Angus swear. "*Hiyah!*"

Both men urged their mounts into a gallop.

For Briar Renfrew, his bride, his beloved wife, was hanging from the primeval turret, and from the look of it, she was slipping.

There was someone else at the top with her, lying down and holding her hands, trying to pull her back up.

"Loghain," Wren breathed.

But as they drew nearer the broch, a man ran out, waving his arms. It was Loghain.

Who was at the top of the tower? And why the bloody hell was it not Loghain up there with Briar?

"Thank God you have come..." Loghain began, his face flushed.

"What is the meaning of this?" Angus bellowed. "What the bloody hell is the lass doing up there, mon?"

"And why are ye no' with her? Why are ye standing about below, waving yer arms like a chicken with its head cut off?" Wren demanded furiously. "Who is up there? Who is with my wife?"

He was sliding off his horse, even before it had come to a standstill, and racing into the tower, not even waiting for an answer.

He thought he already knew.

The young whelp might be their salvation in the end.

"Don't let go, Percy," Briar begged. "Don't let go." She choked back a sob.

"I won't," Percy promised. But she could see the strain in his face.

What was worse, he was sliding, too. He had braced his feet, wedging the tops into cracks between some flagstones that had remained intact. Now in horror, she saw one of his feet starting to come loose.

"If Loghain would get here, we could have you up in no time at all," Percy muttered. "What is taking him so long?"

Briar stared into his eyes.

"I don't think he's coming, Percy," she whispered.

Percy looked back at her, then nodded almost imperceptibly. "That changes this, doesn't it?"

He closed his eyes, a look of fierce stubbornness crossing his face, and then she felt him pulling on her arms as hard as he could.

"It's working, Percy, it's working," she cried.

If she could just get hold of a solid flagstone, she might release poor Percy and pull herself the rest of the way up and over. But right now, her bottom half was holding her hostage.

If she could just get her waist over the edge again...

Percy was straining, pulling, and then she was sliding in the right direction.

"That's it, Percy, I'm over," she cried.

Percy's expression was sheer relief. He had not let go of her hands. Both of them simply lay, too exhausted to move, flat against what remained of the top of the broch.

A huge chunk had fallen away, leaving a toothy gap where Briar had nearly met her end.

Now Percy finally let go of her hand and shakily pushed himself to his feet.

Briar stayed where she was, quite near the stairs, she saw to her relief.

"He must have known," Percy was muttering to himself. "It's completely unsafe. He must have known. Where the hell is the man?"

"Wren will deal with him. We must find Wren," Briar said tiredly. "Once I can move." She felt as weak as a kitten and still utterly terrified. Part of her did not want to move. Did not want to go back down to where Loghain surely waited for them.

What on earth would happen then?

Percy was looking down at his feet. "All of this could go. At any moment. It makes me dizzy. Come, Briar. Let's get you down..."

He moved toward her, as if to help her up.

And then the other half of the tower fell.

***

The sound of Briar screaming was something Wren knew he would never forget.

The scream reverberated through the stones, echoing across the keep, and piercing his eardrums until he thought his mind would surely fracture from the torment.

"Go, mon, go," Angus was shouting from behind him.

The loyal Scot said nothing about the stones pouring down on them from above. Nothing about the fact that the tower was likely to fall atop them both.

No, Angus simply followed.

But Wren would not subject him to this. Very likely he would climb to his death, and it would be too late.

He turned his head back, just for a second. "Stay with Loghain," he commanded, his voice a guttural growl as he saw the fair-haired man standing behind Angus. "Dinna let him out of yer sight, Angus."

And then he was bounding up the steps, hardly paying attention to where his feet landed, his urgency, his desperation so great. Fortune was with him that day. His feet found solid footing. He raced up the circular steps toward the top.

The screaming had stopped. He did not know which was worse.

Had she fallen then? Was that the last sound he would ever hear her make?

He was praying, but later he could not recall any of the words. He chanted her name to himself at one point—he could recall that much —for his teeth were fairly chattering in terror so badly he could hardly form the sounds.

And then he was there. His head poking over the top.

His heart lurched again as he saw half of the top of the tower had fallen away to nothing, pebbles in the sea.

There was a figure lying on the flagstones quite near the steps, motionless.

Only one figure.

It was her.

"Briar!" He stepped over and felt the tower shudder. "Briar, come to me, love. Come to me."

He saw her turn her head slightly where she lay. Her face was dirty and soaked wet with tears.

"Percy," she sobbed.

Then he understood. The figure he had seen at the top with her, helping her.

Saving her.

Percy Quintrell. Lost and found, only to be lost again.

He briefly closed his eyes, then took another step forward.

"Stop, Wren," she sobbed, her eyes wide as she watched. "We'll both die. Go back down. Please. I beg you. Leave me."

"Never in a hundred thousand years," he growled, his jaw clenched so tight he thought it would break. "Never, Briar. Dinna ask it of me. If ye die, so shall I. Anything but leave ye."

He looked down at where she lay on the flagstone and came to a quick decision.

"But ye're no' going to die today, mo chridhe," he promised. "Ye will live. With me. For many years. Until ye are sick of me. I swear it."

"Never, Wren," she whispered, and he saw her smile faintly. The sight wrung his heart. "I'll never tire of you. Not in a hundred thousand years."

"Good. Then let's get ye down from this blasted heap of rubble."

And he reached down and picked up his wife.

Chapter Nineteen

"I'll bloody well see my own wife if I wish to, now get out of the damn way," Wren snarled, pushing the shocked physician, who had come all the way from Inverness, up against the wall and opening the door.

The room was quiet.

Briar lay in the bed, very still, her eyes closed. Her chest was rising and falling softly, which Wren saw with relief.

Esme Grant stood across the room near a table, preparing a tincture of herbs. When she heard Wren enter, she turned. Her face was very white.

"Are ye going to try to make me leave, too?" Wren demanded, glaring at her.

"Nay," she whispered, shaking her head slowly. "Are ye?"

"What?" He looked at her, not understanding.

She took a step toward him, wringing her hands.

"'Tis my fault. All of it. If ye wish me to leave, I'll understand."

"What do ye mean?" Wren stared. "Ye were no' even at the broch."

"Aye, but I..." Esme licked her lips nervously. "I told Loghain. About the..."

"About the what?" Wren asked sharply. "Told him what, Esme?"

"About the bairn," she whispered.

He felt the blood drain from his face.

Esme put a hand to her mouth. "Did she really no' tell ye yet? All the women say they willna tell their men, but they always do."

"What are ye saying? How can this be?" Wren looked at the bed. "Nay, she didna tell me."

He was quiet a moment. Briar with child. Could it truly be so? "Did she lose it?" he demanded of Esme.

The healer put up her hands, her expression helpless. "Who can say for certain?" She bit her lip. "But I dinna think so. She has not bled."

"I see." Wren crossed over to the bed and looked down at Briar. Her face was very pale, the white of her skin contrasting with the rich dark red of her hair. He brushed a strand of it gently off her forehead, then leaned down to kiss her cheek.

Perhaps that was a mistake. He felt the tears coming to his eyes.

He stood up, brushed a hand over his eyes, then sank into a chair beside the bed, resting his head in his hands.

"I'm so sorry... So verra sorry, Laird," Esme was saying softly. She had come closer.

He lifted his head and studied her coldly. "Do ye wish her harm, Esme? That is all I want to ken. Do ye truly mean her malice? Or are ye here to heal?"

"I am here to heal," Esme said. "I wish her no harm."

Her face was solemn and stubborn, just like the woman herself.

He came to a decision, based on all the years he had known her, based on what he believed her to be, truly be. "Yer word is good enough for me."

She began to turn away but hesitated. "It shouldna be." Then more loudly, "My word shouldna be enough for ye. I broke it once, did I no'? And I broke it again, when Loghain made me tell him what yer lady wife had confided about the babe."

He stared at her, his head foggy. "Ye wish to discuss all that? Now? Here?"

She bit her lip, nodded, looking determined. "Perhaps 'tis best. Perhaps it will help ye understand."

"Understand Loghain, ye mean?" Wren frowned. "Let us have

something clear between us, Esme. Yer husband denies putting my wife in danger intentionally. He says it was all a tragic accident, and he begged her not to climb those steps. He claims Percy Quintrell goaded her into doing so, and she chased after him. By his account, Briar is simply a stupid woman who refused to heed his warning. And if we accept his account, then Percy Quintrell died a foolish, pointless death."

Esme bit her lip harder and shook her head. "Nay, nay."

"I dinna believe a word he says," Wren continued. "No' for one moment. Percy Quintrell was a good man. Moreover..." He paused, thinking of a time when these words would not have come so easily. "Moreover, Quintrell was no fool. I believe he was up there saving my wife's life." He ran his hand over his face as he looked at the healer. "But ye, Esme. Ye are Loghain's own wife. Are ye telling me ye wish to betray yer husband in what ye are about to tell me?"

Esme looked at him for what felt like a very long time.

"I never wished him to be my husband," she said quietly. "I had no choice."

"What are ye..." Wren began, but she held up a hand.

"Please," she said, taking a deep breath. "Let me speak and then let me leave." She nodded toward the table. "Give her the tincture when I go. It will help her sleep calmly and without pain. Tomorrow, God willing, she will awaken and speak to ye. But for now, let me speak. Have I not waited years so I might do so?"

Wren was speechless. He gestured to a chair near him, but Esme merely shook her head and folded her hands over her dress. She took a deep breath.

"I didna wish to marry Loghain. I had no choice." She looked up at the ceiling. "While ye were away, he had a leave from the army. He came home. We were all overjoyed to see him, though I wished it was ye instead. He paid me special attention, too much attention, I thought. But he has always been a flirt, a charmer. So, I thought nothing of it at first. Then one day, just before he left, he got me alone." Wren's eyes narrowed. He watched Esme draw a deep quavering breath. "I willna say more about that day."

Wren let out a low growl and clenched his hands into fists. Esme ignored him and continued, her voice growing steadier.

"We heard the war was over. That ye would be returning. Loghain said he would tell ye the truth. His truth. That I was to blame, for was I no' a daughter of Eve?" She gave a wry laugh full of pain. "He said I couldna marry ye now. No' in my... condition. That I must marry him instead. I agreed. What else could I do?"

She looked at Wren then, her eyes suddenly condemning, and repeated her query. "What else could I have done? What would ye have had me do?"

He said nothing, merely shook his head, looking at the woman who by rights should have once become his wife.

She was a beautiful woman, clever and even wise at times. But she was not Briar. And he did not love her, though he pitied her, aye, from the bottom of his heart.

"Ye must end this," Esme said, startling him from his reverie. "Challenge him. Challenge him to trial by combat." Her eyes burned with intensity. "Free us from his lies, once and for all."

"Trial by combat? Ye mean a duel?" Wren asked with surprise. "With Loghain?"

"Aye, Loghain," Esme replied doggedly. "He'll be forced to accept. He's confident. Overly so. He'll believe he can best ye." She began to walk toward the door. "He's sly. Ye willna take him otherwise. Face-to-face is best. Aye, that's the way."

"A duel," Wren mused. It was not a terrible idea. Would he have preferred to throw Loghain into the Renfrew Castle dungeon? Or better yet, off the nearest cliff? Of course. But once again, he had no proof. Only circumstantial. Briar was asleep. If she could speak... If she could say what had really happened...But what if she never could?

"Will she wake?" he demanded of Esme as she reached the door. "Tell me true. Will she really wake?"

She paused at the threshold, her eyes not on him but on the woman in the bed. "Aye, I believe so," she said finally. "Her body must heal. She had a shock. A terrible fright. But it has been only a night and a day. I believe... I believe she will come back to ye. Let her rest. Stay by her side. Let her hear yer voice. So she is no' afraid when she returns." She hesitated, then added, "Ye might speak of the babe. Reassure her about it."

"Aye, I will do that," Wren promised. "Thank ye, Esme."

She gave a small smile and turned away.

Only when she was gone did he allow himself to dwell on all she had told him. He imagined Loghain demanding Esme tell him all Briar had said. Was the man truly so threatened by Wren's wife and the prospect of a Renfrew child—a new legitimate heir—that he would go to such lengths? Or did Loghain simply hate Wren so very much that the idea of his cousin having anything he did not already have was unbearable to him?

The man had assaulted the woman Wren was to marry. Then instead of repenting of his terrible crime, he had blackmailed the poor girl into becoming his own wife and destroyed her prospects of happiness. Little wonder that Esme, so strong ordinarily, had told her husband whatever he wished to know. Wren could only imagine the torment her marriage must be to her.

Wren felt his hands curling into fists again. Fists he longed to drive into a familiar face.

Loghain was no kin. He was a monster. A rabid dog. Unpredictable. Uncontrollable. And worst of all, simmering with deceit.

It was time to put him down, once and for all, before he could harm another woman or child again.

When Briar awoke the next afternoon, Wren had a brief and terrible moment where he almost wished she had not.

For as she slept, she had been at peace. She had not had to recall the awful moments spent atop the broch. But as she began to awaken, they came flooding back, and she woke crying in terror and screaming for Percy.

Wren held her, wrapped tight in his arms as she wept.

"He is really gone then," she said dully after a while. "How? How is it possible?"

Wren was silent a time.

"I was no' there," he said carefully. "No one saw what happened with Percy, besides ye, Briar. Can ye... Can ye recount it for me?"

She looked up at him with amazement. "No one saw? But Loghain... surely, he told you."

"His account is verra different from what I believe ye will tell me," Wren said shortly. He hesitated, then added, "He says ye wouldna heed his warning no' to go up to the top of the broch, for one."

"What?" Briar stared in disbelief. Then her face turned dark and angry. "His warnings? What warnings? He urged us to go! Oh, that bloody bastard!"

Wren had never heard such language from his sweet wife's lips. "Aye, I'm inclined to think so as well."

"He bloody well *murdered* Percy as far as I am concerned," Briar cried. "He promised us it was safe to go to the top, and more than that, he insisted I do so or the people would think I was a coward." She shook her head, tears coming to her eyes. "Fool that I was, I actually believed him. Oh, I knew he was taunting me, in part. But I thought there was truth in his words, too. I thought he was a bully but never that he wished us real harm."

She looked at Wren, her face full of misery. "Perhaps it is all my fault that Percy died. If I had not listened to Loghain... if I had not gone up, Percy would be alive now."

"Nay," Wren shook his head stubbornly. "Not yer fault but mine. I should have warned ye both what Loghain was." He amended, "What I suspected he was." Now confirmed beyond a doubt. "Percy followed ye up, then?"

She nodded. "He was excited to see the view that Loghain had said was simply marvelous from the top of the broch. But when I got to the top... part of it simply sheared clear away. Wren, I thought the entire tower would crumble to the ground then and there." She shuddered.

Her hands were trembling where they lay on the bedclothes, and he took them in his, squeezing gently.

"I fell, slid off the side." She paused. "It was the most terrifying moment of my life. Worse than that night we were attacked. I thought I would surely die. And yet somehow, I found a handhold. And then Percy was there, pulling me up." Her voice broke. "Oh, God. Poor

Percy. He was so incredibly brave, Wren. How shall I ever tell his mother how brave her son was? She must know." She sobbed, then hiccupped. "She must know, Wren."

"Come here," Wren instructed. He drew her against him as she wept. "She will ken. Ye will tell her. Never ye fear. She will ken."

His wife was confirming everything he had suspected. Percy Quintrell had indisputably proven himself a good man in the end. He had done what Loghain should have done were there any goodness in his heart. As Wren's kinsman stood waiting for Briar to die, Percy had saved Wren's beloved wife—and lost his life in the process.

"He saved me," Briar whispered, sniffling against his shoulder. "He pulled me up and then... he fell. It happened so quickly. I could not even reach for him. He should never have been there in the first place."

Wren ran his hands over her back soothingly, but she pulled away, her expression bleak. "I shall have nightmares about that moment all my life, I believe," she said quietly. "Percy standing there, speaking of how the tower was unsafe, then the floor collapsing beneath him. Killing him where he stood."

"No wonder ye could hardly move when I got to ye," Wren murmured. "The broch should be pulled down. 'Tis a wonder no one has perished there before now."

"I suppose everyone was wise enough not to go up those stairs." She looked up at him. "He lied to me, Wren. Blatantly lied. He plainly wished me ill. Why?"

Wren looked at his wife, her eyes brimming with fury and sorrow, her cheeks tinged pink, her hair cascading around her shoulders like a vengeful cloud. She would boil over in her hurt. He knew just how that felt.

His wife needed to be reminded there was more to life than death and mourning and that not all men's hearts were so corrupt. Despite the loss of her friend, there was much to live for.

He leaned forward and pressed his forehead against hers tenderly.

"Let us put Loghain from our minds for a spell. Tell me about our child, Briar," he whispered, putting a hand carefully against her belly. "How long have ye kent?"

Chapter Twenty

In the end, he borrowed Angus's cavalry sword for the duel, as his own was back at Blakeley Manor with Laurel and Marigold.

Pistols would have been easier. Cleaner. Faster.

But Wren was known as an impressive shot, and so he had no delusions that Loghain would agree to a duel by pistol.

No, Loghain fancied himself a swordsman. He believed swords would give him the advantage.

So be it. Wren was confident he could put the rogue down with any weapon placed in his hands—or none at all.

"This is still the stupidest stunt I have ever heard of," Briar muttered from where she was walking a few steps behind.

Wren stopped and turned. "He tried to kill ye, Wife. And probably no' for the first time, if ye consider the bandit attack. What else could I do?" He had finally shared with her all of Angus's beliefs regarding Loghain's true culpability. Understandably, she had been upset for not having been told in the first place. From now on, he decided, he would make sure to always bring his wife into his confidence. That was part of a good marriage, was it not?

"You could not duel," she said, tossing her fiery hair over her shoulder. She was wearing it down and loose, for Esme had said she should wear it simply and not strain her head with heavy braids or knots while she recovered. Wren preferred it like this. She looked like a medieval maiden.

He drew her to him, wrapping his free arm around her waist, and kissed her long and hard.

When he was through, her hands rested on his chest lightly, and she looked up at him.

"Kissing does not end the disagreement," she pointed out.

"No, but it was an enjoyable interlude." He grinned.

"On the way to your..." She shook her head, unable to even finish the jest. If a jest was what it would have been.

"I am no' going to die," he promised. "I may be a wee bit hurt. A few scratches, aye. But it isna as if I have no' fought with swords before. Or in greater battles."

"Yes well, you were younger then," she said petulantly.

"Oh, verra nice encouragement," he complained, but he was still grinning.

He felt optimistic. Refreshed.

His love was by his side. Awoken like a princess in a fairy story. She was shaken but whole.

And after today, they would be free of the heavy cloud of gloom that had hovered over them from the moment they returned to Renfrew Castle.

Today, that threat would disappear once and for all.

Loghain would meet his maker. There was no other way this could go.

Not simply because Wren believed God was on his side in this medieval and albeit outlawed exercise, the trial by combat, the duel. But because he was the better swordsman.

Very well, he acknowledged to himself, he was also on the side of right, and most of all, he wanted to win. Nay, had to win. What he *wanted* was to pummel Loghain, see him bleed, rub his face in the dirt, and then do it all again.

He had been merciful. He had tried to forgive, to move on. But it was not to be.

And when Loghain had tried to murder his wife and his unborn child out of spite and jealousy? Well, he had written his own death warrant that day.

"Och, ye're looking braw this fine morning, Laird," Angus crowed, coming up to them. "That's the spirit. It'll be over in no time."

"Not too quickly, I hope," Wren replied and received a hoot of appreciation in response.

"Stop encouraging him, Angus," Briar protested. "It is still not too late to call this foolishness off."

"Och, all the womenfolk say that," Angus confided, leaning close to Wren. "But if ye were to do as she says, she'd never..."

"What are you telling my husband?" Briar demanded, crossing her arms over her chest and stepping between them. "That I'd think less of him if he called off a duel which may claim his life?"

"Bah! The Renfrew willna die. He'll be fine. A scratch or two, mayhap," Angus declared.

"That's what I told her," Wren admitted.

"You sound awfully sure. Are you able to tell the future, then, Angus? I had no idea that was one of your skills," Briar said dryly.

"He's simply confident in my abilities, Wife," Wren said soothingly. "Angus doesna fear for me, and neither should ye."

Briar bit her lip. "This is all my fault."

"Really?" Wren scratched his chin. "I dinna see how."

"Yes," Briar said resignedly. "If I hadn't married you. If I hadn't asked you to come with me to the Brewers in the first place. If I hadn't..."

He silenced her mouth with a kiss.

"Shush now. The same could be said in reverse. I've nearly gotten ye killed more than once." He frowned. "Today we end this and move on with our lives." He glanced at her belly before he could stop himself.

Briar said nothing but took his arm in hers.

They walked toward the sparring yard.

A crowd was already assembled. All the inhabitants of the castle and the nearby villages seemed to be there, or so it seemed to Wren.

"Loghain isna well-liked," Angus murmured. "I think it's safe to say the crowd is well-favored to ye, Renfrew."

Loghain was already inside the wooden fenced ring which would be their battleground. He was dressed entirely in white and gold.

"Better to show the blood as ye spill it, eh?" Angus said, elbowing him in the ribs. "Daft colors for a duel."

Loghain was talking animatedly to someone near the fence. When he moved aside, Wren saw it was Esme. She did not look happy.

When she caught sight of Wren and Briar, she nodded at them, then said something to Loghain, who turned and nodded a greeting as well.

"That's right. Be polite to one another before you fight like raging barbarians," Briar muttered rebelliously.

"It is about justice, mo chridhe," Wren said, refusing to be put off or to feel any guilt over what he must do. "It will be over soon. Ye need no' watch if ye..."

"If you think I am going to hide under a blanket while my husband fights for his life, you have another thing coming, Robert Renfrew," Briar said hotly, stopping in her tracks and putting her hands on her hips.

Wren grinned. "Aye, that's what I figured ye'd say. Come and stand by Angus, then."

⁓

Loghain looked remarkably sanguine for someone about to fight a duel with a man considerably larger than he was, Briar thought. But perhaps size did not matter so much as speed and skill when it came to swords.

She watched as the man who had tried to kill her raised his hand and smiled in greeting. Despite her efforts to be cheerful for Wren's sake, a knot of worry was growing in the pit of her stomach.

What right did Loghain have to look so optimistic? So cheerful? He had tried to kill his rightful laird and his laird's wife.

Not to mention their future child, should the baby thrive. With that thought, Briar put a hand on her belly, then quickly drew it away. She did not wish for Esme to see. Though Wren had explained what Esme had told him, Briar had been unable to fully forgive the other woman so easily. She trusted her as a healer, certainly. But as a friend? Briar was not so sure.

She wished to forgive. But she found it was easier said than done.

Now Esme stood, watching her husband as he made small talk and banter with the onlooking crowd. She looked lovely and pure, with her pale-yellow braid falling over one shoulder and a high-necked dress of white wool adorning her tall, slender figure.

Loghain glanced appreciatively at his beautiful wife, a bright smile on his handsome face.

Did he have a reason for his optimism? Something up his sleeve that Wren did not know about?

She watched Esme tug at Loghain's sleeve and whisper something in his ear. Loghain smiled more broadly and nodded his head.

"Wren, something isn't right," Briar imagined herself saying. And then? What could she follow that up with? "I don't trust Loghain." Well, that was why they were all gathered there today, wasn't it?

And besides, it was too late. The trial was beginning.

She watched as Angus clapped an older gray-haired man on the shoulder, then stepped back to allow him to enter the ring. Cormac Grant was the older man's name, and he was something of an elder and advisor at Renfrew Castle. He was also related to both Wren and Loghain, as were most of the people gathered there.

Cormac walked to the center and held up his hands until the crowd quieted.

In a daze, Briar listened as Cormac spoke about right and wrong, about honor and truth, and about how the ancient practice of trial by combat would settle once and for all this disagreement between the laird and his kinsman, in the eyes of all these witnesses—and in the eyes of God.

Briar was trembling. She clutched Wren's arm, feeling like a fool. He looked down at her, smiled, kissed her forehead, and gently released himself from her grip.

And then he was entering the sparring ring and standing across from Loghain.

The next sound Briar heard clearly was the sound of clashing steel, and the two men drew their weapons and engaged.

Both men were excellent swordsmen as far as she could tell. They moved with such speed and grace she could hardly keep track of the lunges and parries, the stabs and feints.

When Loghain drew the first blood, the crowd around her gave a collective gasp, and she covered her mouth. Wren had been slashed on the forearm. She could see blood trickling down onto the earth, splattering the dust, and felt faint.

A strong hand gripped her shoulder.

"'Tis a flesh wound, lassie. Nothing to trouble over," Angus murmured in her ear. "Take yer hand away from yer mouth now, darling. Dinna let them see yer fear."

Don't let *him* see it, was the unspoken implication. Briar quickly did as Angus said.

She looked across the ring at where Esme stood, all alone. Their eyes met.

Esme was afraid, too, Briar realized. She was gripping the wooden fence with both hands, her knuckles white.

What was she so afraid of? That Loghain would lose?

Or that he might win?

There was suddenly a collective cheer, and Briar realized Loghain had been hit. His wound was more serious than Wren's, she saw with delight, then felt guilty as she watched him wincing and holding his shoulder. But she recalled Percy and hardened herself. No, she would feel no guilt, she decided. The ruthless and bloodthirsty one was not her nor Wren but Loghain himself.

There was a pause in the fighting. Wren had given his opponent the opportunity to rest.

But instead of coming over to Briar, Wren moved to speak to Angus, Cormac, and some other men who stood on the side. They conferred in low voices, but there was chuckling and smiling, too. They did not seem particularly worried about their laird, Briar noticed with relief.

She glanced over at Esme and Loghain. Esme was holding up a wooden mug to Loghain. She seemed to be urging him to drink. To Briar's surprise, Esme was smiling a little. There was a sparkle in her lovely blue eyes. Loghain was grinning back. He seemed very confident and not at all put off by the injury he had sustained. He took the mug eagerly, and as Briar watched, tipped his head back and drained it, then shook it a little and held it up, as if asking Esme if there was more.

Esme shook her head, then took the mug back, and gently put a hand to Loghain's shoulder just where the wound was.

To Briar's surprise, Loghain did not wince or brush the hand away, but rather he smiled even more broadly. He said something excitedly to Esme, and she nodded and pointed back to the ring.

The break was over, and the two men stood once again in the center of the yard, swords poised.

Cormac raised his arms, called out something in Gaelic, and the clashing began once more.

To Briar, Loghain looked even more energized than he had before being wounded. He surged toward Wren as if fueled by some unknown power, and Wren had to move quickly to dodge and block.

The movements were repeated until Briar felt dizzy from observing the men spin and feint, spin and feint. She was desperate for it all to be over.

And then Loghain lunged, stabbed, and Wren did not whirl away in time.

The shining sword breached his leather cuirass, sliding through it like a knife through butter, in and out.

For a moment, Briar was not even sure Wren had been wounded. Until he staggered a little.

He hid it well. Perhaps Loghain had not noticed how bad the wound was.

Then she saw the half-smile the golden-haired man wore. He knew, he knew.

Loghain moved as if his own shoulder injury were nothing more than a scratch. But the wound was freely bleeding now. Esme had not even bothered to bind it. Briar wondered why.

From time to time, an odd look crossed Loghain's face. He would brush it away, and Briar saw his serenity temporarily return. But then his face would freeze, his smile vanish.

When Wren struck a second blow to his foe, Loghain seemed more shocked than anyone else. Wren's blade penetrated Loghain's other shoulder. He had time to look at the blade as it slid in, then out.

Briar half expected he would drop his sword. After all, he was wounded on both sides now. Surely the pain must be immense.

But instead, to her shock, Loghain held his sword aloft and, turning to Esme, shouted something she could not hear. Briar watched the other woman smile slowly and put her hands together, as if she were clapping.

When Loghain turned back to face Wren, he was smiling and looked as fresh as when he had begun the fight.

Briar saw Wren frown in confusion. He was not the only one.

All around the ring, there came the buzz and chatter of people discussing Loghain's incredible, almost inhuman reaction.

"One might think he were fey-touched," Angus said crossly, coming up beside her. He shook his head. "Something's no' right. He canna go on like this. The mon is sorely wounded, smile or no."

Briar's eyes widened. "Wren?"

"Nay, no' Wren. Loghain. He's wounded in both shoulders. The bleeding isna stopping. He just isna feeling the pain, see? Verra odd." Angus's scowl deepened.

"But Wren can still win the fight?" Briar asked, her voice low.

Angus glanced at her. "Aye, he'll win. Never fear."

The two men had resumed their frantic pace. Around and around the ring they went.

And then Loghain finally stumbled, going down on one knee before swiftly rising back up.

But he was beginning to falter, Briar saw with excitement. He stumbled again, then again.

Now Loghain was no longer smiling. His face was pale, and his smile had dropped away.

She saw his eyes go to his wife, who was watching intently. She smiled at him encouragingly, but he did not return her smile.

A moment later, Loghain sank to both knees, one hand resting in the dirt for balance. For a moment, Briar thought he was about to faint.

She saw Wren pause, then say something to Loghain in a low voice.

But Loghain shook his head, an ugly scowl crossing his face. He pushed himself upright and lifted his sword.

But his hands were shaking as he held it.

A ripple went through the crowd. She was not the only one who had noticed.

Wren said something again, more urgently this time. Briar could see the frustration on his face. He wanted this finished, she knew. But he had no wish to kill a man who could not face him fairly in a fight.

This time Loghain ignored Wren entirely, and to her shock, hurtled himself forward toward his opponent, bellowing a wordless battle cry of fury.

Wren parried the attack, blocking Loghain and spinning.

He caught Loghain in the side, thrusting through his cuirass once, then quickly a second time.

For a moment, Loghain stood, looking down at the blood dripping to the ground as if he could not believe it.

He turned to Esme and shouted something, then looked down at himself again.

And then, he fell.

His wife did not go to him.

Wren crouched beside his cousin. The man's face was ashen-gray, and he could hardly see the rise and fall of his chest.

What did one say to a man dying from a blow you inflicted intentionally upon him? Loghain was Wren's kin. His childhood companion. And yet the man had tried to kill him—and worse, destroy everything he held dear.

And so, he said nothing. Just waited. Surely death could not be long now. Surely Loghain must know it, too.

Angus and Cormac approached behind him, as well as some other men from the castle. Good warriors, all veteran fighters of the king's wars in France. They had seen their share of death.

"'Twas a strange battle," Angus said, his voice low in Wren's ear. "Verra strange. Ye offered him the chance of surrender?"

"I did," Wren said shortly. "Should I have done more?"

"Ye tried twice, did ye no'? Nay, there was no more ye could do. He was intent on fighting ye. The mon seemed to think he was invincible." Angus was quiet a moment. "What was he saying to his wife? Did ye hear it?"

Wren nodded. "He was saying, 'I canna feel the pain.'"

"That happens to some in the heat of battle, aye." Angus nodded, but his face was troubled. He said something to Corman, who crouched down beside Loghain, touching his chest.

"Is he dead?" Wren demanded. The waiting felt interminable.

The older man shook his head. "No' yet. But it willna be long now."

Then, to all their surprise, Loghain's eyes opened.

He searched the faces of the men around him and, when his eyes found Wren's, spoke with what seemed like great difficulty.

"She... did... this."

Wren scowled and leaned down. "My wife? My wife did nothing to ye."

Loghain seemed to be trying to shake his head. "No... pain. No... pain... she... said."

"He means Esme," Angus said suddenly. "He means *his* wife." He crouched down quickly beside Loghain. "Do ye mean Esme, mon? Speak up."

But Loghain was gone.

Angus stood up. "That treacherous wretch. What did she do?"

"Hold, Angus," Wren tried to command, but the older man was already striding over to the fence where Esme Grant still stood, watching.

"What did ye do?" Angus shouted at her. He grabbed the woman and pulled her through a gap in the fencing, then drew the knife from his belt and held it to her throat. "Have ye no' betrayed enough men for one lifetime? Did ye do this to yer husband, woman? Speak!"

"Angus," Wren said sharply. "Remove yer knife. Gently, mon. Gently."

"She's lied to us all. She betrayed ye once, Laird, dinna forget," Angus bellowed accusingly. "Now she poses as a healer, but does this? What did ye give him, woman? What was in the mug, Esme?"

He shook her shoulder, but Wren saw the man had put his knife back in his belt. Good. If Angus knew the truth of what Esme had suffered at Loghain's hands already, Wren knew he would be ashamed for his rashness.

"Calmly, mon," Wren said soothingly. "Esme, answer Angus. What was in the mug? Ye may settle this easily."

Esme was staring down at her husband. "He is really dead, then?"

"Aye, he is dead," Wren replied.

He was not prepared for what she did next.

Coming up beside her husband, she looked down at his lifeless gray face, then spat upon it.

"Here now," Angus cried, pulling Esme back and looking shocked. "Do ye need more proof than that? She hated the man, 'tis plain to see."

Wren struggled not to point out that Angus had not precisely viewed Loghain with benevolence himself.

"I did hate him," Esme said, nodding. "Angus is right."

Briar had come up to the group. She studied Esme, her voice gentle.

"Esme, tell us, please. Did you harm Loghain? Or did he die by my husband's blade? The latter is far more likely, Angus," she added more sharply. "And I'll thank you to keep your knife away from my friend from now on."

Esme seemed startled by Briar's defense. She looked at her for a moment, then shook her head. "'Twould be best if ye no' defend me," she said quietly. "I dinna deserve it."

Briar glanced at Wren. "What do you mean, Esme?"

Esme drew a deep breath. "I mean, I hated my husband. I never wished to marry him in the first place. But he had... dishonored me. Forced me. He lied to me, told me Wren—our laird—dinna wish to wed me any longer, that he was the only man who would take me."

"And so ye killed him?" Angus asked in disbelief. "Ye expect us to believe this story?"

Esme was quiet. "Believe what ye will, Angus Macleod. Ye always have. Ye have never liked me. I dinna ken why."

"Because ye broke my friend's heart," Angus said hotly. "Played him for a fool. Then played the loyal wife. And reaped the benefits when Alec and the old laird died. Verra conveniently."

"Aye, what else would ye have had me do? I was Loghain's wife, was I no'? What else could I do but support the man?" Esme retorted. "I nursed Alec when he was ill. The verra best I could. It wasna my fault he died."

"Nay? What about the old laird? Did ye poison him like ye did yer verra own husband just now?" Angus spat back viciously. "For 'twas poison in the mug, was it no', Esme?"

Esme said nothing. She looked down at Loghain's body, then nodded slowly. "Aye."

"Ye see," Angus crowed. "I kent it!"

"I had nothing to do with the old laird's death," Esme interjected. "Nothing." She gave a hard laugh. "Though Loghain would have gladly had me poison old Donnell, hasten yer grandda's death, aye. But I wouldna do it. And punished bitterly for saying no I was, too."

Angus looked flabbergasted. "Ye are saying ye poisoned one man but no' the other?"

"Aye." Esme took a deep breath and, ignoring Angus, met Wren's eyes calmly. "Aye, that's what I'm saying, Laird. Believe what ye will. I ken Angus will, no matter how much truth I speak."

Angus threw up his hands with a bitter laugh.

"Esme," Wren said carefully. "Ye are confessing to murdering a man. Are ye sure ye ken what ye are saying? Why would ye wish Loghain dead?" He glanced at Cormac Grant, who was watching all that transpired quietly from where he still stood beside Loghain's body.

Esme looked at him steadily. "Aye, 'tis a confession, if that is what ye wish to call it. 'Twas aconite in the tea. Wolfsbane. I told Loghain it would give him the strength of ten men, ye see. And that he would feel no pain. Aconite numbs the flesh. Ye feel nothing at first. Then yer heart begins to slow."

"I see." Wren felt his heart growing cold. "So ye let me finish the job? Kill a mon who was already dying?"

Esme did not flinch. "Would ye have preferred I give the wolfsbane tea to yer lady wife?" she asked bluntly. "For *he* would have." She nodded at the body on the ground. "He wished me to poison her. He wished her harm from the day he laid eyes on her, simply because it was plain ye cared for her. When he learned she might be with child, his rage knew no bounds. God pity any man who dared have something Loghain wanted and could not possess himself. The idea of ye returning as laird with a healthy wife, and soon a bairn on the way, was more than he could stand. But if wishin' harm to the laird's own wife isna enough for all of ye," Esme said, raising her voice a little. "Perhaps this will help ye all to understand."

Her face twisted with pain as she yanked down the shoulders of the white gown she wore, exposing the expanse of skin on her shoulders, her back, and her chest up to the tops of her breasts.

Briar put a hand to her mouth as Wren let out a string of curses.

Even stout Angus's face paled. "Good God, lass," the man choked out. "Why'd ye no' tell us? How'd ye bear such a thing?"

Esme was covered with bruises and cuts, some old, some very fresh. She had wrapped bandages over herself, beneath the white dress, but in some places the blood had already begun to seep through. Beneath the new injuries were a mishmash of crisscrossing scars, some very deep. It was astonishing, Wren thought grimly, that the proof of her husband's cruelty had lain just beneath the surface of a lovely white gown.

"This is just above. Would ye like to see below, Angus Macleod?" Esme demanded. "He commanded me to bear him a child, then he beat me until I could hardly stand. And ye ask me why I hated him? After the manner of our marriage and the way he laid hands upon me whenever things did not go as he liked? Everything evil was in him, and he wished for me to become the verra same as he."

"I didna ken, Esme," Angus stuttered. "If any of us men had kent..."

"Ye'd have what?" Esme challenged. "Done what the laird just did and fought him?" She shook her head, her expression turning bleak. "I doubt it. I have no family here. There was no one on my side. Ye didna trust me." She shrugged. "No' that I blame ye."

"I..." Angus began.

"But ye did poison him, Esme," Wren said quietly.

"Aye. I did. He tried to kill yer wife. Kill yer unborn babe. He would have killed me someday. Of that I have no doubt," Esme replied, her voice tense. "Aye, I helped to hasten his death along. But I also had no doubt who would have won the fight. Ye are the better mon. God was on yer side, Robert Renfrew."

"Well, we'll never ken now, will we?" Wren said wryly.

He sighed and ran a hand over his face. This was the worst position to be in. He found he had no desire at all to punish Esme for what she had done, God help him.

Briar's hand slipped into his and squeezed. He looked down at her and saw her eyes echoed his thoughts.

He glanced around. Thankfully, the crowd had mostly drifted away. A few older folks had lingered, watching all that had transpired in silence. Now Wren saw Cormac Grant murmur a few words, and they, too, began to step away, careful not to look at Esme.

Cormac stepped forward, his face grave. "'Tis a terrible thing when a hale man's heart becomes corrupted by envy and greed," he said slowly, looking around him. "But the trial by combat revealed all, and the unworthy has fallen today. There is no doubt in my mind, no doubt at all, that our laird, Robert Renfrew, fought nobly today in the eyes of all his clan and the eyes of our Lord. Loghain Grant perished by his blade. And so far as I am concerned, that is all needs be said on the matter."

Angus stepped forward next. "Aye, what Cormac said is nay more than the truth. I concur. Let no more be said on the matter. The matter should be closed." He spoke firmly and did not look at Esme.

There were nods from the last of the folk who had lingered. No one disagreed.

It was settled then. No more would be spoken about the means of Loghain Grant's death.

His wife was a widow now and entitled to all the solicitude and care a Renfrew clanswoman was due, henceforth.

Wren felt his heart clench with gratitude. Let no one say that the Scots were a hard people. He felt a terrible tenderness toward Esme and all she must have endured. The years had separated them irrevocably, but he would always feel pity for the woman he had once thought he loved. He had believed himself betrayed, but all this time so had she.

Now the man accountable for all that heartache and more was dead.

He and Esme were both responsible. Perhaps that was as it should be.

He turned to look at his wife, but she was already distracted. All her concern and compassion were directed toward Esme, who stood looking small and solitary and utterly perplexed. As if she could not believe her friends and neighbors were not about to castigate her, to punish her in some way.

"Come back to the castle with me, Esme," Briar murmured, putting her arm through the other woman's. "Come up to my room and let us sit awhile, just you and I. Perhaps Wren will brew us some nettle tea."

Chapter Twenty-One

Three days later, Renfrew Castle

Wren traced the smooth skin on his wife's belly, the outline of her navel.

Everything about her was perfect.

"Can there really be a babe in there?" he asked, looking at her stomach skeptically. He didn't wish to point it out, but the surface was still rather flat. He put his ear against her skin. "I dinna hear anything."

Briar giggled. "What do you expect? To hear a baby crying?" Her face sobered abruptly. "You must not... get your hopes up, you know, Wren. For Esme says..." She bit her lip. "She says many women lose it, the first time."

"Aye." Wren nodded. "That is the way of nature." He felt his heart clench as he thought about their unborn child. "But 'tis easier said than done."

"Yes," Briar agreed, placing a hand protectively on her belly. "Our baby."

He grabbed her hand and kissed it. "Ours. Yers and mine."

He sat up in the bed. "I had a thought. For a name. If ye approve."

"What is it?" Briar asked curiously.

"I thought perhaps Percy if it is a boy," Wren offered.

"Percy," Briar murmured, her face becoming sad. "That would be a lovely name. Or Percival, for I believe that is what it was short for."

Wren was not as sure about Percival, but he decided not to say so. "A knight's name."

"Sir Percival, yes." Briar nodded. "And if it is a girl?"

"I had no' thought of that," Wren admitted.

"Your mother's name was Lara, which is a very pretty name," Briar mused. "Or if we wish to honor Percy, regardless of whether it is a boy, then there is Persephone, I suppose."

"Was she no' the wife of Hades?" Wren asked uncomfortably. "It seems an ill-omened name for a wee lassie."

"But she was also the goddess of spring. Rebirth. New life," Briar murmured.

Wren quickly decided what his wife wished to name the baby would be good enough for him. "They're braw names. Percival or Persephone."

"Persephone Lara Renfrew sounds lovely, doesn't it?" Briar smiled and sighed.

Wren rose from the bed and began to pull on a clean shirt.

"Ugh, stop that," Briar said crossly, wrinkling her nose as she watched him. "Take it off."

"So ye can have yer wicked way with me again?" Wren grinned and winked.

"That, too," Briar said, smiling in a way that made his heart flutter and his cock stir. Then she frowned. "I cannot believe we are about to honor... that... that goddamned *man*."

"Loghain. Aye." Wren looked about for his plaid. "*Honor* is putting it too strongly. I prefer to think of it as stowing him safely below ground." Better Loghain than anyone Wren loved. "Besides," he reminded her. "Yesterday was when we honored a truly worthy man. Dinna forget it." The day before they had held a service in the small chapel for Percy Quintrell before sending his body home to England. Percy's funeral had been conducted with much more pomp and ceremony than would be given to Loghain today. There had likely been much more weeping for the young man than Loghain was bound to receive today, too.

Wren had a thought. "Did ye send a letter to his mother? Percy, I mean."

Briar nodded slowly. "I did, yes."

"What did ye say?" Wren asked, curious. "There must have been much to tell."

"There was, yes," Briar said, with a sigh. "You have no idea how I agonized over just what to put in and what to leave out."

Wren was quiet a moment. "I hope ye mentioned his bravery."

"Of course, I did. I wonder what she will make of it all. To hear of her son being kidnapped, and then coming to the rescue of his kidnappers and befriending them by the end. I told her of how he went to Angus's aid during the attack that night. I told her of how the men loved his bannock, of how skilled he was at digging for spoots. I told her of how he died valiantly, saving me. It was a very long letter by the end." She was quiet a moment. "I wonder if she will hate me now. For living while her son has died."

Wren crossed over and put a hand on her shoulder. "Nay, she will likely be verra proud. And verra grateful for the length of the letter."

Briar tried to smile. "I should like to visit her, after the baby is born. And Bessie, too. She must be very close to her time now. I mentioned Bessie, of course, to Percy's mother. But then, she must be aware. Percy had made arrangements for Bessie before he... passed."

"He truly had changed a verra great deal," Wren murmured.

"Part of that was thanks to you, I think, Wren," Briar began.

There was a sudden pounding on the outer door of their suite of rooms. Wren looked at Briar. She shook her head.

He stepped into the sitting room as Briar quickly rose and slipped into a heavy wool robe.

"Who is it?" Wren called. He couldn't help it. His eyes went to the cavalry sword, which he had not yet given back to Angus. It was sheathed, leaning against a table in the corner, but if necessary, he could reach it in an instant.

The door pushed open and a familiar dark head appeared.

"Angus!" Wren scowled. "Why are ye banging on the door like a mad mon? Did Loghain rise from the dead?"

Angus snorted. "He'd better no', or we'd have to put him down again." He glanced at Briar who had just stepped in, her robe snugly fastened. "Pardon me, milady."

"Oh, please. I would be the first to commend you," Briar said brusquely.

"What is the reason for the ruckus, then?" Wren demanded.

"It's Esme. She's gone."

"Gone!" Briar stepped closer to Angus. "What do you mean she's gone? It's the day of her husband's funeral."

Angus cocked an eyebrow. "Aye. Perhaps that's why she chose today."

"She hasn't been abducted, then? Oh, Angus, you gave me a fright. I thought it was our own history repeating itself for a moment," Briar complained.

"Speak clearly, mon," Wren said. "Did she tell anyone she was going?"

"She left a note, aye." Angus looked distressed. "For ye. Here. Read it for yerself." He pulled a crumpled paper from the pocket of his plaid and handed it to Wren, who held it low so Briar could read along with him.

He scanned it, then glanced up at Angus.

"Aye, I read it," Angus admitted. "I was worried about the woman."

Wren nodded his understanding and turned back to the note.

"My laird, ye offered forgiveness, but I find it is too great a gift to accept. Ye might have banished me. Perhaps ye should have. Either way, I find this can no longer be my home. I wish ye and yer lady good health. Esme Ross."

"She signs it with her maiden name," Wren observed. "I suppose that is understandable." He sighed. "Well, what would ye have me do? She is a free woman. She may go where she wishes, Angus."

Angus frowned. "I wish to be excused from my obligations today at the funeral. I aim to leave Renfrew Castle within the hour."

Wren was aghast. "Ye wish to go after her? But why? Ye canna force her to return, Angus."

"Nay, but I can persuade her," Angus said stubbornly.

"But..." Wren was beginning to argue when he felt Briar's hand gently light upon his arm. He looked down and saw her shake her head.

Wren swallowed what he had been about to say. "Verra well. All the best to ye, then. We shall make do without ye. I'm sure we can find another mon to help carry the casket."

"Even if ye have to pay him," Angus said, smirking. "Aye, well. I'll return soon." He began to step out into the hall.

"Ye had better," Wren said quickly before the man could vanish. "A castle needs its steward."

Angus turned around, a look of surprise on his face. "Steward?"

Wren nodded. "Aye. Donnell should have appointed ye long ago. I willna be so remiss. Angus Macleod, will ye serve as my steward and help me to oversee the Renfrew lands and to care for our people? I ken of no better mon."

"Well done," Briar murmured, squeezing his arm.

Angus's face twitched suspiciously. He swallowed hard. "Aye. Steward. I should be happy to oblige, Laird." He grinned, then shook a finger. "When I return, that is."

He stepped out into the hall, then turned back one more time. "A castle needs its healer," he said seriously.

And then he was gone.

"What was all that about?" Wren asked, looking down at his wife. "Since when does Angus care anything about Esme Grant? Esme Ross, I mean," he corrected.

Briar's expression was thoughtful. "I believe he always has. Cared, that is."

"Angus?" Wren shook his head. "Nay, he never liked her. Neither did Alec."

"Your two friends didn't like the prettiest maiden around when you were all growing up here together?" Briar raised her eyebrows. "How very odd. And convenient."

"What are ye saying?"

Briar sighed. "I'm saying that Angus knew you and Esme were sweethearts, so of course he would not look at her in such a way. And later, he had convinced himself he disliked Esme, perhaps until very recently. But at the duel, when he learned how Loghain had really been treating her, he was appalled. His heart went out to her. Anyone could see it."

"Aye," Wren said slowly. "But he also pulled his knife on the poor woman..."

"Never mind, Wren," Briar said impatiently. "Just wait and see. If I am right, well." She shrugged and smiled. "I hope he does convince her to come back. I can understand why she felt she must go away, of course. But I don't agree with her. Esme's place is here. After all"—she patted her stomach nervously—"who will help when my time comes?"

Wren drew her to him and kissed her. "I'll be there. I'll deliver the babe myself if need be." He grinned. "I've brought calves and lambs into the world. What's one more?"

Briar shrieked, but she was laughing. "Our baby is not a calf! And it had better not be as big as one, either. Oh goodness, can you imagine..." She let out a mock groan.

"Come and get dressed," he said, nuzzling her neck. "And come down to see us off." The men would carry the coffin in a burial procession, away from the castle to the little cemetery which lay down by the sea. "And then come back with me and get undressed. And let us no' think of Loghain Grant ever again."

He kissed her collarbone, and she made an appreciative little mew.

"Let us think only of each other and the family we are making, Briar. Growing like the branches on a beautiful tree, one by one."

"Mmm." He felt her smile. "I like that. How lovely."

Wren's heart was brimming, fuller than he could bear. "Ye are lovely. And I love ye."

He kissed her lips and looked down at her. The future was bright and full of joy and love.

THE END

Thank you for reading *Lady Briar Weds the Scot*!

. . .

Follow up with Dare's story in book 2 in the Blakeley Manor series: *Kiss Me, My Duke*!

Lost: One duke's sister. Found: The unexpected love of a lifetime.

The handsome duke and a young housekeeper with a mysterious past must venture into the dangerous London underworld... only to belatedly discover that the bedroom may be the most perilous place of all.

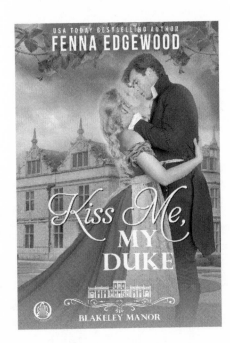

Also by Fenna Edgewood

The Gardner Girls Series

Masks of Desire (Prequel Novella)

To All the Earls I've Loved Before

Mistakes Not to Make When Avoiding a Rake

The Seafaring Lady's Guide to Love

Once Upon a Midwinter's Kiss

Must Love Scandal Series

How to Get Away with Marriage

The Duke Report

A Duke for All Seasons

The Bluestocking Beds Her Bride

The Brazen Belles

The Brazen Belles Anthology

About Fenna Edgewood

 *USA Today* bestselling author Fenna Edgewood writes swoon-worthy, humorous stories of love, family, and adventure. In other words, the most important things in life! She is an award-winning retired academic who has studied English literature for most of her life. After a twenty-five-year hiatus from writing romance as a twelve-year-old, she has returned to the genre with a bang. Fenna has lived and traveled across North America, most notably above the Arctic Circle. She now resides back on the Prairies with her husband and two tiny tots (who are adorable but generally terrible research assistants).

Connect with Fenna:

https://fennaedgewood.com

facebook.com/fennaedgewoodbooks

instagram.com/fennaedgewood

bookbub.com/authors/fenna-edgewood

amazon.com/stores/Fenna-Edgewood/author/B0929KJV52

Made in the USA
Columbia, SC
12 January 2024

30401832R00152